You

JO PLATT
You Are Loved

CANELO

First published in the United Kingdom in 2017 by Canelo

This edition published in the United Kingdom in 2020 by

Canelo Digital Publishing Limited
Third Floor, 20 Mortimer Street
London W1T 3JW
United Kingdom

A CIP catalogue record for this book is available from the British Library.

Print ISBN 978 1 78863 734 3
Ebook ISBN 978 1 911591 59 7

Look for more great books at www.canelo.co

Printed and bound in Great Britain by Clays Ltd, Elcograf S.p.A.

Prologue

Aiden hesitated, his hand resting on the latch of the unopened front door.

I gazed at him, feeling strangely detached and wondering if this would be the moment when he would blame, or explain, or apologise and attempt some sort of situation retrieval. I also wondered what my reaction might be if he did.

He turned and looked over his shoulder at me. 'Solicitors then,' he said quietly.

His expression left me uncertain whether it was a question or a statement, but I said nothing in reply. I wasn't being strong, or playing a part. I simply didn't have anything more to say. He had broken my trust, broken my heart and shown no remorse. This ending, this exit, might, I reflected, actually be the least painful part of the process to date.

He glanced at the stairs. 'I'll email about the rest of my things.'

So, no situation retrieval then.

He turned, opened the door and left without another word.

I'm not sure how long I remained standing in the hallway, staring at the glossed white surface of the front door, but I moved only when my mobile rang. I took it from my pocket and looked at the screen. It was Simone.

'Hi, Sim.'

'Hi, Grace. Is it OK to talk?' Her tone was gentle and uncertain.

'Yes, he's gone.'

'Did you agree anything?'

'We agreed that it's over.'

There was a pause before she spoke again. 'Guy is home. Shall I come round? Or you could come here? Stay over, if you like.'

I shook my head.

'Grace? Are you still there?'

'Yes, sorry, I'm here,' I said. 'Thanks for the offer, but I'm really tired tonight. Maybe another night? Would that be OK?'

'Of course. Shall I call you tomorrow morning and we'll fix something up?'

'Great,' I said.

Another pause. 'Are you OK? How are you feeling?'

I smiled into the phone, as if the unseen facial expression would make what I was about to say sound more convincing. 'I just want to draw a line under it all, and I can do that now. So I actually feel OK.'

'That's good to hear,' she said.

I thought I heard a note of relief in her voice, and I was pleased for her sake that she seemed to believe me. There was no point, I decided, in telling her that I didn't think I'd ever be able to draw a line under Aiden. And as we said our goodbyes and my forced smile fell away, I knew there was certainly no point in telling her that what I actually felt was unloved.

Chapter 1

'Now, Grace.' Neil looked at me over the top of his tortoiseshell glasses before turning and smiling his thanks to the waitress. She glanced at him appreciatively and placed a large pot of tea, a jug of milk and two cups on the table in front of us. 'Let's talk about this latest book of yours.'

His whitened orthodontic smile was as bright as ever, but I detected tension behind it. He would usually have given me his initial comments by email, but on this occasion he had suggested 'a catch-up over a cup of tea', on the pretext that we hadn't seen each other, or spoken, for a couple of weeks. He clearly felt that today there were matters to be confronted in person. I couldn't claim to be surprised and was pretty sure that a clash, however gentle, was imminent.

'Yes, let's,' I said, whilst actually wanting to delay the conversation as long as possible. 'Shall I pour, or would you prefer to let it stand for a while?' I reached for the teapot.

'I'll wait for a moment,' he said, shifting slightly in his chair and adjusting his impeccably tailored tweed jacket, 'but you carry on. So, this book...' He extracted multiple pages of notes from his brown leather messenger bag and placed them to his right on the table.

'Nice bag,' I said.

'Gavin gave it to me,' he said, unable to resist smiling at the mention of his partner. 'It's an anniversary present.'

I smiled. 'Four years. That's flown. And what did you get him?'

'I'm taking him to Paris for New Year,' he said, now sounding a little strained. I knew he was torn between wanting to tell me about the planned trip and the pressing need to get down to business.

'Paris!' I gasped and clapped my hands. 'Oh Neil, he'll love that. How romantic.'

'Yes, it will be,' he said, before adding drily, 'Rather more so than your book.'

I cursed myself for so carelessly giving him a route into literary discussion. I poured my tea and added a splash of milk. 'You're sure you don't want me to pour yours?' I looked up at him. 'It's quite strong.'

His pale brown eyes narrowed. 'You're very talented, Grace.'

I put down the teapot and sighed, realising that further attempts at procrastination and distraction would be pointless.

'You *are*,' he insisted, running a thoughtful finger round the rim of his empty cup. 'You have talent, you have a number of books behind you and, if you want it, a long career ahead of you, but…' he peered at me again over the top of his glasses, now appearing fatherly despite, at thirty-five, being two years my junior, 'this draft isn't quite there yet.'

'That's no surprise. The first draft never is.'

He pursed his lips, as if to stifle a hasty response. 'Yes, but *this* draft,' he said slowly, 'is further away from where it needs to be than usual.'

'Really?' I maintained a neutral expression. 'How far away?'

He removed his glasses, placed them carefully on the table and leaned back in his chair. 'Well, to use an analogy, let's say that the book needs to be in Edinburgh.'

'OK.'

'Well, at the moment, I'd say it's in—'

'Glasgow?'

'Zimbabwe.'

'Oh.'

He smiled sadly. 'You know I can't take this to publishers.'

I nodded. 'Of course. I always expect you to suggest changes.'

'You're dodging the issue and that's not helpful,' he said, his tone a mixture of patience and candour.

I opened my mouth with the intention of issuing a denial, but thought better of it. Neil had been my literary agent, and good friend, through six years, four moderately successful novels and one very painful marital breakdown. He had been brutally honest, gently coaxing, stern and supportive as required, and it was thanks to him that I was able to maintain a comfortable lifestyle as an author, working from a two-bedroom period flat in north-west Bristol, rather than managing commercial property from a soulless open-plan office in Swindon, as I had been when he had first agreed to represent me. He was right: dodging the issue wasn't helpful and he didn't deserve it.

'I just wanted to try something different,' I said. 'To reveal a little more of me.'

'This is too different. You've revealed too much of you. Put your knickers back on.' There was no hint of a smile now, sad or otherwise. He picked up the teapot and poured himself a cup.

'It's not *completely* different,' I ventured. 'It's not like I'm writing sci-fi.'

He replaced his glasses and reached for his notes. 'Do you know the most frequently repeated word in this little lot?' he asked, not looking at me but instead leafing through the bundle, which I could see was a mixture of typed and wildly scrawled comments.

'*The?*' I suggested.

'*Cynical,*' he said, refusing to acknowledge the quip. '*Cynical* is the most frequently repeated word in my notes, along with *cynic* and *cynicism*. Your latest novel is a bitter little pill. And the worst of it is that the first seventy per cent gives no hint of the sting in the tail.'

'That's life for you,' I interjected brightly.

'Loyal readers of Elizabeth Canning novels – *your* readers, *your* novels –' he continued, without pause, 'will be sitting in bed, gulping red wine and munching their way through Ferrero Rocher...'

'Who's being cynical now?'

'... being happily reeled in by the handsome million-aire and the feisty, perfectly formed heroine...'

'And loving it.'

'... only to discover,' he slammed a hand down heavily on top of his notes, making me jump slightly, 'that the hero of the piece is sleeping with quite a few other women, including our heroine's best friend.'

'Ah, but,' I protested, holding up a finger, 'that all started before he met our heroine.'

'But he carries on sleeping with the best friend for quite a while, doesn't he?' said Neil, clearly exasperated. 'And what's more, the best friend doesn't try to end the relationship with him, even though she is already married *and* is fully aware that our heroine has fallen for Mr Not-So-Right.' He began to scan and remove sheets from the pile. 'Oh, but that's OK, actually, because it turns out that our heroine isn't averse to a revenge bonk or two – *with her best friend's husband.*' He smiled, whilst looking far from happy. 'It's neat, Grace; I'll give you that. And there's no denying the element of surprise. But,' he looked up at me at last, 'your readers don't want surprises.'

'Don't they?'

'Not nasty ones – no.'

'My couple still get together in the end.'

He shook his head. 'Only in a they-deserve-each-other kind of way. We don't like them. They're not nice people. They deceive their friends, they deceive each other, and *you*,' he jabbed a finger at me across the table, 'deceive your reader.'

'Actually,' I said defensively, 'I feel like this is the first time I'm *not* deceiving them. This is real life – apart from the butler and the mega-yacht, of course.'

'It's one version of real life – a highly *cynical* version – and it's not,' he picked up his notes and carefully replaced them in his bag, 'an Elizabeth Canning novel. And that is your established market. Your readers want a millionaire with emotions in need of resuscitation and a beautiful woman in need of a hero. They want romance and escapism. They do not want an unreformed calculating bastard getting together with an unrepentant scheming bitch. They would choke on their strawberry creams, retreat traumatised under their duvets and, far more importantly, they would never buy a book by Elizabeth Canning ever again.'

He paused, and I noticed two small red patches on his cheekbones – a sure sign of stress. He picked up his tea with both hands and took a sip. When he continued, his tone was calmer, but just as serious.

'I'll be your friend forever, Grace,' he said, replacing the cup carefully on its saucer and leaning towards me. 'But when it comes to business, I am in the business of selling books. If you've had enough of selling books—' he held up his hands, 'and maybe you have; maybe you want to go back to leases and landlords, or to sell your flat and attempt to eke out an existence on future royalties – that is fine. We can stay friends and end our business relationship. But,' he smiled, and his tone became more gentle, 'if you want to keep selling books, then you must listen to what I say and take my advice.'

I took a deep breath, looked down into my teacup and remained silent. He reached out and squeezed my left hand with his right.

'That book,' I said quietly, 'is me, Neil.'

'I don't actually believe that,' he said, releasing my hand. 'Or if it is you, then it's the current you. And the current you clearly needs to take a break.'

I rolled my eyes. 'From what? I sit at home all day, on my own, on my arse, making stuff up and writing it down.'

'And that's exactly what you need a break from,' he said. 'Including this latest effort, you've written five novels in six years. That's quite a schedule, and as much as I care about my twenty per cent, I care about you more. You need a sabbatical.'

'You mean you want me to go away and then come back and write a happy novel.'

'You are just so, *so* cynical, Grace,' he tutted, shaking his head. 'But yes. That's exactly what I mean. So get off your arse, go and do something different and, for God's sake, cheer up.'

Chapter 2

I closed the door of my flat behind me, dropped both my bag and coat on the floor and headed down the long, narrow hallway towards the kitchen. Once there, I made straight for the fridge, taking out the remains of the bottle of wine I had opened the previous evening and placing it on the work surface. I then checked the use-by date on a lonely tub of custard, sole occupant of the top shelf, before dismissing it as too dangerously antique to eat. The three cherry tomatoes that rolled forlornly around the crisper drawer as I slid it out were equally unappealing, and after a moment, I slammed the fridge shut, grabbed the bottle of wine and a glass and sat down at my eight-seater dining table, a legacy and reminder of my failed marriage. Then, feeling as lonely and appealing as the tub of custard, I wondered what on earth I was going to do next.

Neil was, I knew, quite right: the book was unsellable. And he was also right, I had decided during a two-hour post-meeting mooch around the shops, when he said that I needed to stop writing books, stop thinking about writing books and take a break. Because although my immediate urge was to switch on my laptop and try to produce something publishable, I had a horrible suspicion that whatever I came up with might turn out to be just as bitter, and every bit as cynical, as my last effort.

I sighed miserably and picked up the bottle of wine.

'I thought I heard the door go.'

I jumped and put a hand to my chest, replacing the bottle with a clatter on the table. 'Dear God, Rose.' I laughed with relief at the sight of my cleaner, smiling benevolently across at me; a pleasantly plump fairy godmother, with a feather duster substituted for a wand. 'I didn't know you were still here.' I checked my watch. 'And why *are* you still here? It's almost six.'

'Is it only six?' She placed the duster on the table and nodded, with a hint of disapproval, towards the bottle of wine. 'When I saw you with that, I thought it must be nearer to eight.'

I bit my lip guiltily. 'Tough day at the office,' I said.

She nodded and began to unbutton the blue overall she always wore for cleaning. 'Well, I'm all done here,' she said. 'I was running late because I had to take Archie to the vets this morning.'

'Oh no. Is he OK?'

'Yes he bloomin' well is, the stupid dog,' she tutted. 'But our bank balance isn't. One hundred and twenty quid to discover he's pulled a muscle. Pulled a muscle! The fat numpty. I don't know what my Tony will say. That dog has cost us more than either of the kids ever did, and neither of them left home until their mid-twenties.' She shook her head despairingly.

'Do you have pet insurance?' I asked hopefully.

'Doesn't cover the first eighty pounds,' she said. 'Still, I suppose that's better than nothing. Anyway,' she folded the overall and placed it in her green National Trust tote bag, 'I'll be off now. Oh, but I found an open box of Maltesers under your bed. They looked past their best, a bit green like, so I've thrown them out. Hope that's OK.'

I nodded. 'Thanks.'

She smiled. 'See you next week then, Gracie.'

'Yes... oh, unless,' I looked up at her, suddenly desperate not to be alone, 'you'd like a cup of tea? After your stressful day? I've got some biscuits somewhere.' I turned and glanced over my shoulder towards the spotty biscuit tin on the kitchen counter, which I knew full well was empty, having devoured the contents the previous evening while drooling over Harrison Ford in *Witness*.

I turned back towards Rose and she shook her head. 'You know I usually love nothing more than a cup of tea and a natter with you, but,' she glanced at the kitchen clock, 'it's so much later than usual.'

I nodded and forced myself to smile whilst actually, ridiculously, wanting to cry.

She looked at me, hesitated for a moment, then put down her bag. 'But it's so much later than usual,' she repeated, 'that what I'd really like is a glass of that wine you've got there.' She pointed at the bottle.

'Really?' I asked, delighted at the prospect of her company.

'Really,' she said gently, and smiled. 'So you go ahead and pour me one, and I'll just phone my Tony and tell him that I'm going to need a lift home.'

—

'Well it's hardly surprising, is it?' said Rose, as I topped up her glass half an hour later, having brought her up to date about my meeting with Neil. 'I mean, how are you supposed to write romantic stuff about perfect men and perfect relationships when…' She shook her head and picked up the glass.

'When my own man and my own relationship turned out to be so crap,' I said, completing the sentence for her and attempting a smile. 'She's had the baby, you know,' I added.

She nodded grimly. 'Thought she must have, but I didn't like to ask.'

'Three weeks ago. A little boy. They've named him Warren,' I said. 'Which is appropriate, seeing as they were at it like rabbits for so long.'

Neither of us smiled.

'Seen him lately?' she asked after a moment.

I sighed. 'I saw him at his dad's funeral. When was that?' I looked at the Cats in Sweaters calendar, a gift from Neil's partner Gavin, which was hanging next to the fridge, and frowned. 'I guess a couple of months ago now. But I've spoken to him on the phone since then. And he's coming round tomorrow evening, actually,' I added, still focused on the calendar and draining my glass. 'Apparently he has something he needs to ask me.'

'He's coming *here*? Why couldn't he just ask you over the phone?' Rose's lips thinned disapprovingly.

I shrugged, stood up and walked to take a second bottle of wine from the rack. 'Don't know. But he's got a meeting round the corner, so he's going to drop by after that.' I opened the bottle and poured myself a second glass.

Rose shook her head. 'Maybe it's none of my business, but we've been sharing our ups and downs every week for seven years now, Gracie, and…' she hesitated, her expression darkening, 'and I saw what he put you through.

You're within your rights to have nothing to do with him at all, and if you were my daughter, that's what I'd tell you.'

I returned to the table with the bottle of wine, sat back down and leaned forward to give her a hug. 'It is absolutely your business, Rose. You've been such a support to me.'

She patted my back. 'You've done well,' she said gently.

'With a lot of help from very good friends. I don't know what I would have done without you,' I added, releasing her. 'And I know that if Mum and Dad were still around, they'd feel exactly the same way about Aiden as you do. But the divorce went through two years ago and things work for me now. I don't hate him. I don't hate her. I accept the situation and I move forward,' I smiled, repeating out loud my daily internal mantra.

Rose nodded but looked justifiably unconvinced.

I picked up my wine glass and waved it blithely. 'It's all good,' I said, forcing another smile. 'Anyway, enough about me. How are you? Looking forward to *les grandes vacances*?'

She frowned. 'To what?'

'To your holiday. To seeing Violet,' I beamed. 'Two whole months of Spanish autumnal and winter sunshine with your sister. Imagine that.'

Rose smiled hesitantly.

I put down my glass. 'There's not a problem, is there?' I asked. 'It's all going ahead, isn't it?'

'Well, it's all booked,' she said. 'I was to fly out a week Monday and then return just in time to be home for Christmas with the boys. Tony was going to join me for the middle bit.'

'That's right,' I said, nodding as I sipped my wine. 'Your plans haven't changed, have they?'

'Eileen's put her back out,' she said, staring forlornly at her glass.

'Oh dear,' I said sympathetically. Eileen was, I knew, Rose's best friend. They had met over forty years earlier, when both working as housekeepers in a Bristol hotel, and had been friends ever since. They had gone on to start families at around the same time and had each returned to hotel work, before Eileen retired and Rose went into part-time domestic cleaning. They were very close, but although I was sorry to hear that Eileen was unwell, I was also unable to see what the state of her back had to do with Rose's holiday plans. 'I'm sorry,' I said. 'Poor Eileen. But her husband will look after her, won't he?'

Rose looked up at me. 'Yes, of course.'

'So why does that make a difference to you going to Spain?' I asked.

She heaved a sigh. 'Well, who's going to clean your flat while I'm away?'

'Oh, don't be silly,' I laughed, as I remembered that Eileen had agreed to fill in for Rose. 'I can manage without a cleaner.' I drank my wine and waved a hand. 'You mustn't worry about that.'

Her expression remained unchanged. 'I knew *you'd* be understanding,' she said. 'I said to Tony you'd be fine about it, and he said, "Course she will."' She managed a smile. 'But it's James and Emily, isn't it?'

'James and Emily?'

'My other clients,' she said mournfully. 'I do six hours for them, since Emily moved in with her allergies: three hours Monday and three hours Thursday – sometimes more on a Friday, if they've got people coming. And then on top of that I do quite a bit for Percy who's next door to them.' She sighed. 'And they go hand in hand.'

I nodded along to the details, which meant nothing to me. 'But they'll all cope – or get someone else in,' I said when she'd finished.

She sighed. 'That's the problem right there. They *will* get someone else in. And not someone like Eileen, who'd let me have the job back. Someone new, someone younger, with organic bleach and a degree. And they'll stay on. And then that's me out of a job, isn't it? I'm sixty-nine, with white hair and a bum bigger than… well, bigger than it should be. It'd be hard for me to find new clients around here these days. Impossible, I reckon.'

Her lower lip wobbled and I leapt in to reassure her. 'I'm sure you're wrong, Rose. You're so great and so reliable. James, Emily and Percy will have you back the moment you're home. They won't want to lose you.'

She shook her head. 'It's kind of you to say so. But busy people like James don't want to be hiring and firing cleaners every five minutes. It's a problem he can do without. He's got enough on his plate and I don't want to put him to that bother. And besides, it wouldn't be fair on the new cleaner. If I was away for two weeks it'd be different. But I'm off for two months, and a lot longer than that by the time I start back in the new year. That's too long to be without a cleaner when you're busy, or you've got allergies, or you're elderly, and quite long enough for a new one to get nicely settled.' She heaved another sigh. 'But never mind. Tony and I have discussed it. He said stuff the job, but I've already decided that if I can't find a friend to fill in, I'll just go to Spain for a couple of weeks.'

'But you've been looking forward to this since last year!' I exclaimed. 'You can't change your plans now.'

She shook her head. 'I don't earn a fortune, but it keeps us in little treats – and some bigger ones; like this visit to my sister, for instance. Plus I do really enjoy my job, Gracie. I'd miss it. And the people I clean for.' She picked up her drink and cleared her throat before taking a sip. 'It can't be helped. These things happen and I'll still get a holiday – just a shorter one.' I watched with admiration as her features transformed from deep unhappiness to philosophical acceptance. 'There are some people who don't get any holidays at all, aren't there?'

'I'll do it.' It seemed to me that the words were out before I had even thought about saying them.

Rose looked at me. 'You'll do what, love?'

'I'll...' I hesitated for just a moment before completing the sentence. 'I'll do your cleaning job while you're away.'

She looked around the kitchen. 'You mean here?'

'No, no,' I said, shaking my head. 'You need someone to cover James, Emily and Percy for a couple of months...'

'Longer than that.'

'That's right, and I need something to do – to get me out of the house and keep me occupied...'

She stopped nodding and simply stared at me.

'So,' I smiled, 'I'll do your job while you're away. And you can have it back when you get home.'

'But...' she began uncertainly, 'I'm not sure it's really your kind of thing.'

'Why not?'

'Well, you don't really... enjoy cleaning and tidying. I'm just thinking of the Maltesers,' she added.

I thought for a moment. 'That's cleaning my *own* house and not getting paid to do it. This'd be different. I'd be earning money, plus you know how nosy I am. It'd be perfect!' I said.

Rose looked pained. 'You're so lovely,' she began slowly, 'and it's a kind offer – *very* kind – but I wonder if people might be a bit uncomfortable having an author cleaning for them. Would it seem... quite right? I think they might expect me to find them a... well, an actual cleaner.'

I felt my face fall and realised that at some point in the past two minutes I had gone from trying to help Rose to being desperate to help myself. The idea of having a routine, a purpose and a physical occupation appealed hugely. It seemed like the beginnings of an answer – a tiny lifeline.

'But I do appreciate you trying to help me,' continued Rose. 'You know, I don't think there's another person in this world who would have offered to do that for me at the drop of a hat like that.'

I looked up at her. 'We wouldn't have to tell them that I'm an author, would we? And you could show me round and train me up before you go.' I tried not to sound pleading. 'Ooh, and when I was a student, I cleaned in a hospital one summer,' I added. 'So actually I already have genuine professional experience of cleaning to a high clinical standard. That's all they have to know, isn't it? The relevant stuff? I'd just keep shtum about my day job.'

Rose looked at me. I could tell she was weighing things up and, I hoped, weakening a little. I pressed home what I thought might be an advantage. 'I'll mop in a figure of eight, damp-dust, wear yellow gloves for the sinks, red gloves for the loos and always flush the brush. That's what we did in the hospital.'

She continued to stare at me for a moment or two and then smiled. 'Would you honestly be happy to do my little job?' she asked.

'I'd love nothing more, Rose,' I said.

'Well in that case,' she held her glass out towards me, 'thank you very much. You're a lifesaver.'

'And I feel just the same way about you,' I said, clinking my glass against hers. 'Just the same.'

Chapter 3

It was around 7 p.m. the next evening and I was checking my reflection in the circular hallway mirror when the sound of the buzzer made me jump. I tutted at myself, walked towards the front door and pressed the intercom.

'Hello?'

The response was broken by static and, I thought, slight anxiety. 'Hi, Grace... It's me... er... it's Aiden.'

'Come on up,' I said, attempting to keep my voice light. I pressed a button to unlock the main front door and then hurried back to the mirror for another quick check, adjusting the collar of the white shirt I had selected with great care in an attempt to look good whilst appearing not to have made any effort at all. I had adopted the same approach to my hair and make-up, and the carelessly put-together look had taken me some considerable time to achieve.

It was an effort I went to every time I saw my ex-husband, and not one of which I was proud. We had been divorced for two years and he had been sleeping with his current partner for at least three, and probably longer. So the fact that I still cared what he thought of my appearance wasn't something I really wanted to analyse. I sometimes tried to excuse it by telling myself it was a matter of self-respect to make an effort whatever the occasion, and whoever I was meeting. But deep down, I knew this wasn't the case. I often went make-up-free with friends, and Neil's partner, Gavin, had said that my unkempt hair at a recent literary lunch had resembled a roadkill hat. But for Aiden, for whatever reason, I always wanted to look my best. I was certain I didn't want him back, but perhaps I did want to stir in him a feeling of regret, no matter how small, regarding his infidelity. Something he had, so far, shown no sign of whatsoever.

I had just carefully repositioned a casually stray lock of hair when he knocked on the flat door. I closed my eyes, inhaled deeply, exhaled slowly and went to let him in.

'Hi, Grace,' he said, smiling broadly as I opened the door. 'Found you.'

'Quite an achievement,' I said drily, beckoning him in, 'what with living less than ten minutes' drive away and having my full address, including postcode.'

He continued to smile as he stepped into the long, narrow white hallway, looking around approvingly as he did so. 'This is great,' he said. 'I remember you saying it needed quite a lot of work. I love that you've gone for white against oak floorboards. Is the cornicing original?'

I looked at him for a moment, my face expressionless.

He raised his eyebrows questioningly and then, allowing them to fall, he sighed. 'Sorry,' he said. 'I guess we're past small talk.'

I nodded. 'Way, *way* past it. But come on through and you can admire the stripped floorboards in the lounge and the kitchen while I get you something to drink. Tea or coffee?'

He looked at me with a weariness and an unfamiliar vulnerability that left me teetering dangerously on the brink of feeling something approaching pity towards him. This was the first time in well over two years that we had been alone together in anything other than the neutral territory of a solicitor's office. All other encounters had taken place at weddings, funerals, parties and the odd, awkward dinner hosted by well-meaning friends, parading their determination not to take sides. At all such events Summer, Aiden's new and much younger partner, was present and, quite literally, hanging off his arm. As a three-some, we restricted ourselves to brief, polite, outwardly good-humoured exchanges about work, house renova-tions and holiday destinations; nothing personal was ever discussed. So to find myself now standing opposite him with no spectators or spectres present, and therefore no reason to stick to being polite or impersonal, was strangely unsettling.

'What would you like to drink?' I asked again, a note of impatience in my voice, as we made our way through the lounge and into the kitchen.

'Hang on, yes,' he said, and I turned in time to see him produce from behind his back a Sainsbury's bag, from which he then extracted a bottle of one of my favourite wines. 'I brought this for us,' he smiled. 'For you, really.'

I frowned at the bottle and then at him. 'What is this, Aiden?' I asked.

'It's Rioja Reserva,' he said, looking puzzled.

'I don't mean *that*,' I said, jabbing a finger at the wine. 'I mean this situation. I mean, why are you here? And without Summer. I'd almost forgotten what you look like without her clinging to you like a barnacle on the bottom of a boat. Did you have to have her scraped off?'

'Grace...' He put the bottle down on the kitchen counter.

I checked my watch. 'Just cut to the chase, Aiden.'

He sighed and took off his jacket, throwing it casually across the back of a kitchen chair, almost, I thought with resentment, as if he was in his own home. 'Look, how about I pour the wine and then we can talk? Unless you'd prefer a cup of tea?' he added.

I hesitated for a moment, before deciding that whatever he had to say, it would probably be easier to bear with a glass of wine in my hand. 'I need a drink,' I said, taking two glasses from the cupboard.

He opened the bottle of wine. 'Good, because so do I.'

I handed him the glasses and watched as he poured, taking in his appearance, which was distinctly less well-groomed than usual. His dark hair was in need of a trim, by his exacting standards, and there were distinct streaks of grey at the temples. At forty, he was, I admitted to myself, still undeniably attractive. But today he looked knackered, and there was no doubt that fatherhood was taking its toll.

I nodded towards the glasses, now full almost to the brim. 'You're not in charge of the night feeds, then?'

'Summer is at her sister's with Warren until Friday.' He handed me a glass. 'So I've got two nights off.'

'Lucky you.' I walked through to my temporarily immaculate lounge and sat down on the long red sofa, this evening adorned with the scatter cushions, which were more usually scattered everywhere but. I glanced briefly at the built-in cupboards either side of the fireplace, fearing that they might at any moment ping open and vomit forth the paper and clutter I had stuffed into them just minutes before Aiden's arrival.

I looked back at him as he, to my surprise, sat down just a few inches away from me on the sofa, rather than in one of the armchairs opposite. He sipped his wine, leaned back and looked around.

'The place does look great, Grace,' he said. 'And that's not insincere small talk.' He turned to me. 'You look great too.' He frowned and hesitated. 'And that's not small talk either. You always look great. I suppose I just don't ever feel I have a right to tell you that.'

'You don't,' I said flatly, frustratingly pleased with the compliment but far from enjoying a situation I didn't understand. I decided to force an explanation. 'So come on. What brings you here?' I demanded.

'God, yes.' He raised a hand and rubbed his forehead. 'Well, to get to the point, Summer wanted me to invite you to Warren's christening.' He blurted out the sentence as if it were an unpleasant taste in his mouth of which he couldn't wait to be rid.

I had just raised my glass to my lips to take a sip, but now lowered the wine untouched. 'I'm assuming that's a very poor joke,' I said quietly.

He closed his eyes. 'Christ, I wish it was, believe me.'

I stared at him. 'I take it you agree that the suggestion is an appallingly inappropriate and insensitive one?'

He nodded, his eyes still closed. 'I do.'

'And yet you still put it to me.'

He opened his eyes and turned to me. 'I put it to you so that she didn't pick up the phone and put it to you herself.' I opened my mouth, ready to explode, but he held up a

24

hand. 'I've put it to you. You've said no. That's it.' I glared at him. 'Please, Grace,' he said. 'Can that just be it?'

I lifted my glass a second time and drank as an alternative to speech, my head full of venomous thoughts and feelings towards the woman who had not only shagged my husband, but who now wanted me to dote upon the fruits of their labour.

'Thank you,' said Aiden after a moment, 'for not exploding.'

'Don't be too grateful,' I muttered. 'I might not be ranting, but I am thinking all colours of malevolent stuff.'

'I can imagine, and I don't blame you. It was a ridiculous idea. All I can say in her defence is that she meant well.' His shoulders sagged slightly. 'I think.'

We sat in silence while I continued to seethe and Aiden stared at the French doors which led out onto my small balcony overlooking the shared back garden. When he eventually spoke, it was clear that *his* thoughts, at least, had moved on from christenings.

'I walk past this place at least once a week, you know,' he said absently, his gaze still fixed on the view outside. 'I have a project in Butler Place. We're raising a roof.' I didn't reply, and he turned suddenly to look at me. 'Grace, I regret...' he began, before hesitating. I stared back at him, and realised that I was holding my breath. 'I regret that I can't knock on your door.'

I exhaled. 'Yes, well, I regret that you slept with your bimbo of a PA,' I snapped, before taking another gulp of wine. 'We all have our issues.'

'I'm sorry,' he said.

I looked at him. 'Care to be more specific?'

He heaved a sigh and lowered his eyes. 'I'm sorry for the betrayal. For the choices. For the mistakes… the huge mistakes.'

I curled my left hand into a fist, digging my nails hard into the palm in an attempt to distract myself from tears.

'I've been sorry for a long time.' He looked up and shifted his position so that he was now facing me. 'But I lacked the strength of character to tell you. I'm here this evening not to pass on the infantile suggestion that you should come to the christening – I could've done that over the phone. I'm here to apologise. And to tell you that I hugely regret the completely understandable loss of your friendship and to ask…' he hesitated, 'to ask if I can knock on your door sometimes for a coffee – or even just a five-minute conversation. I know I don't deserve that from you, but I'm asking just the same.' He turned his head again towards the French windows.

I continued to stare at him, the hurt welling up inside me. The hurt of, to use his word, betrayal. And not just any old betrayal. He had bedded a woman who could not have been more different from me: ten years younger, five inches shorter, two cup sizes bigger and named after a bloody season. She had been the youthful, blonde, fluttery-eyelashed perfection to my mid-thirties, unruly-mopped brunette muddle. This particular betrayal had been a rejection underlined in bold.

I opened my mouth to begin the withering speech I had been waiting for over two years to deliver. 'Well thank you for that *eventual* apology, Aiden, but…' I paused and looked at him as he continued to stare into space: exhausted, defeated, greying. And what had he just done? He had apologised. And what was I about to do? I was about to reward him for that with a good kicking. I looked down at my wine. I was, I decided, better than, and beyond, that.

'It's not something I want to discuss,' I finished. I watched as his head dropped slightly. 'And getting back to christenings, why don't you tell Summer,' I continued, 'that I said thank you for the offer, but that I'm not free that day. Or any other day.'

He lifted his head and looked at me.

'Just tell her that I said thanks – but no thanks,' I said quietly. 'Tell her anything, and in any way, that makes it easier for everyone.'

'Thank you,' he said, smiling sadly. 'Again.'

I shook my head. 'I'm still thinking all the malevolent stuff.'

'And I still don't blame you.'

There was a moment's uncertain silence before I said, 'My latest book is shit. Neil told me yesterday that it was marginally less uplifting than reading obituaries in an abattoir.'

He nodded slowly. 'Good to know he's still pulling the punches.'

'Nothing much changes.'

He smiled and pointed at my half-full wine glass. 'How about a top-up?' And then, without waiting for a reply, he took the glass from me, stood up and headed for the kitchen.

Chapter 4

I looked around the immaculate bedroom. A king-size double bed, dressed in varying shades of cream and olive green, took centre stage, whilst above it, three framed pen-and-ink drawings of skeletal leaves had been hung with to-the-millimetre precision on pristine off-white walls. Two cream-shaded lamps were equally perfectly positioned on mirrored cabinets either side of the bed. I marvelled at the latter, wondering how on earth they could be touched without leaving fingerprints. I could assume only that the occupants wore white cotton gloves at all times.

It was just over a week since I had offered to take on Rose's cleaning duties, and today, with just four days to go before her departure for Spain, she was showing me the house I would be responsible for while she was away. We had been in the high-ceilinged, five-bedroom, Georgian Clifton semi for half an hour now, with Rose talking me through the detailed three-page cleaning schedule she had prepared. And I was horrified to discover that each room we entered seemed more perfect than the one before. This was, I decided, the home of a clinically certifiable neat freak.

'But there's nothing to do here, Rose,' I protested. 'And aren't you due to clean tomorrow? I feel as if I'm making the place look untidy just by being here.'

She laughed. 'It does seem a bit like that, doesn't it?' she said. 'But with James and Emily it's all cleaning, no tidying.'

I nodded absently and picked up a framed black-and-white photograph from a glass table situated between two floor-to-ceiling windows. In it, a couple, arms linked and wearing winter walking gear, stood looking directly into the camera. She was grinning broadly, as if on the point of laughter, whilst he was giving only the merest hint of a smile. 'Is this them?' I turned the picture towards Rose.

'Yes,' she said, nodding. 'Aren't they a handsome pair?'

'Certainly are. What's the age gap?' I asked, focusing first on the gamine doe-eyed blonde and then for rather longer on the man with the penetrating gaze, who I guessed was several years older.

'Ooh, now Emily did tell me,' said Rose, looking fondly at the picture. 'She's twenty-six and I think she said there's over ten years between them. Interesting, isn't it? Not sure of the story behind that.'

I nodded and resisted rolling my eyes at yet another case of a man approaching forty opting for a twenty-something blonde in preference to a woman nearer his own age. 'And how long have they been living together?' I asked.

Rose placed a thoughtful finger to her lips. 'She moved in not long after he stopped seeing Kirstie.'

So hot on the heels of the last one then, I thought disapprovingly.

Rose's nose wrinkled. 'You know how I don't like to speak ill of anyone, Gracie, but I did not like Kirstie one little bit. And Percy next door certainly didn't either.' She nudged me with her elbow. 'She didn't live here but was here often enough, and whenever James wasn't around she behaved like it was her house and I was riff-raff. Nice as pie in front of him, though. But anyway, she's gone now. Suffice to say, I was very relieved when he gave her the old heave-ho.'

'But you like Emily?'

Her face brightened. 'Oh yes, she's a really sweet girl. She calls James her best friend, which I think is lovely. She's changed career because...' She paused and cleared her throat. 'Anyway, now she's working part-time and studying too. She's so gentle. And lovely to chat to – just like you. Couldn't be nicer.'

Compliment aside, I felt myself disappointed with this response. 'And how long has she been living here?' I asked again, reluctant to let the topic slide.

'Full-time since towards the end of last year,' smiled Rose. 'That's when I upped my hours because of her allergies. Let me think...' She paused and counted on her fingers. 'Ooh, she's been here ten or eleven months now. Nearly a year.' She sighed and looked again at the picture, this time a little sadly. 'I shall really miss seeing her every week. She's moving out in January.'

I looked up sharply. 'So she's not a permanent fixture, then?'

She put a hand to her mouth. 'Ooh, now James told me that in confidence. So don't mention it, will you, Grace? He hasn't talked to her about it yet.'

I frowned. 'She doesn't know?'

Rose shook her head. 'I don't think he wants her worrying about it before she has to. And whatever happens, I know he'd like her here for a second Christmas. He really enjoyed last year. And their Easter together was lovely too,' she added.

She took the picture from me, gave it a rub with the sleeve of her cardigan and replaced it on the table.

'But…' I began, before stopping short, feeling slightly at a loss regarding Rose's acceptance of her client's apparent tendency to date – and give women 'the old heave-ho' – on such a cold, calculating, festivity-related basis. I wondered why he didn't just dump Emily the day after Halloween and get in some fresh meat for Advent. Rose looked up at me questioningly and I decided against an openly critical approach. 'Is James nice?' I asked.

'Oh yes. No side to him. Very straightforward. Just like my Tony,' she said, pushing up her sleeve and checking her watch. 'Now, as time is pressing, shall we pop into one of the bathrooms? I don't think we need to look at all the bedrooms. You've seen the two largest. They're the important ones, and I'd really like to go over mould prevention with you.'

Chapter 5

'Sorry? You're doing what?' Neil frowned at me as I accepted my second cosmopolitan from him with a grateful nod. He had called three hours earlier to tell me that he and Gavin were going out for cocktails on a whim and would I like to come. It was an invitation he regularly extended, and one I often declined, due to sheer laziness and a Saturday-night preference for my PJs and Netflix. But this evening he had been reluctant to take no for an answer. I knew he wanted to check up on me after our difficult meeting the week before, and in the end, I accepted the invitation. And as I smiled up at him and picked up my cocktail, I was pleased that I had. He and Gavin were good company individually, and fabulous company as a pair; Gavin's salt-of-the-earth south London humour and sense of fun perfectly balancing Neil's rather more risk-analysis approach to life.

'I'm cleaning,' I repeated. 'Or I will be. I've just been telling Gavin about it. From Monday, I'm filling in for Rose while she's on holiday. I'm doing ten weeks for her.'

'You're filling in for ten weeks?' queried Neil. 'That's not a holiday. That's a—'

'Oh, *shhhh*,' said Gavin, frowning and flapping a hand as Neil sat back down next to me. 'Let her speak.' He looked at me, his bright blue eyes wide with anticipation, a broad grin stretching across his slightly rounded, lightly bearded face. 'Carry on, Grace.'

I smiled. 'It's definitely two mornings, but probably more. I went to have a look round the other day. It makes a show home look like a squat.'

'But I don't really—' began Neil, before being silenced by a further interruption from Gavin.

'Wait till she tells you about the OCD bastard.' He grinned excitedly, turning and placing his hand on my arm. 'Tell him about the OCD bastard, Grace.'

I laughed, but Neil looked less amused. 'Have you really thought this through?' he asked, picking up his cocktail and looking at me askance.

'Will you just *stop* being such a misery?' Gavin slapped him lightly on the back of his hand. 'It's all *soooo* interesting.' He looked at me, his eyes widening yet further into almost perfect circles. 'Have you checked for CCTV yet?'

I nodded. 'That was the very first thing I asked Rose about. There are no cameras. Just a burglar alarm.'

'Better and better,' said Gavin, toasting me with his glass. 'Snooper's paradise.'

I raised and clinked my glass against his. 'I know!'

'You two are unbelievable,' said Neil, putting down his drink, placing his elbows on the table and resting his head in his hands. 'And in the interests of plausible deniability, I don't want to hear anything more about snooping. But do you know how much trouble you could get into, Grace? I can smell the litigation from here.'

'You worry too much,' said Gavin. 'She's just doing a spot of cleaning, for God's sake. You're going to have an ulcer by the time you're forty if you carry on like this.'

'And can I just remind you that this whole thing was your idea?' I added.

Neil looked up and frowned. 'Sorry, but at no point did I tell you to become a cleaner.'

'You said to get off my arse and try something new.'

'When I said that, I was thinking literary lectures, Open University courses, Mediterranean retreats. I was not thinking mopping floors.'

Gavin turned to him, his face now serious. 'I hope you're not being a snob about this. Because you'll remember that Auntie Tina cleans the salon for me. Which reminds me,' he said, returning his attention to me, 'when are we going to see you to sort this out?' He reached out and began to play with my shoulder-length and extremely curly hair. 'The last time you had a cut was over three months ago. You look like bloody Bellatrix Lestrange.'

I pushed his hand away. 'Everyone says she's very sexy, actually.'

'Do they? OK, you don't look like her then,' he said. 'But come in for a cut, for God's sake.'

Neil, meanwhile, was looking hurt. 'I'm hugely respectful of cleaning as an occupation, and you know how highly I think of Tina. It's just, well…' he hesitated, looking at me and then back at Gavin, 'well, you've seen her flat,' he said, lowering his voice.

Gavin nodded. 'Fair point, well made. And that crossed my mind too, but…'

'Er, excuse me, but I'm not deaf,' I began indignantly, keen on defending the state of my home. Gavin continued without pause, apparently oblivious to my interruption.

34

'... it'll keep her busy and it's all so interesting.' He rubbed Neil's back soothingly. 'The house is owned by a handsome evil devil who's planning on binning his girlfriend as soon as the poor love's helped him take down the Christmas tree.'

Neil smiled. 'It does sound quite an intriguing situation. But not,' he added, his face falling as he turned towards me, 'a very uplifting one. And we need uplift. Remember?'

I stared at my cocktail and sighed. 'I remember.'

'Uplift isn't a problem for sexy Bellatrix, though, is it?' said Gavin, placing an arm around my shoulders and squeezing. 'I mean, just look at those boobs.' His eyes lowered to my chest, which was that evening encased in a black polo-neck sweater. 'They look great. New bra?'

'Same old bra,' I said, before adding in a rush, 'But Aiden has apologised. Does that count as uplift?' It was a fact I had been desperate to share since the moment I arrived, but I had delayed the telling, uncertain how Neil in particular would react.

I noticed Gavin flick a look at his partner before smiling at me and kissing my cheek. 'That's definite uplift in my book,' he said.

Neil, however, wanted more information before passing judgement. 'Apologised for what, exactly?' he asked.

I looked at him. 'For his behaviour. For her. For the whole shebang.'

'Wow!' exclaimed Gavin.

Neil appeared equally surprised, but more sceptically so. 'What brought that on?'

I shrugged. 'I really don't know. He seems sort of...' I hesitated, 'sort of lost. He wants us to be friends again. He's working a stone's throw from my flat and has asked if he can pop in for coffee sometimes.'

'And did you agree to that?' asked Neil.

'I ignored the request,' I said.

Neil frowned. 'Why didn't you just say no?'

I rolled my eyes at him and Gavin gave my shoulders another squeeze. 'I think it's fab that he's apologised. You should feel very good about that. But Neil's right to be a bit nervy about it all.'

I attempted a careless laugh. 'I'm not planning on falling for him, you know.'

'Course you're not,' said Gavin. 'You're way too smart to want him back,' he smiled, adopting the tone my father had used when attempting a softly-softly approach to my teenage party-going. 'He's a self-centred, lying scumbag and you know it.'

'I do,' I said. 'But—'

Neil shook his head. 'I think I'd prefer you not to finish that sentence.'

I looked at him and sighed. 'I'm lonely, Neil.'

'Oh don't say that,' wailed Gavin. 'We all know it's complete bollocks, but you're still breaking my heart.'

Neil leaned back in his chair and studied me for a moment. 'You don't really mean that, do you?' he asked.

'I'm not saying I haven't got friends. I've got lots of lovely friends. You two especially,' I said, looking at him and then turning to Gavin and patting his knee. 'I'm just lonely like you two would be lonely without each other.'

Gavin bit his lip and Neil nodded. 'I get that,' he said quietly. 'But I don't think Aiden is the answer.'

36

Gavin nudged me. 'Much as I hate to admit it, he's right again,' he murmured.

'I know he is,' I said, smiling and picking up my cosmopolitan. 'But Aiden's OK, familiar company and currently a hell of a lot needier than I am. And right now, that's a huge and much-needed boost to my ego.'

There was a pause before Gavin spoke. 'Well, so long as you go careful, I think it'll be fine.' He looked at Neil. 'Won't it?' he asked pointedly.

Neil smiled. 'Of course,' he said after a moment, picking up his drink and toasting me with it. 'This is Grace we're talking about. What could possibly go wrong?'

Chapter 6

I looked again at the various aprons hanging on the wall of John Lewis's homeware department, feeling hugely drawn to one patterned with oversized poppies and another covered in waddling geese. But neither seemed to scream *professional*, and I suspected I should opt for the plain bottle-green tabard, of the kind the dinner ladies at school used to wear when shovelling chips onto my plate. I sighed resignedly, unhooked the tabard and placed it in my basket, alongside the six pairs of rubber gloves, two bottles of granite cleaner and single large tub of Hob Brite I had already picked up.

There were now less than twenty-four hours to go before I returned to number 3 Bennett Park, home of James Brooke, this time not merely to view but to clean. Rose had already handed over her blue carry-crate of cleaning products and cloths, with her preferred granite and hob cleaners being the only products currently running low. She had also offered me overalls and gloves from the Costco stockpile she kept at home, but I had refused, telling her it was about time I invested in a new apron for use at home, as my current one – black, emblazoned with the words *Back off, I've got a knife* – was now almost a decade old and had been a gift from Aiden; two excellent reasons for replacement.

Rose's offer of workwear had been made that morning over the phone, along with a last-minute opportunity to opt out of our arrangement if I wanted to. I suspected the latter was the real reason for her call, and had reassured her that I was looking forward to having a fixed occupation and a routine over the coming months. She was leaving for Spain the next morning and I was determined that she should head off carefree, untroubled by doubts about either my happiness or, most importantly, the security of her job. I didn't therefore share with her the fact that actually I was feeling rather nervous about the weeks ahead; an anxiety not helped by Neil's misgivings, expressed over cocktails the night before. The vacuuming, dusting and polishing didn't bother me at all, but I was a little nervous about possible encounters, however brief, with my new employers. I had been assured by Rose that this was unlikely in the case of James, who was primarily office-based. But I was, she had told me, almost certain to bump into Emily.

She had presented this to me as a positive, and under any other circumstances I would have been delighted to meet and chat to new people – especially ones of whom Rose spoke so warmly. But in the current situation, I was very wary of dropping her in it, even slightly. She took her responsibility to her clients very seriously, and I knew she would hate anyone to think that she had made a substandard, hasty arrangement to meet their cleaning needs while she was away. She had told them only that I was a reliable, well-trusted friend with professional cleaning experience, and such was their trust in her, they had asked nothing more. And as Neil had emphasised and re-emphasised to me the previous evening, it wasn't in anyone's interest for me to tell them any more than that for the moment. He reminded me of my tendency to talk rubbish under pressure and had therefore advised a policy of minimal information, at least initially, should any conversational exchange extend beyond a brief hello.

Thankfully, my drive to the Mall and unhurried Sunday-morning shop for cleaning accessories had, for the past hour or so, proved a calming distraction from the worries so effectively thrown into relief by Neil. However, as I continued to linger over the aprons, my temporary sense of calm was disturbed by a quiet 'hi' close to my ear and an unexpected hand on my shoulder.

I jumped and turned quickly to discover Aiden standing behind me, smiling broadly. 'Sorry to startle you,' he laughed. 'Hey, but now I know why your home is so immaculate these days,' he added, pointing at the contents of my basket.

'What?' I frowned, flustered by his sudden appearance, then looked down at the basket and understood. 'Oh, this? This is…' I paused and looked up at him. 'I just needed a few bits and bobs.'

'Well that little lot should keep you going for a while,' he smiled.

'Yes.' I put a hand to my hair, suddenly wishing I had checked my reflection more recently than four hours ago, as I had blearily cleaned my teeth while regretting letting Gavin talk me into a fourth cocktail. 'Well,' I said, attempting to regain my composure and trying not to care, 'what brings you to John Lewis at this time on a Sunday? Is Summer…' I began before correcting myself. 'Is your family with you?'

'Summer and Warren are at home.' His smile flickered and his tone was unmistakably clipped. 'I did the night feeds and she had the morning off. Now it's my turn.'

'Right,' I said, slightly at a loss as to how to respond to a statement which, for reasons I chose not to analyse, had lifted my mood considerably.

'Yes, so,' he said, his smile recovering, 'where else would a man with a free afternoon go other than the Mall?'

'Almost anywhere else, I would have thought,' I said.

He sighed, and there was an awkward pause before we both said 'Anyway' at exactly the same moment.

'You go first,' said Aiden.

'I was just going to say enjoy your afternoon and that I'd better be getting on.'

He nodded. 'I was going to say something along those lines myself. Hope to see you soon for that coffee.'

I smiled noncommittally and, offering him a small wave with my free hand, turned and walked over to the tills to pay for my domestic haul.

A few minutes later, I had made my purchases and was just exiting the store for the car park when I felt a hand on my shoulder a second time. This time, I didn't jump and realised that I had actually been waiting for it – expecting it.

I turned to face Aiden.

'I wasn't entirely truthful earlier,' he said.

'You weren't?'

He shook his head. 'I wasn't going to wish you a nice afternoon.'

I looked up at him and waited.

'I was going to ask whether you'd eaten,' he said. 'And whether you fancied heading back into town for a late lunch. My treat.'

I continued to look at him, remembering Neil's repeated instructions to treat this man with extreme caution. 'I have to—'

'Or just a coffee, if you've already eaten,' he interrupted, his eyes now betraying something close to desperation.

I heaved a sigh and decided to take pity on him, or on myself, I wasn't quite sure which. 'I haven't eaten,' I said, and watched him relax. 'But let's go Dutch.'

–

It was almost 5 p.m., and we had finished our very late lunch at The Cow Shed an hour or so earlier, when Aiden suddenly raised a hand, beckoned our waiter over and asked him for a second bottle of wine.

'One moment,' I said, reaching out and touching the waiter's arm as he nodded at Aiden. 'Can you just give us a minute to discuss a choice?'

'Of course. I'll come back in a moment,' he said and walked away.

'You'd like something different?' asked Aiden.

I looked at him and shook my head. At several points during the course of the afternoon it had crossed my mind to ask him what time he was supposed to be home. It had not escaped my notice that he had switched his phone to silent, following a string of texts received in quick succession at around four o'clock. And I didn't have to be Sherlock Holmes to have a pretty shrewd idea as to their author and content. Aiden had sent only one text in response, which could not have been more than a single, short sentence.

I had noticed all this but said nothing. It was not my job, I had told myself, to remind him of his fatherly duties, or to interfere in any way in his new relationship. Besides, a long lunch in The Cow Shed, even with Aiden, was a much better way to spend Sunday afternoon than doing my laundry, with only my fears about starting a new job the next day for company.

We had, by mutual undeclared consent, avoided all risky topics associated with our recent past, and had instead reminisced about more distant, less contentious times and updated each other regarding our careers, Aiden confiding the difficulties of finding a new work–life balance and me confirming that I was taking a little break from writing, but not sharing any details of my arrangement with Rose. It had been a surprisingly pleasant afternoon, but now my conscience, or something similar, kicked in.

'What time are you expected back?' I asked.

He looked at me across the table and ran a hand through his hair. Then, taking out his phone, he tapped and swiped the screen, scrolling, it seemed, through a considerable list of missed messages. He appeared to type something and then returned the phone to the pocket of his jeans.

'I haven't had an afternoon this enjoyable for months,' he said quietly, now gazing at the table. 'Maybe not for years.'

I said nothing and, after a moment, he looked up at me and smiled sadly. 'I just don't want it to end. Simple as that.'

'Yes, the food was great,' I said, keeping the compliment determinedly impersonal.

We remained in silence, looking at each other across the table, until interrupted by the return of the waiter.

'Have you made your choice?' He smiled down at us questioningly.

'Well, I'd like another bottle of the red,' Aiden said, his expression serious. 'But how about you, Grace? Do you want something different?'

I looked at him for a moment longer, weighing up the situation. My conscience was clear, I told myself. I hadn't invited him out for lunch, or encouraged him to stay, and I had given him every opportunity to leave. In fact, I had done more than that: I had actually prompted him to go home. However, he clearly didn't want to, and why should I feel responsible for or bad about that? He was, after all, a grown-up and his life choices had been nothing to do with me for a very long time now. As for myself, well, I had absolutely nothing and absolutely no one to hurry home for.

'I'm fine with the red,' I shrugged, draining my glass and refusing to acknowledge any possible shallowness or selfishness in my decision.

'Great,' said Aiden.

'Perfect,' said the waiter, and he went to fetch the wine.

Chapter 7

I had set my alarm for 8:15 the next morning, with the intention of showering, eating a leisurely breakfast, going through Rose's schedule, packing the car and being at Bennett Park in good time for the agreed 9:30 start.

But as I yawned, stretched and finally squinted at the small white readout on my alarm clock, I realised to my horror that I must have unconsciously hit the snooze button – and more than once; more than three times, in fact, because it was now 8:55.

I sat up quickly, before immediately regretting the move, putting a hand to my forehead and flopping back down on the pillow. Despite having had over eight hours' sleep, I felt terrible. Never great with alcohol at the best of times, I was definitely paying the price for the second bottle of wine Aiden and I had polished off at The Cow Shed.

I sat up again, this time more slowly, pulled back the covers and swung my legs round so that I was now sitting on the edge of the bed. I felt that if I could just make it to the bathroom and, more specifically, to the Nurofen in the corner cupboard, I would be on the road to recovery. I forced myself to my feet and, walking like an octogenarian in need of a Zimmer frame, made my way into the bathroom.

Thirty minutes later, I was carefully reversing my Mini into a parking bay outside the home of James Brooke, feeling slightly out of body but congratulating myself for somehow being on time. I had even managed to squeeze in a shower and a light breakfast of a banana and a Tunnock's wafer, consumed as I drove.

I turned off the engine and looked down, adjusting my pristine green tabard, before taking a moment to check my reflection in the rear-view mirror, in the forlorn hope that I might look better than I felt. When I found I didn't, and instead resembled a damp corpse, I sighed resignedly and exited the car.

It took me another few minutes to transport my cleaning caddy, plus bucket, microfibre mop, grout brush and extendable duster from the car, down the path and up the five broad, shallow steps to the front door. But finally, at 9:29 precisely, after ringing the bell to make sure no one was at home, I turned my key in the deadlock, opened the front door and, pushing the tools of my new trade across the threshold with my foot, shuffled inside.

I had closed the door behind me and picked up my bucket before the significance of the slow but persistent beeping dawned on me and I remembered that there was a burglar alarm to be deactivated. A brief wave of panic swept over me before I recalled Rose's schedule, which had the alarm code handily emboldened and highlighted on the very first page.

I grabbed the schedule from the caddy, homed in on the code and entered the numbers 2125 onto the keypad situated on the wall to the left of the front door. The beeping immediately ceased and my shoulders sagged in relief at the disaster averted.

It was approximately one hundredth of a second later that the alarm went off, emitting a wail which seemed to me, in my fragile state, to exceed the boundaries of what I had previously considered sound. My head felt as if it was a basketball being repeatedly slam-dunked, and I screwed shut my eyes and stuck my fingers in my ears in an instinctive attempt to prevent my brain, which I was certain was being liquidised, from leaking out. After a few seconds of complete immobility, I opened my eyes and shouted at myself inaudibly to get a grip. I picked up Rose's schedule from where it now lay at my feet and attempted to focus on the alarm instructions once again.

To deactivate the alarm…

Yes.

Press the unlock symbol…

Shit – hadn't done that.

Enter 2125…

Yes.

… and then press the unlock symbol a second time.

Hadn't done that either.

To turn off the alarm and reset the code…

Yes! My eyes bulged with concentration as I followed the instructions, and finally, after two attempts, beautiful, blissful, luxurious silence was restored – save for what I hoped was a temporary ringing in my ears.

I dropped the schedule, fell to my knees, curled myself into a tight traumatised ball and remained in that position for a minute or two whilst I waited for normal brain and body function to return. Then, when I felt as good as I thought I was ever going to get, I uncurled, stood up, picked up my things and headed into the kitchen.

By the time I had finished cleaning the top-floor wet room fifty minutes later, I was feeling much better. As a result of the alarm debacle, I was now concentrating fully on Rose's instructions and following them to the absolute letter, including using a toothbrush around the taps and donning the elasticated plastic shoe covers she had provided so that I didn't have to mop floors in my socks or risk leaving footprints. I was making good progress and, having spent the first half-hour after my hearing returned singing along to Adele's latest album, I now had Radio 4 on my iPhone and, with my earphones in, could hear every word of *Woman's Hour*, even when vacuuming.

All things considered, the morning was now progressing reasonably well and, alarm issues aside, the only minor problem I had encountered was my hair, which, in my haste to leave home, I had failed to pin up or tie back. Whilst this was fine for hoovering and mopping, it proved enormously irritating whenever I bent over to clean sinks and surfaces. But after failing to find string or an elastic band in the kitchen, I had struck on the idea of using one of Rose's elasticated shoe covers as a mob cap. This worked perfectly and as I moved on from the wet room to the study next door, and bent down to plug in the Dyson without hindrance from my hair, I congratulated myself on the innovation.

I straightened up and looked around the study, deciding as I hit the one-hour mark to sit down for a moment before affixing the duster-brush attachment identified in Rose's instructions and pressing on. I removed Jenni Murray from my ears and flopped down onto the grey wheeled office chair, which, I thought, like everything else in this house, appeared untouched, unused and unloved. My eyes roamed across the sparse gunmetal-grey walls and along the high-shine white shelving units and expansive desk – bare, save for a Mac, a printer and a tall white lamp. Nothing in the room seemed to offer up any clue as to Mr Brooke's personality or occupation, and I now regretted not asking Rose for more details. But as I continued to scan the room, slowly revolving in the office chair as I did so, my interest was caught and piqued by three grey box files, which stood on one of the lower shelves on the back wall. I definitely had my new employer down as a paperless-office kind of guy, but as each file was dated, I thought them unlikely to be for aesthetic purposes only. Intrigued, I stood up from my chair, walked across the study, reached out a hand and took hold of one of the files.

'Hello.'

At the sound of the voice, I snatched back my hand as if burned by the surface of the file and whirled around. In the doorway stood James Brooke. I recognised him immediately from the photograph I had seen the week before, although today he was dressed rather differently. A blue shirt and dark trousers replaced the warm walking gear and, of course, he now stood an undeniably intimidating four or five inches taller than me, rather than being an easily dismissible three-inch image in my hand. But that aside, he looked exactly the same: his stance assured, his stare unblinkingly penetrating and his expression one of half-hearted compliance with a social requirement to smile.

'Hello,' he repeated, taking a moment to pointedly transfer his focus from me to the grey box file and then back again. 'I'm James.'

I nodded and smiled far too enthusiastically, experiencing a continuing panic at being caught with my hand on the file, and wondering whether I had, at ten-thirty a.m. on day one, already let Rose down to an irretrievable degree. I found myself mentally scrabbling for an explanation as to why I might have been about to remove the file from the shelf. *To dust it?* But where was my duster? *To reposition it?* Why? *To examine its contents in order to satisfy outrageously inappropriate curiosity?* Suppressing an urge to whimper, I suddenly recalled Neil's advice to restrict my conversation to minimal factual information.

'I'm a cleaner,' I said through clenched teeth, my facial muscles seemingly locked in a maniacal grin.

James Brooke's head tilted slightly to the right and he studied me for a moment before replying. 'Yes, I know,' he said, his cold blue eyes lowering to my bag-clad feet before moving slowly upwards and coming to rest once again on my face.

I felt myself redden and tried to relax my mouth into a smile less reminiscent of the Joker. 'My tabard is from John Lewis,' I offered after a moment, finding the silence unbearable but determined not to stray from a cleaning theme. 'It's new.'

He pointed at the shoe cover on my head. 'And is that...' he hesitated, '*hat* from John Lewis too?'

'It's a shoe cover,' I said, sticking to indisputable, closed-ended facts.

'Ah yes, I can see it's a shoe cover now,' he said, looking again at my feet. 'I'm afraid I didn't recognise it…' another pause, 'out of context.'

He said nothing more and I began to feel sick, due to a combination of anxiety, embarrassment and, I suspected, the lessening effects of the Nurofen. 'Well,' I said, attempting a casual air, 'best be cracking on.' I looked at the Dyson and then moved towards it, taking three highly self-conscious, over-long steps to reach it, in the manner of a hurdler badly misjudging her stride.

My employer glanced again at the box files. 'I'm home because the burglar alarm went off,' he said. 'My neighbour called me. Apparently she tried knocking and ringing the bell but there was no answer. And you'd put the chain on the door, so she couldn't get in with her key. I had to use the kitchen door.' He looked at me and raised an eyebrow questioningly, the token effort smile now gone.

My face fell into open-mouthed horror. 'Oh my goodness, I'm so sorry,' I gasped. 'I was deaf and then,' I held up my earphones, 'Adele. I'm so sorry,' I repeated.

His expression remained unchanged. 'Well, now that I'm here,' he said, 'I'm going to stay and work from home for the morning.'

'Oh, right.' I looked at the Dyson. 'Shall I hoover in here later then?'

He shook his head, walked over to the chair and sat down in front of the Mac. 'Don't worry,' he said. 'Just forget about the study today. And in the future,' he added.

'Oh,' I said, my heart sinking for both myself and Rose. He clearly had me pegged, quite rightly, as a snooper – possibly worse.

'Emily doesn't work in here; she prefers the kitchen table,' he continued, looking up at me. 'So the dust isn't so much of an issue. And I know how to use a vacuum cleaner when I have to.'

'I see. Well in that case I'll just, er…' I bent down and unplugged the Dyson, 'move on to the bedrooms.'

'OK, Grace.'

I looked up at him, for some reason surprised by his use of my name.

He had been studying something onscreen, but now turned towards me. 'Everything all right?'

I nodded and began to exit with the Dyson. 'Yes, James,' I said, abandoning Neil's factual policy and instead lying through my teeth. 'Everything's great.'

Chapter 8

Still wearing my tabard, I flopped down in my favourite armchair and took out my phone. I had felt it buzz multiple times in the back pocket of my jeans during the course of the morning, but had chosen to ignore it. This was at first because I was anxious to press on and guessed it was probably Gavin, pestering me for snooping updates; and then later, when I would, under different circumstances, have enjoyed a text natter with him, I ignored it because of my severely flattened mood and the lingering presence of James Brooke.

A new fact I had discovered about Mr Brooke, to add to my list of previously discovered facts (namely that he was unsmiling and had a ruthlessly cold-hearted attitude towards relationships), was that he had the ability to move about his home with all the silence, stealth and charm of a Dementor. From the moment I was aware that he was in the house, I had consigned my earphones to the pocket of my tabard and worked on in silence. But this didn't prevent me from being taken by surprise three more times by his sudden appearance: first of all in his bedroom, when he came in to retrieve his jacket from the bed – no doubt to prevent me from stealing his wallet – and then twice in the kitchen, the second of those occasions being just as I was preparing to leave.

During each encounter, he had seemed to have difficulty tearing his gaze from the shoe cover on my head, which, in my calmed state, I knew he found ridiculous but which I determinedly left in place for practical reasons and in the strange passive-aggressive hope that it somehow irritated him. Under different circumstances, I would have given him a full light-hearted explanation as to how I came to be wearing it. But confronted with his icy personality, and wary of giving myself any further opportunity to put a foot wrong, I restricted my conversation to simple, straightforward responses to any and all enquiries. I didn't attempt to initiate conversation, or to deviate from domestic issues, with the consequence, no doubt, that he now considered me 'special', with possible tendencies towards obsessiveness and criminality.

Whilst this didn't at all bother me in terms of ego, and I actually took some satisfaction in the idea of not being liked by a man of whom I so disapproved, I did worry about how his opinion of me might reflect on Rose. I just hoped that the fact that I had worked my fingers to the bone that morning polishing, mopping and sweeping his house to clinically clean standards meant he felt that on a professional, if not personal, level she hadn't been completely hopeless in her choice of me as her replacement.

I sighed and looked down at my phone. I had seven new messages: five, as I had suspected, from Gavin (all variations on the *What have you broken/found out?* theme), one from Aiden and a much longer text from Rose, which I decided to save until last.

Aiden's text turned out to be a jovial apology for taking up so much of my time the day before and an enquiry as to whether I was available to meet for lunch later in the week. I hesitated for just a moment before deleting his text. I hadn't had a moment to think about him so far today and I didn't want to think about him now. I had enjoyed our long lunch, but at the same time I recognised that that might not actually be a good thing. Even as a friend, Aiden came with more strings attached than a shopful of marionettes. And I didn't need Neil sitting next to me and frowning to know that backing off was the sensible thing to do.

I sighed for a second time, opened Rose's text and read.

> Dear Gracie, I've arrived safe and sound in Spain and the sun is shining. It's a very lovely 24 degrees here, which is perfect for me. I'm by the pool and Violet has just gone inside to get us some drinks. I'll be tipsy by teatime. I was just wondering how you got on this morning with the cleaning. Hope you didn't work too hard and I hope I didn't forget to tell you anything. Did you meet Emily? She's usually at college on a Monday but every now and then something's cancelled and she has a cup of tea with me on my break. If not, you might see her on Thursday. If you need anything it's best to email me – Vi will show me how to pick them up on her computer. My email is rosefortune1947@hotmail.com. Can you let me know yours? Lots of love to you and thank you for helping me out again. I've told Vi all about you and she thinks you're marvellous too. Rose xx

I alternately smiled, bit my lip and felt tearful at Rose's text, hoping yet again that I hadn't let her down too badly this morning and resolving for her sake to be as smiley and look as normal as possible next time I encountered either James or his girlfriend. I now felt that Rose was probably justified in her conviction that should he find another cleaner to replace me, her job would be lost forever, and I was desperate for that not to happen. I stared at the phone for a moment before tapping out my reply.

> Hi Rose, you're already sounding so relaxed and that's wonderful. Things went very smoothly this morning and I really enjoyed myself, listening to music while I worked. I think this is an arrangement which will suit us both very well. Enjoy your well-earned break with Violet and don't go falling in the pool! Much love, G xx And my email address is gbwaterhouse@blueyonder.co.uk x

I hesitated before pressing send, wondering if I should tell her that I had met James. But deciding that that might prompt questions and concerns as to why he was at home, I sent the text as it was. Then I leaned forward, slid my laptop from under my armchair, where I hid it for safe-keeping when out of the house, and opened it up.

From the moment Rose had accepted my offer to step into her domestic shoes, I had decided to keep a diary of my foray into cleaning. Neil was right that I needed to take a break from trying to write publishable fiction, but he and I both knew I didn't simply write to be read. Writing had been my therapy and my release, as well as my occasional torment, for as long as I could remember, and it was an addiction I couldn't break, even if I had wanted to. And for now, the cleaning diary was my drug of choice.

I had already written about my first visit to Bennett Park with Rose, and had tipsily brought things up to date in bed the previous evening with an account of my slightly anxious excursion to John Lewis, and the welcome distraction from my worries that had been lunch with Aiden. So far, the process of committing details of everything job-related to my laptop had steadied any nerves over my impulsive offer to fill in for Rose and helped me to focus on the positives of the domestic deal, for both of us. Consequently, I was now very keen to write down my Day One experiences, in the hope of achieving some sort of calm and clarity and, as Neil would put it, uplift regarding what at that moment felt like an unmitigated disaster of a start. I began to type.

Monday 17 October: A new broom

Today was my first day in my new job. And to start with the positives:

1. I was bang on time.
2. Cleaning a three-storey house in three hours is an excellent physical workout.
3. It was great to have clearly defined goals, no matter how simple, and the sense of purpose I felt was something I realise I have been lacking for quite some time.

I read and reread my three undeniable plus points before, in the interests of balance, moving on to the more challenging aspects of my morning.

However, it was not quite all plain sailing because:

1. I had a hangover.
2. I set off the burglar alarm.
3. James Brooke came home unexpectedly and caught me in the study just about to open a box file. Obviously I wasn't intending to rifle through it, photograph the contents and pass the pics to MI5. I merely wanted to look at the top sheet and see if it gave any clue as to who or what he is. But actually I needn't have bothered because I found out exactly what he is without ever opening the file: he is a cold-hearted corporate cut-out. Our encounter in the study was utterly one-sided. He had all the advantages of home turf and employer authority, while all I had was a maniacal grin and a shoe cover on my head. A more feeling person would have taken pity on my first-day nerves, but he made no attempt whatsoever to put me at my ease. Instead he seemed determined to make me feel as uncomfortable as possible by constantly staring, unblinkingly, at my shoe-cover hat. He's really good at staring, I'll give him that. In fact, if he hadn't spent the entire morning tracking my every move, I'd have sworn he had two glass eyes. He kept popping up

everywhere, hell-bent on unnerving me into a second slip-up, like Columbo after a GQ makeover.

I stopped typing, aware that my final point was now more boulder than bullet and that my balanced account of the morning had degenerated into an unhinged rant. I took a deep breath and, without amending anything that had gone before, began a new paragraph.

> James Brooke is not a pleasant individual, but neither is he responsible for my dreadful start. I would love nothing more than to dump all my failure, anger and frustration at my new employer's door, but I can't. This morning was my fault entirely: the hangover, the alarm and worst of all, the box file nosiness and a lack of self-control – all my own shortcomings. I failed to take my responsibilities both to Rose and the client seriously enough and I have come away today feeling hugely disappointed with myself and with an increased consciousness of the fact that Rose's reputation is now inextricably linked to mine. She entrusted me with a job she both needs and loves, and I've let her down already.

I paused again and this time abruptly closed the laptop, realising that on this particular occasion, far from cheering me up and calming me down, reliving the day was simply lowering my mood even further. I looked absently around the room, desperately scrabbling for some additional positives to take away from the morning.

After less than a minute, I was grateful to be distracted from this doomed objective by the buzzing of my phone – another text, probably from Gavin, I thought. However, on checking the screen, I was surprised to discover that it was from Aiden, saying that he had had a meeting cancelled and was letting me know that he was free to stop by for half an hour or so at 3 p.m., 'on the off chance' that I was at home.

I stared at my phone, shook my head despairingly and then, still feeling utterly miserable, texted my reply.

> What a coincidence. I've also had a meeting cancelled. See you at 3.

And then, refusing to let myself dwell on anything more troubling than my desperate need for a cup of tea, I shoved the laptop back under the chair and went to put the kettle on.

Chapter 9

'Oh my God, Grace.' Gavin looked at me in the mirror and continued to laugh. 'He thinks you're a nutter *and* a klepto!'

'I know, I know,' I sighed, settling myself into a chair in the now empty salon. Gavin had called an hour earlier to tell me that his last client of the day had cancelled and to ask whether I was free to come for a haircut – or, as he put it, a shearing. I had jumped at the chance, not only of sorting out my hair, but also of a chat with Gavin. He always cheered me up, and despite a lingering misery over my disastrous first-day-at-work experience, he had me giggling within minutes of my arrival.

'I'll tell you what,' he continued, recovering slightly and dabbing at his eyes with a tissue plucked from a nearby box. 'I'd have paid anything to be there when you set that alarm off.' He began to laugh again as he gently combed through my newly washed hair. 'And when he asked you about the bag on your head.'

'Shoe-cover,' I corrected. 'And how about I wear it next time we go out?'

He pointed at me with his comb. 'I'm gonna hold you to that. Oh my God, but anyway,' he cleared his throat. 'Did you clean again today? You're doing Mondays and Thursdays, aren't you?'

I nodded. 'That's right. Today was my second morning and it was fine. No sign of him or his girlfriend and no repercussions over the box file,' I put a hand to my chest, 'which I'm *so* relieved about.'

'Bet you are,' said Gavin, resuming his combing. 'So overall, is the job cheering you up?'

I thought for a moment. 'Well,' I began, 'it definitely takes my mind off me. And I love the feeling of completion. Writing a book can be such a lengthy, open-ended process. It doesn't offer—'

'That's nice, but you're getting arty-farty rambly now,' interrupted Gavin absently, crouching down to check where my hair fell. 'Keep it simple. Overall, is the job fun?'

I nodded. 'Yes, it's fun. The best bit is being on your own in someone else's house.'

'I'd *love* that,' he said, standing up and rubbing his hands together. 'I'd be reading all the notes on the fridge and checking the labels in any clothes left lying around. You know like when you go to someone's house for dinner and they pop out of the kitchen for a moment, or you go off to the loo and do a sneaky detour into their bedroom?'

I frowned. 'Is that what you do when you come to my flat for dinner?' I asked.

He shook his head. 'Not any more. It was all bin-collection reminders and huge M&S knickers that would have put me off my tea if it had been edible in the first place. When was the last time you took yourself shopping for undies?' He looked disparagingly at my grey hoodie. 'Or for clothes in general, for that matter?'

I opened my mouth to reply, but he didn't pause for breath.

'And so what about Aiden?' he asked.

I turned my head to look up at him over my shoulder. 'What about Aiden?'

He tutted. 'You know full bloody well what. Are you being a good girl and being careful like Neil said?'

'I haven't even spoken to him since I last saw you!' I protested.

'You are *such* a crap liar,' he said, running his hands through my hair. 'I know you've seen him at least once for lunch.'

'How on earth did you know that?' I asked, wondering if I had failed to spot him in The Cow Shed.

'Didn't,' he said, winking at me in the mirror.

I scowled at him. 'Devious.'

He smiled. 'Just… be… careful,' he said, tapping the top of my head lightly with his comb.

'I… am… being… careful,' I insisted. 'I've had a quick lunch and a coffee with him, that's all. It's just interesting to catch up, and it's been great to discover he's miserable.'

Gavin shook his head. 'You can't fool me. I know you're way too nice to hang around with someone just to gloat.'

'There are no feelings there, Gavin,' I insisted. 'He's helped to fill a few hours' downtime. Nothing more.'

'Yeah, well,' he said, looking sceptical, 'how about you keep me updated on Aiden, as well as on the snooping?'

'OK.' I patted his hand, which was now resting on my shoulder.

'And if you fancy lunch or a coffee with someone with a bit more integrity, I'm always around, you know. Which reminds me, do you fancy dinner Saturday? At ours. Neil's got some booky spod coming round and said to ask.'

I smiled. 'Thank him very much for the invitation, but I'm going to have a quiet weekend. I drank too much and had late nights Saturday *and* Sunday last week. That's what got me into trouble on Monday.'

His eyes widened. 'Drinking on Sunday night too, eh? Who was that with then?'

I looked down to avoid eye contact, needlessly adjusting the cuffs of the black salon robe. 'With Simone Beringer.' I cleared my throat. 'We went to the pub on Whiteladies, the one with the barman you fancy who looks just like Neil. We got taxis there and back,' I concluded.

He looked at me expressionlessly. '*Such* a crap liar,' he sighed. 'That was way too much detail; going on about taxis and telling me Simone's surname like we know more than one person called Simone. You got pissed up with Aiden, didn't you?'

I tutted. 'OK, well yes, it was with Aiden. But so what?'

Gavin shook his head sadly.

'Don't do your disappointed dad face at me, Gavin,' I protested. 'I'm actually seeing Simone for dinner in couple of weeks' time.'

He held up both hands in a gesture of confusion. 'And that's relevant because…?'

'Because I wasn't telling a complete lie. It was a future truth.'

He laughed. 'You spout such Bertie bollocks some-times, you know,' he said. 'Just don't do anything silly,' he added more gently.

'Thank you for caring,' I said, again placing my hand on his. 'About me and about my hair.'

'You're a gorgeous person.' He squeezed my hand, then bent down and kissed the top of my damp head. 'But your hair looks like shit, so what,' he continued, becoming suddenly brisk, 'are we going to do with it?' He looked up and smiled.

I shrugged. 'I suppose you could always put a shoe-cover on it.'

'You may laugh, Bellatrix,' he said wearily, 'but that's an option I'm definitely keeping in reserve.'

Chapter 10

As I pressed the unlock symbol, entered the code and then pressed the unlock symbol for a second time, it struck me that I was actually, on this my fifth visit to Bennett Park, now feeling rather more in control: I knew what to do, I had my routine established and I was no longer referring to Rose's notes.

For the past two weeks, with the exception of my brief encounter with my employer, I had had the house entirely to myself. This had surprised me, not only because Rose had said she usually saw Emily at least once a week, but also because after James Brooke's blatant distrust of me on my first day, I had felt sure that he would suddenly be working from home every Monday and Thursday in order to keep a wary eye on me. When this turned out not to be the case, it crossed my mind that he might have installed cameras. And after Neil sent me an online article about a homeowner who had calmly watched two plumbers rifling through his bedroom drawers while he recorded the whole thing from his desk at work, the idea had become a genuine, if somewhat paranoid, concern. I had therefore taken to scanning every room I entered in search of CCTV and carrying out my cleaning duties with the utmost professionalism whilst displaying theatrical disinterest in any object which I didn't intend to wash, wipe, dust or polish.

As far as my personal life went, however, I was not, despite Gavin and Neil's advice, being quite so cautious. I had met Aiden twice more for coffee since my salon appointment and, although I was reluctant to admit it to myself, I had actually begun to look forward to seeing him. And our texted conversations had become more regular, to the point where it was a surprise if a morning or afternoon went by without hearing from him. What was more, I had now taken to consciously suppressing any underlying misgivings about the situation, choosing to focus instead upon the positives of our detente. It was, I told myself, evidence of a healthy willingness on my part to move towards forgiveness, and of a new-found maturity and humility on his. Besides, his interest in me was a bolster to my ego and self-confidence which I was reluctant to give up.

These were just some of the thoughts occupying my mind when I heard the front door creak open and then quietly click shut as I cleaned the downstairs cloakroom of Bennett Park that Monday morning. I sighed, flushed the loo, removed my rubber gloves and walked into the expansive entrance hall, ready to say a polite hello to either James or Emily.

But it wasn't James, and it wasn't Emily either.

Instead, I was greeted by the sight of a petite, slightly stooped elderly woman toting a black patent-leather handbag so enormous that I feared she might overbalance at any moment. She was standing side-on to me and absently fingering a double string of pearls which hung around her neck, whilst flicking through the pile of mail

I had earlier picked up and placed on the single-drawer bureau which stood against one wall of the entrance hall. I watched her for a moment as she continued to examine the mail.

'One from HMRC. How very dull,' she said quietly. 'But what's this?' She held up a beach-scene postcard addressed to 'Ems', which I had already read in full, under cover of dusting the bureau. 'Barbados. My goodness.' She turned it over and began to read.

I cleared my throat but she gave no indication of having heard me, instead calmly replacing the postcard on the table and continuing her examination of the pile. I had just decided she was deaf and was about to announce myself more loudly, when she spoke. 'I do so love going through other people's correspondence,' she said, turning her head to look at me. 'Don't you?'

I blinked at her, taken aback by the total disregard for social norms. 'Can I help you?' I asked after a moment. It didn't feel like quite the right thing to say, but it ticked as many boxes as seemed possible in the circumstances.

'No thank you.' She smiled and tapped the pair of half-moon glasses perched on the end of her nose. 'I remembered my spectacles today, so I needn't trouble you to read anything for me.' She returned her attention to the mail.

I decided there was nothing for it but to stop worrying about offending this person and be direct. 'I'm sorry, but can I ask who you are and what you are doing here?'

She pushed the glasses to the top of her head, placed a hand on her chest and laughed in the manner of a tipsy Miss Marple. 'Oh my darling, I am so sorry,' she said. 'How funny.' She laughed again and put down the white, hand-written envelope she had just picked up. 'I'll finish going through those later,' she murmured, as if to herself, and then walked towards me, holding out her hand.

'I live next door,' she said, her tone indicating that this information should be enough to clear up any confusion as to why she was in someone else's home and rifling through their post. I took her hand and shook it. 'I thought you knew,' she continued. 'But my goodness, I expect you thought I was one of those bogus workmen who inveigle their way into homes and prey so heartlessly on dimwits such as my friend Arthur. He was burgled by a scoundrel who gave him a quote for sanding and repainting his window frames – which are plastic. Not only that, the quote included scaffolding costs, and Arthur lives in a bungalow.'

She smiled up at me and continued to shake my hand as I racked my brain for anything which might make sense of the current situation. However, in the end I thought it best to come clean and admit defeat. 'I'm so sorry, but I'm afraid—'

I was cut short by the front door opening and the arrival of a young woman with silky poker-straight blonde hair and pale blue eyes. She was slim and casually elegant in skinny jeans, long brown boots and a brown suede jacket, and I recognised her immediately as James's partner Emily.

'Well hello!' she cried, smiling broadly at both myself and the mail snoop. 'How lovely not to come home to an empty house.' She crossed the hall and kissed her next-door neighbour on the cheek. 'I'm so glad you could come. How are you?' she asked.

'Oh, I'm just marvellous, beautiful girl.' The older woman reached up and affectionately cupped the new arrival's face in her hands. 'And thank you for inviting me. I was just sorting out your post for you. You've got a postcard here from a Henry. He says he's very drunk and terribly sunburnt.' She picked up the postcard and handed it over. 'Is he ginger, perhaps? My Patrick was ginger. He once burnt in Widnes on the second of October.' She sighed at the memory.

'Henry is strawberry blonde, actually,' smiled Emily and then turned to me. 'And you must be Grace. I'm Emily. Wow, I love your hair. I've always wanted curls. It's so nice to meet you.'

I blinked a little at the sing-song gentleness of her voice, combined with machine-gun-rapid speech. 'Thanks,' I said, raising a self-conscious hand to my head, on top of which my hair was messily piled. 'My hairdresser friend isn't quite so kind about it. He wants to chop it all off.'

'Oh no,' she frowned. 'Don't let him do that. It makes you look dangerously attractive.'

I shook my head. 'I think that's the tabard.'

She laughed. 'Rose said you were funny, didn't she, Percy?' She nudged her neighbour.

'Oh you're *Percy*!' I exclaimed, suddenly understanding. 'Rose did tell me about you but I'm afraid I assumed you were a man.'

Percy laughed. 'Euphemia Percival, hence Percy. Can't abide the Euphemia, so I try to forget about it. Makes me sound like a musical instrument or a bronchial infection. But poor Grace,' she said, turning to Emily and laying a gentle hand on her arm. 'I frightened the poor creature half to death. She mistook me for a scaffolder, of all things.' Emily looked at me and frowned slightly.

'Well, I—' I began, but Percy didn't pause for breath.

'Ooh, now...' She opened the handbag and began to delve. 'I'm returning your spiraliser and a whisk and a screwdriver, Emily. I popped in yesterday to borrow them.'

Emily smiled. 'Thank you. Shall we go into the kitchen? Grace,' she looked up at me, 'do you fancy a coffee?'

'Thanks, but I should be getting on,' I said, assuming the suggestion was more polite than serious.

Her face fell, and Percy looked up from her bag. 'Oh please do join us, dear,' she said. 'I've actually got a little favour to ask of you and I could explain it all much more fully over a cup of Earl Grey and...' she reached into her bag once more, this time extracting a small plastic box, 'I've made shortbread!'

—

Twenty minutes and one piece of tooth-crackingly hard shortbread later, I was sitting at Emily's kitchen table still none the wiser as to the favour required. I was, however, warming very much to both Percy and Emily. They were relaxed, inclusive and unselfconscious. And although Emily, as evidenced by the smiles she attempted to hide behind her mug of coffee, clearly found Percy's conversation as entertainingly off-the-wall as I did, she determinedly bought into the topics raised by her neighbour.

'So you didn't like the locum?' she asked as Percy pulled a disgruntled face over a recent doctor's appointment.

'It was pity rather than dislike, my darling. You see, he was so terribly young and his hands shook the whole time. Like this.' Percy put down her cup of tea and did jazz hands at Emily. 'I did feel for him. I pointed out the tremor and asked him what his condition was.' She picked up and sipped her tea. 'He said he didn't have a condition, but, well, his hands shook more than ever after that.'

'Oh dear,' said Emily.

Percy shook her head. 'Do not trouble yourself, dear. I made sure to mention it to the receptionist on the way out. I told her all about his shakes and that I thought the poor boy might need some support. And then a lovely elderly gentleman on the far side of the waiting room called across that if the boy wasn't disabled then he was probably an alcoholic. And another lady said she had read an article in the *Daily Mail* just that morning which said that most young doctors are dreadfully depressed drug abusers these days and that that might be the cause of his shakes, if it wasn't a fondness for the bottle.'

'Hmm...' said Emily noncommittally, her mug again hiding her mouth from view. 'Well let's just hope that, as you say, he gets some support.'

'Oh, I'm sure he will,' said Percy brightly. 'And as I was leaving, there was a little crowd of people who had appointments with him, all asking to see a different doctor in order to take the pressure off the boy. Wasn't that kind? People can be so thoughtful when it matters,' she added, clearly oblivious to the surgery chaos she had left in her wake. 'But enough about that. How are you and James, Emily?' she continued briskly, without pause. 'Oh, and I do of course want to find out a little more about Grace here.' She turned to me and smiled. 'Do you live far away, dear? Is it a trek for you to get here?'

Feeling mildly anxious at the prospect of a grilling, I shook my head. 'Not at all. I'm in Henleaze, so it's ten minutes in the car, unless there's a jam on the Downs.'

'Oh, I do so love all those little shops in Henleaze,' beamed Percy. 'When I was thinking about moving, I looked at a very lovely bungalow there, but then,' she sighed, 'I realised that my heart is in Bennett Park and here I must remain. Have you lived in Henleaze long, my darling?'

'I've been in my flat for over two years now and I'm very happy there.'

'That's marvellous,' said Percy, reaching out and placing her hand on my arm. 'And are you like me, my darling? Do you live alone?' She glanced at my left hand, looking, I guessed, for a ring.

I smiled at her, but despite the unmistakable kindness of her interest, I was far from keen to discuss my love life – or lack of it. 'I do,' I said, clearing my throat. 'Just me and two pot plants I haven't quite managed to kill yet.' I paused, and then, in a bid to change the subject, asked, 'Are you green-fingered, Percy? These houses have such lovely gardens.' I gestured out of the kitchen window at the large lawn and immaculate borders.

'They do,' she agreed, turning towards the window. 'Patrick and I used to do all the gardening ourselves in our younger years. Now, of course, I can't quite manage it, so I have help. A lovely young man comes and tends the lawn and I look after the patio pots,' she continued, still gazing into the garden. 'Patrick didn't like pots, of course. He said that they were cages and that plants should be allowed to range and roam – that was how he put it.

He said he wanted our garden to teeter on the brink of beautiful mayhem.' She smiled at the thought.

'I rather like the idea of beautiful mayhem,' I said.

Percy turned back towards me, still smiling. 'Like your hair,' she said. 'It is a beautiful storm of curls. Patrick would have approved.'

I laughed and felt myself blush, touched and taken unawares by the sudden compliment. 'Thank you,' I said. 'Some days are more stormy than others.'

'Well I think it's simply wonderful,' she said and looked at Emily. 'Isn't it wonderful?'

'It is.' Emily smiled and nodded. 'James thought so too.'

I looked at her and felt myself frown, not at the flattering lie but at the sudden mention of James and the equally sudden recollection that this pretty, kindly, vivacious young woman was living with a man who, according to Rose, planned to pack her bags for her before the twelve days of Christmas were up.

Emily replaced her mug on the table and leaned towards me. 'Oh, I'm sorry, I've embarrassed you,' she said. 'I just think it's nice to know when someone has paid you a compliment.'

I forced a smile. 'No, no, it's fine,' I said. 'It's just that when I met James, I had a shoe cover on my head.'

It was her turn to frown. 'Really? He didn't mention that. Why did you—'

'And how *is* darling James, Emily?' interrupted Percy. 'He seems to be working incredibly hard. And I thought he looked a little tired when I popped in on Tuesday to return the drill.

Emily's face cleared and she smiled. 'Oh, he's all right. He'd just been up late finishing a report and that put him in a really grumpy mood. He gave me lots of advice yesterday on how to better organise my time and then asked dozens of questions about the new guy in the office. He tried to disguise it all as casual conversation, but I knew exactly what he was up to. He talks to me as if I'm a teenager sometimes.'

I felt my lips purse involuntarily, but Percy, by contrast, seemed to approve of such controlling chauvinism. 'That's because he cares so much, you see,' she smiled. 'He is such a lovely boy. I do so love having you both living next door. I feel blessed.'

She looked a little emotional, and Emily edged her chair closer to her and placed an arm around her shoulders. 'Oh Percy, and I love being here too, with such a wonderful neighbour. And as for James… well, I feel grateful for him every day.' She smiled and then looked up at me. 'Sorry, Grace, we're getting soppy.'

I attempted to return the smile whilst feeling a renewed dislike for James. Emily was clearly smitten and totally oblivious to his lack of attachment. 'Not at all,' I said, pushing back my chair and standing up. 'But I must get on, or I'll be with you till midnight.'

Emily sighed. 'I wouldn't mind if you were,' she said. 'I'm dreading starting this essay on the dismantling of British colonial rule.'

'You have an essay to write?' exclaimed Percy, now also rising to her feet. 'Well in that case I must get out of your way, darling. Ooh, but Grace, dear, are you able to clean for me next Friday? I'm having one of my soirées on the Saturday and I know Fiona Saunt will be running her fingers along my credenza, so I need everywhere spick and span. And would you be free to come along and help me take coats and top up drinks, as a paid guest? I usually rely on Rose for that. I struggle with the running back and forth these days, you see. I'm so decrepit.'

I hesitated slightly whilst formulating an excuse. I had no problem with the extra cleaning work, but the idea of being a waitress for the evening at a house party didn't appeal one bit. 'I can clean for you any time next Friday,' I said. 'But I'm afraid I'm not free on the Saturday. I'm having dinner with friends.'

Percy appeared only momentarily downcast before rushing to reassure me. 'That's perfectly fine,' she said, reaching out and squeezing my arm. 'It was extremely short notice. And silly of me to think you wouldn't have plans.'

'I can come and help, Percy,' offered Emily.

Percy tutted and wagged a finger at her. 'I'm not so old as to have forgotten that you have a getaway planned for next weekend.'

Emily shook her head. 'There's nothing booked and we could come to your party instead.'

I looked at Emily, willing to sacrifice a weekend away with her evil lover to help out an elderly neighbour, and contrasted that with my refusal to miss out on an evening sofa-slobbing with my best bud, Mr Pinot Grigio. A wave of guilt swept over me and I removed my phone from my tabard pocket and began to tap at the screen. 'Hold on a moment,' I said. 'I think I may have got my weekends muddled. It's *this* Saturday that I'm having dinner with Simone. So yes,' I put the phone away, 'I'm free to help.'

Emily smiled and Percy clapped her hands. 'Wonderful!' she said, walking to my side and rubbing my arm. 'And I shall introduce you to all my friends.

Except Fiona,' she added. 'You wouldn't want to meet her. She's terribly annoying and I invite her only because it's always good to have someone to loathe.'

Chapter 11

'Come in!' Guy, Simone's husband, beckoned me into their home with his usual bonhomie. It was a quality which, together with his kindness and integrity, made him one of the few people I had met through Aiden whom I actually liked – loved even. Aiden's other friends had always seemed slightly reserved, or as if business was never quite off the agenda, but Guy, despite being a former colleague, was most definitely more focused on pleasure than business.

'And may I just say how particularly lovely you are looking tonight, Grace?' he said, bending his tall, willowy frame low and kissing me on both cheeks.

'You may,' I smiled. 'Especially since I have tried a lot harder than usual.' And it was true. I had taken Gavin's throwaway comment about my wardrobe somewhat to heart and had splashed out not only on some new undies, but also on new boots, new jeans, a cowl-neck sweater and a black midi dress. The dress I was debuting this evening, and I had trialled the boots, sweater and jeans earlier in the week, when meeting Aiden for a drink after work.

'Well it's certainly paid off,' said Guy, his dark eyes dancing. 'You look Tony the Tiger grrrrrrreat! Doesn't she, Sim?' he added over his shoulder as Simone emerged from the lounge into the hallway.

'She certainly does!' she exclaimed, walking towards me and opening her arms for a hug. She was as warm and effusive as her husband, and I felt proud, as I did every time I saw them, at the part I had played in bringing them together. Simone, a former surveyor, and I had become friends during the years I had worked in commercial property, and it was I who had introduced her to Guy, feeling sure that, despite one or two marked differences in personality and temperament, they would get along. And they did, moving in together within just three months of meeting and marrying two years later.

As couples, we had spent an awful lot of time together, and the aftermath of Aiden's affair and our break-up had been almost as difficult for Simone and Guy as it had been for us. But they had managed our friendships in the wake of the divorce with typical kindness, as well as unfailing tact and diplomacy, something made all the more astonishing by the fact that neither of the latter two qualities came naturally to Guy. But somehow, no doubt under Simone's strict management and guidance, they had avoided causing either Aiden or myself any awkwardness in their company over the past three years – which was why it now came as such a shock to see my ex-husband emerge from the kitchen carrying two glasses of red wine. He was clearly as surprised to see me as I was him, and his reaction didn't go unnoticed. Simone put a hand to her mouth and then, recovering, looked sternly at Guy.

'Please tell me you asked them about this,' she hissed.

Guy's face fell and he ran an anxious hand repeatedly through his thick black hair. 'You know, I meant to, but...'

Simone groaned. 'For God's sake, Guy,' she muttered, beckoning Aiden to join us by the front door. 'I'm so, so sorry about this. We set aside a date for dinner and Guy and I invited you two independently,' she explained quietly. 'When I realised what had happened, I wasn't happy and said we'd go ahead only if we could clear it with you both and,' she looked up at Guy malevolently, 'he told me that he had.'

Guy, looking mildly panicked, his hair now sticking out at all angles, cleared his throat. 'I forgot to text, and then time marched on and then when I remembered I thought I would be in trouble for forgetting, so—'

'You *are* in trouble,' said Simone flatly. 'Big trouble.'

I looked at Aiden, feeling slightly sick at the thought of an evening in the company of new mother Summer but at the same time not wanting to make the situation any worse for a clearly mortified Simone. 'It's not at all a problem for me,' I said. 'Really.'

Aiden attempted a smile but looked far from comfortable. 'Of course, it's fine.'

'Good man,' interjected Guy brightly, looking relieved, clearly taking Aiden completely at his word and slapping him on the back. 'My fault entirely. Can't say sorry enough. So won't even try.' He winked at Simone, in response to which she shook her head and sighed heavily.

'About as perceptive as a two-year-old,' she murmured.

'It is honestly *not* a problem,' I insisted, looking again at Aiden for confirmation.

This time his smile appeared more genuine. 'It's not. I was just surprised to see Grace.' He looked at me. 'But it's a very nice surprise, actually,' he added, leaning forward to kiss my cheek. 'Hello.'

Simone studied him for a moment, her expression slightly puzzled, and then linked her arm through mine. 'Well, I'm sorry. But come on into the living room and I'll introduce you to everyone else while Guy fetches you a drink...' she glanced up at him, 'and finds a comb. What do you fancy?'

'A glass of red would be great, please,' I smiled.

Aiden held out a glass. 'Here,' he said, 'have mine. Simone can give this one to Summer and I'll get another.'

After a moment's hesitation, I took the glass, smiling my thanks, and then, as Aiden and Guy returned to the kitchen, Simone led me into the living room.

–

As it turned out, Summer's shock at the situation put anything displayed by either Aiden or myself into the shade. She looked up from the sofa as I entered the lounge and turned a shade of red which made her skin almost indistinguishable from the thin, billowing fabric of the dress she was wearing.

'Grace!' She stood up and hugged me. 'What a surprise,' she said, in a way which indicated that this particular surprise was right up there with the cat bringing in a decapitated mouse.

Simone spoke up immediately. 'I forgot to circulate a guest list, Summer,' she said, handing Summer a glass of wine whilst graciously taking the blame for the situation.

Summer took the glass, forced a smile and sat back down, examining me from head to toe with uncharacter-istically tired eyes. After a brief but uncomfortable pause, Simone cleared her throat and spoke again. 'So, Grace, this is my little brother, Matt. I think you knew *he* was coming.'

'Yes, I did.' I turned and raised my hand to a bearded man with a rugby player's frame ensconced in a large armchair to my right. 'Hello.'

'Hi,' he said, smiling and raising a bottle of beer in my direction. 'And I'm thirty-four, Sim,' he added with a sigh, 'only a few years younger than you. So maybe it's time to drop the *little*. I don't want Grace thinking you're talking about my anatomy.'

I laughed and Simone rolled her eyes. 'Anyway,' she said, turning back to the couple sitting next to Summer on the sofa, 'these are our friends Jasmine and Callum. I was at university with Jasmine and they're with us for the weekend from Canterbury.'

'Hello.' I smiled at the balding, bespectacled Callum before turning my attention to his wife, who was beaming up at me. She looked, I thought, remarkably similar to Simone; slightly heavier, but sharing the same dark bobbed hair and rosy, outdoor complexion. 'I think I remember Simone telling me about you, Jasmine,' I said. 'Did you busk together at university?'

Jasmine laughed, stood up and kissed my cheek. 'That's right!' she exclaimed. 'We did. About half a dozen times at the Bullring Shopping Centre. Each time we made about two quid before being moved on, on account of being absolutely dreadful.' She laughed again and sat back down next to her husband, moving along the sofa to create a space for me between herself and Summer. 'And you're a famous author, I hear,' she said with a smile.

'Hardly,' I said, sitting down. 'But I've written a few books. How about you? What do you get up to?'

'Nothing anywhere nearly so exciting,' she said. 'I work part-time in an art gallery.'

'Sounds exciting to me,' I smiled.

'Jasmine works part-time because she has children,' chipped in Summer. 'She's a mother. We were just discussing motherhood when you arrived.'

I turned to look at Summer and then back at Jasmine, whose eyes widened slightly as she shifted in her seat. Simone had clearly made her aware of my relationship to Aiden, even if Guy had forgotten to tell us that we would be spending the evening together. I looked up at Simone, who had remained standing next to the sofa. Her expression had taken on a slightly glazed quality, and Aiden, who had just re-entered the room carrying a replacement glass of red wine, offered me a slow, despairing blink.

'I just *love* being a mum,' persisted Summer. 'I feel like I've been really missing out until now. And I'm so pleased I've had a baby while I'm still young and able to enjoy every moment of it all.'

I turned to her again. This was, I thought, a new approach. She was usually polite and patronisingly benevolent towards me, secure, I assumed, in the knowledge that she had taken my husband from me – or at least that he had followed her. I had, from the outset, apportioned blame equally between them for the disintegration of my marriage. But this evening, perhaps due to being unable to prepare for our encounter, she was different; her pitying, magnanimous cat-who-got-the-cream air had disappeared and she was clearly anxious to highlight and underline her superiority – and my shortcomings. I took a deep breath and, for Simone's sake, bit back a retort involving Summer's voluminous red dress and the Moscow State Circus tent currently pitched on the Downs.

'And motherhood agrees with you, Summer,' I said. 'You look great.'

I heard what I thought was an exhalation of breath from Jasmine, and Simone smiled down at me, looking as relieved as Jasmine sounded. Summer, meanwhile, was talking again. '... because before Aiden and I had Warren, we were clueless as to what it must be like to have children. I mean, you can *imagine* what it might be like to have a child, but you can't possibly *know*. And then you have a baby and it's like joining a wonderfully secretive club.' She leaned across me to squeeze Jasmine's arm conspiratorially. 'Like the Magic Circle.'

I felt Jasmine stiffen as she managed an awkward smile in return.

'A magic endless circle of pee, poo and sleeplessness,' murmured Callum wearily.

'God, yes,' said Simone. 'Harry didn't sleep through for months.'

'Same with Ellie,' Jasmine nodded and then looked at me miserably. 'That's why you look half our age, Grace. No sleep deprivation.'

'I have to say that having children does age women generally,' said Matt, resting his beer on the arm of his chair and leaning towards us.

'And *why* exactly do you have to say that, Matthew?' frowned Simone. 'Is it because you enjoy offending people, or because you're on the spectrum?'

He grinned up at her and shrugged. 'You and Jasmine said it yourselves this afternoon. "Everything goes south",

84

you said.' He looked at Summer and winked. 'And Aiden said the same thing about you earlier.'

His comment was clearly intended as a joke, but instead of laughing along, Summer's response was to shoot a look at Aiden which would not so much have withered a pot plant as vaporised it.

Aiden uttered a low groan and flopped down in a nearby armchair. 'It's a joke, Summer,' he said quietly, not looking at her but instead focusing on the floor. 'He is joking.'

'Yes, he is,' said Simone, bending down and placing her hand on Summer's arm. 'It's just very hard to tell because he's not at all funny.'

Matt glanced guiltily at Simone and took a gulp of beer. 'Of course I was joking,' he said, in a hoarse attempt to reassure Summer. 'I actually think you look really… *un*motherly, Summer. In fact, when you walked in here, I thought, my God, she's not mother material.'

'Hey, everybody!' exclaimed Simone, suddenly and very loudly, in what seemed like a retrospective attempt to drown out Matt. 'I think dinner must be ready by now. So let's go and sit up,' she concluded, with just a hint of hysterical wobble in her voice.

'What's with all the shouting?' A grinning Guy stuck his head round the door. 'And I'm not ready for everyone quite yet, darling,' he said, continuing to smile whilst waving a wooden spoon. 'How about you give me five more minutes?'

'How about I don't,' she said flatly. And then, taking Matt's hand and dragging him to his feet, she led the way into the dining room.

Having been left to devise our own boy-girl seating, I found myself sitting between Matt and Aiden. The former, it turned out, was single, amiable and very entertaining. In fact, it occurred to me more than once that if only the guest list hadn't included Summer, the evening would have been pretty close to perfect for me. Matt was witty, well-meaning and straight-talking, and despite this latter quality veering dangerously close to a tactlessness which clearly irritated his sister on more than one occasion, I found his slight lack of social awareness funny rather than offensive.

'Do you know what,' he said, lowering his voice and leaning towards me as Guy got up to fetch the cheeseboard from the kitchen. 'When Sim said that you and Aiden were both coming to dinner this evening, I panicked a bit. All the divorced couples I know want to rip each other's heads off.'

At this, Aiden turned towards us. 'Yes, well, let's just say I'm always very relieved when we get to the dessert course,' he said. 'No knives.'

'Ah, but I can do dreadful things with a spoon,' I said quietly, before taking a final mouthful of my berry crumble, 'if he doesn't behave,' I concluded in a mumble.

Matt laughed, and then, as Aiden returned his attention to Jasmine on his right, he leaned towards me. 'Can I be blunt?'

'Depends on the subject matter,' I said, smiling my thanks as he topped up my wine glass. 'I don't do well with criticism.'

'You're really attractive,' he said.

I turned to look at him. 'I'm not great with flattery either,' I said. 'I probably should have mentioned that.'

He shook his head. 'It's not flattery.'

'Oh and I meant to tell you, Grace, that I saw Rachel the other day,' said Aiden, suddenly rejoining the conversation.

'Rachel Kington?' I asked, looking over my shoulder at him.

'Yes,' he nodded. 'I was at a breakfast meeting with her. She's a client's party-wall expert. She said to send you her love and to ask when the next book is out.'

'I haven't seen her in ages,' I smiled. 'I must call her.'

'She reminded me of that time we all went punting,' continued Aiden, 'when we were in Oxford for her birthday. Richard Webster fell in. Do you remember?'

I laughed and leaned back in my chair. 'Of course. Poor Richard.'

Aiden grinned. 'He surfaced with a weed wig.'

'Sounds hysterical,' said Matt, sounding like it wasn't really.

Aiden looked at him. 'It was,' he said. 'We couldn't stop laughing.' He continued to look unsmilingly at Matt for a moment, before adding, 'For a really long time.'

Matt held up his hands. 'Hey and I believe you, Ade.'

'It *was* funny,' I smiled. 'But probably only in a you-had-to-be-there kind of way.'

'Had to be where?' interrupted Summer at considerable volume from across the table. Her tone was strangely shrill, and conversation around the table ceased as everyone turned to look at her. She was smiling broadly and, I noticed, swaying slightly in her chair.

'Aiden was just telling me about the time Richard Webster fell into the Cherwell, Summer,' said Matt. He glanced at Aiden. 'I fell about laughing.'

Summer redirected her gaze to Aiden, her eyes lagging behind the turn of her head. 'Who's Richard Cherwell?' she asked, still grinning.

'Richard Webster,' corrected Aiden. 'He's an old friend and it was a long time ago,' he added, clearly wanting to move on.

'I wonder where Guy has got to with that cheese,' said Simone. 'I bet he—'

'But it sounds like such a good story,' pressed Summer. She turned to Simone. 'Doesn't it, Simone?'

Simone said nothing, but instead reached for her wine, taking a sip whilst eyeing Aiden significantly over the top of her glass.

Aiden looked at Summer and sighed. 'OK, well, Richard is an old university friend. We were punting in Oxford when somebody's hat blew off. Richard was trying to rescue it when he leaned over too far and—'

'I was wrong. It's a shit story,' said Summer.

Matt laughed explosively. 'God, you're all so funny,' he said, reaching again for the bottle of wine, this time to refill his own glass. 'I was just saying to Grace, it's great that you can all have a laugh together, instead of oozing tension and wanting to kill each other.' He replaced the bottle on the table and looked up. Summer was now staring at Aiden, clearly with murder on her mind, whilst he in turn focused determinedly on his wine glass. 'Oh, right, yeah,' said Matt. 'I see… that's, er…' He picked up his wine and drank. 'Ooh, that's good. Tastes pricey.'

'Why don't you tell some stories about our son, Aiden?' slurred Summer. 'Instead of really shit ones about your old, really shit friends?'

Aiden rose to his feet. 'Thanks for a lovely evening, Simone,' he said, still looking down. 'But I think Summer and I have to leave now.'

'Why?' protested Summer, her lower lip protruding in a childlike pout. 'Why do we have to leave? I'm still having a great time chatting to Callum here.' She turned to Callum, pulling his face roughly towards her and planting a lingering kiss on his forehead, her lips leaving a messy, deep red smudge. 'We're having great conversations, aren't we, Callum? You don't want me to leave, do you? You're not a bastard.'

Callum looked around the table with the air of a man desperately trying to spot a fire exit. 'Ooh, now,' he laughed nervously, 'I wouldn't want to cause a disagreement between you and Aiden.'

Summer laughed a touch maniacally. 'Oh, you are *such* a gentleman, Callum,' she said, tapping his chest playfully. 'And can I just say how attractive your shiny head is?'

Aiden had by now walked around the table and was standing behind Summer's chair. He placed a hand gently on her shoulder. 'Time to go,' he said quietly.

Summer looked up at him. 'Don't think I don't know what you're up to.' Her teeth were clenched and she seemed to be attempting a whisper, but the statement was all too audible.

Simone stood up. 'Come on, Summer. I'll help you find your things.'

'He's seeing someone, Simone,' blurted Summer, her eyes filling with tears. 'He's late home and I know he's not at work because I've checked. And he disappears at weekends. Goes out to get something and doesn't come back for hours.'

I looked at Aiden, picked up my wine glass and drank a third of its contents. He meanwhile raised a hand to his forehead, glanced briefly at me and then looked at Simone. 'I'm so sorry,' he said.

Simone shook her head at him and took Summer's hand. 'You go and get the coats,' she said softly, pointing into the hallway. He turned and left the room as Simone looked down at Summer. 'You've just had a little too much to drink, Summer, and you're not used to it since having Warren,' she said calmly. 'Hormones plus alcohol make it hard to think straight. I was exactly the same after having my two. Come on.'

Summer nodded dumbly, rose to her feet and then, steadied by Simone, walked slowly to the door. Just before she disappeared into the hallway, however, she suddenly whirled around, raised her right arm and pointed at me. 'You…' she began, jabbing her finger towards me.

I took a deep breath and held it.

'You,' she repeated, raising her voice, her wide eyes further enlarged by rings of smudged black eyeliner, 'you understand.' She looked around the table, sweeping her arm dramatically to point at each guest in turn. 'She can tell you and you and you and you and *all of you*,' she circled her arms in a wild gesture of inclusion, 'what he's like.'

Everyone looked at me as I exhaled and smiled weakly. Summer nodded at me solemnly, offered me a wholly inappropriate double thumbs-up and then exited, brushing past Guy, who had just re-entered the room fully focused on balancing a dangerously overloaded cheeseboard. 'Here we go, all,' he said, beaming and placing the board proudly in the middle of the table as we heard the front door slam. 'We've got more biscuits than you can shake a stick at, plus Stinking Bishop, Connage Dunlop, Wigmore, and a huge chunk of good old Cheddar – hurrah! Now if that doesn't make for the perfect conclusion to a lovely evening with friends, I honestly don't know what does.' He looked at Simone as she returned from the hallway and sat down heavily in her seat. 'Toilet break, darling?' he asked.

Simone looked up at him incredulously, opening her mouth as if to reply, before checking herself and instead taking a deep breath. 'You know,' she said eventually, smiling wearily and reaching for the cheese knife, 'I some-times wish I was as obtuse and oblivious as you, Guy. I really do.'

Chapter 12

When Simone texted the morning after the dinner party to ask if I was free for a walk on Monday afternoon, I wasn't surprised. Neither she nor the evening had ever quite recovered from Summer's dramatic exit, and to say the remaining guests were subdued would be an understatement. Even Guy, once the situation had been explained to him, had lost his bounce and Simone herself seemed to switch to social autopilot, smiling and nodding like the Beatles bobbleheads Gavin had brought back for me from a recent trip to a hair show in Liverpool.

I had arranged to meet her in Leigh Woods at 2 p.m. and as I spotted her car and walked towards it, she lost no time in getting to the point.

'I'm so sorry it all turned to shit on Saturday,' she said without preamble as soon as she opened the car door. She climbed out, gave me a long hug and then walked to the back of the car, opening the boot to allow Katy, her chocolate cocker spaniel, to exit.

I laughed. 'Forget about it.'

'I can't,' she said, shaking her head. 'And astonishingly, neither can Guy. He blames himself. And so do I.' She slammed shut the boot with unnecessary force. 'None of you should have been put in that position without warning. It was unforgivable,' she added as we began to make our way across the car park and towards the woods.

'I actually had a really nice time,' I insisted. 'I was just upset for you and Guy.'

'*You* were a star,' she said, giving me a second brief hug. 'We all noticed the provocation. Apart from Matt, of course,' she sighed. 'God, I wanted to throttle him.' She took a ball from her pocket, threw it for Katy and then threaded her arm through mine.

'Don't be mean. I really enjoyed talking to him.'

'Did you?' she asked, turning to look at me. 'Because he thought you were great. His main gripe about the Summer tantrum was that *even he* realised that trying to chat you up after that might not be the best move.'

'He was lovely,' I smiled. 'I'm not sure I'm looking to date just at the moment, but I did like him.'

She nodded. 'Well, if you change your mind...'

We walked on in silence for a moment before she said, 'One nice thing about Saturday was seeing you and Aiden getting on. I mean, the pair of you have always been very polite and well-behaved in public, but there seemed to be a little bit of genuine warmth there. Or was it all an act?' She nudged me mischievously.

I smiled. 'No, I think things are better than they were. We've cleared the air a little.' I bent down to pick up Katy's ball before throwing it straight into a nearby tangle of twigs and branches. 'And that,' I said, 'is why I never made it onto the rounders team.'

Simone said nothing, and when I turned to look at her, I found that she was frowning at me. 'What is it?' I asked.

'Have you spoken to him since Saturday night?' she asked.

'To Aiden? No,' I said, walking to retrieve the ball. 'Have you?'

She shook her head. 'I did wonder if I should call him. What do you think?'

'I'm surprised *he* hasn't called *you*,' I said, crouching down in an attempt to see the ball.

'Do you think Summer is right? Do you think he could be seeing someone else?'

I shrugged. 'I don't think he's got the energy for an affair these days, if that's what you mean. But then I was never great at spotting that kind of thing, was I?' I extracted Katy's ball from the brush and handed it to Simone. 'Here, you throw it for her.'

She took the ball. 'I'm sorry,' she said. 'I expect Aiden is the last thing you want me gossiping about.'

'Don't be silly,' I smiled. 'What he did to me and what he does to someone else are two totally separate things. I'm not saintly enough for the idea of him cheating on Summer to bother me. And you know I *love* to gossip.'

'Ooh, well if you're sure,' she said, lowering her voice as if the trees were taking note. 'There was something I wanted to tell you. Guy ran into Duncan Sharp, who's working on Aiden's current project, and apparently Aiden has missed a few meetings recently.' She looked at me significantly and I experienced a sudden, indecipherable mix of satisfaction and disquiet.

'What reason has he given?' I asked.

'Various,' she said. 'Duncan was worried that he might be ill and taking time out for medical appointments. But Guy and I don't think that's it. And then on Saturday...' She hesitated. 'Actually, I don't know whether I should tell you this bit.'

'Oh for goodness' sake, Simone!' I exclaimed, throwing my hands up. 'You have to now.'

She bit her lip. 'I suppose I do really. Well, when he and Summer first turned up – annoyingly early, actually – he offered to help Guy in the kitchen and he was in there for a good quarter of an hour talking about…'

I squeezed her arm and laughed. 'What? Nothing can be that bad.'

'Well, he was talking about…' She looked at me uncertainly. 'He was talking about *you*, Grace.'

'Oh.' My disquiet/satisfaction levels went up a notch. 'What did he say?'

'Nothing dramatic. But Guy said there was lots of reminiscing: funny conversations you'd had, your first place together, your writing. Guy said he was definitely looking back, not forward.'

'Right.'

'And I just think that doesn't bode well for him and Summer, does it?'

'Hmm…'

We stopped walking and she eyed me suspiciously. 'You know something, don't you?'

'Simone,' I held up a hand, 'I swear I have no idea whether or not Aiden is having an affair. But,' I sighed, 'I do agree with Guy that things aren't great. Mind you, having a baby can make you feel a bit crap, can't it? God knows, Summer having a baby made *me* feel a bit crap,' I added quietly.

'Oh, Grace,' she said, putting her arm around me.

'It's OK,' I reassured. 'I feel much better now. But the pregnancy did feel a bit like being kicked while I wasn't quite up. You know Aiden and I had just agreed to try for a baby when it all kicked off.' I shrugged. 'At least I thought that's what we had agreed.'

Simone looked pained. 'God, I'm so, so sorry. And all that is precisely why I wanted you to have a chance to opt out on Saturday.'

I shook my head. 'It was really good not to have an opt-out. Otherwise I might have been opting out forever. It was something I needed to get out of the way, rather than keep hiding from.' I took a deep breath. 'So not being given any warning was actually a blessing in disguise. For me, anyway – not so much for Summer. Or for anyone else,' I smiled ruefully. 'Poor, poor Callum. Why on earth didn't Jasmine wipe that lipstick off his forehead?'

'I think she was just too dazed.'

'It felt like a target to aim for when I was kissing him goodnight.'

'It did!' She laughed. 'Are you going to put him in a book?'

'I'd love to, Sim. But people can be stupidly sensitive about being ridiculed in print, you know.'

She laughed again and threw the ball for Katy. 'I know you'd never do that to anyone. But on the subject of books, how's your latest one going?'

'Actually, I'm taking a little break,' I said as we started to walk again. 'My last effort wasn't quite as…' I hesitated, 'quite as positive as it perhaps should have been.'

Simone pulled a face. 'Oh dear. Can you put it right?'

I smiled. 'I think it's more about putting *me* right than the book. Neil thought I should take a break, and he was right.'

'A break from writing? But you love it so much.'

'I do,' I agreed, 'so I'm still writing – except now it's fact, not fiction. I'm keeping a diary about...' I paused mischievously for effect.

'About what?' she asked, turning towards me.

'About my new job.'

I enjoyed her look of surprise as she stopped walking and took my arm, forcing me to a standstill. 'You've got a new job? And you haven't told me about it?' she exclaimed. 'Why on earth didn't you mention it on Saturday?'

'Because it's a bit of a secret,' I whispered. 'I'm going incognito.'

'Ooh!' Her face lit up. 'Sounds exciting. Tell me, tell me, tell me!'

'I'm cleaning.'

Simone's expression of open-mouthed intrigue and excitement became a little fixed. Maintaining it was clearly a struggle. 'Ooh... cleaning...' she said, her mouth still ajar.

'And this Saturday...' I continued.

'Yes?'

'I'm going to be waitressing!'

At that, the effort of appearing excited became too much for her. Her mouth closed and she shook her head. 'Nope, sorry, not getting it. You're going to have to explain.'

'Well,' I said, smiling, 'the first thing you should know is that I've met some very interesting people and I'm enjoying the job. It gets me out of the house, out of my comfort zone and out of myself. I needed all of that.'

She nodded. 'OK, so now I'm getting it,' she said gently, smiling across at me. 'And approving massively, by the way,' she added, as we started to walk again. 'But why incognito?'

'Well, you see,' I said, linking the arm which she now held out for me, 'I'm doing someone a little last-minute favour.' And then, after swearing her to absolute secrecy, I brought Simone up to date, hand-on-box-file and all.

Chapter 13

What I hadn't appreciated when accepting Percy's cleaning commission was that although she owned the house next door to James and Emily, she occupied only the ground floor, the upper floors having been converted into two as-yet-unoccupied flats. So I was surprised when she opened the door to me on the following Friday morning to find myself in a communal entrance hall.

'I'm eighty-two now, darling, and three floors is just too much for me,' she explained, as she pushed open a bright red front door and led me into her flat. 'I decided about two years ago that I needed somewhere smaller. I looked at lots of lovely bungalows but I felt rather afraid of moving. This has been my home for over forty years. That's when James suggested flats. He's so very clever. And it's been marvellous. I'm so cosy here now.'

'James next door?' I clarified, placing my crate of cleaning products on the floor.

Percy nodded. 'They're not quite finished yet, although one is already let, of course. Aaron, my lovely electrician, has to put up a few more lights and then we're away. It'll all be done by Christmas. Anyway, can I get you a cup of tea, darling?' she asked. 'Rose and I always have one before she starts.'

'Well, I've actually just had a coffee,' I said. 'But if you show me round and I make a start, then maybe I could have a cup of tea with you when it's my break. I'd love that.'

'Oh my goodness,' she smiled. 'You're so clever and efficient. Just like James.'

The subsequent tour took rather longer than I'd anticipated; almost an hour, in fact. This wasn't due to the size of the flat or the complexity of the task, but rather to the fact that Percy seemed to have a tale to tell about every single fixture, fitting, painting, photograph and piece of furniture in every single room.

'And this,' she said, pointing at one of half a dozen framed photographs sitting on top of a piano as the tour drew to a close, 'is, or rather *was*, my elder sister, Elspeth. She's sixteen in this picture. It was taken the year before she died.' She picked up the photograph and looked at it fondly. 'Wasn't she beautiful?' she sighed. 'I do miss her still. Even after all these years.'

'She is very beautiful,' I agreed. 'That's so sad that she died so young. I'm sorry, Percy.'

Percy smiled. 'She was quite the eccentric, you know. She used to crochet beautiful little hats and jackets for the cats, and she so, so loved setting fire to things.'

I frowned. 'Setting fire to things?'

Percy nodded.

'You mean she liked making bonfires?' I asked.

'Oh no, dear. She was quite the arsonist,' said Percy, looking up at me benignly.

'My... er... goodness,' I said, struggling for an appropriate response. 'Did she set fire to... big things?'

Percy shrugged. 'Big things, small things. Anything really. She burned down some stables and an outbuilding before Daddy sent her to boarding school. And then, of course, the school burned down, so she had to come home again. A coincidence, Daddy said, but we all knew better.' She nudged me, winked and tapped the side of her nose.

'I see,' I said, uncertainly.

Percy nodded. 'And then,' she continued, rolling her eyes, 'irony of ironies, she dies of hypothermia.'

'Hypo...'

'Yes. Climbed some silly mountain against all advice. Got lost. Hypothermia. Dead.' She clicked her fingers with grim finality.

'Oh no,' I said. 'How dreadful.'

'Indeed,' she nodded. 'But at least we were then able to remove all the sand buckets from the house. So every cloud... Now, shall I go and put the kettle on for a cup of tea?' She looked at her watch. 'You've been at it for a good hour now. You must be ready for your break.'

Once I was finally able to actually start cleaning, the job was finished relatively quickly. And this was despite Percy trailing me with a duster, which she moved in a circular polishing motion – frequently in mid-air – whilst telling me more family tales and briefing me on my role the following evening. I would, she explained, be opening the external door to her thirty or so guests, topping up drinks and having lots of fun. Much as I was beginning to like Percy, I thought the latter was unlikely, but as she chattered away, trying intermittently to ply me with her concrete shortbread, I had no regrets about having agreed to help.

It was almost one o'clock by the time I wound up the flex of Percy's ancient Electrolux Silverado vacuum cleaner – which she had bought as a birthday gift for her husband, Patrick, in 1983 – and prepared to leave, whilst resisting her attempts to give me lunch. 'But you have to eat, dear,' she said. 'You're over six foot tall and I shouldn't think you weigh more than seven stone.'

I laughed. 'I'm five foot seven and I weigh well over nine stone.' She smiled up at me. 'But another time,' I continued, 'I would love to stay for lunch. Or maybe we could go out.'

She beamed delightedly. 'Oh that would be lovely,' she said.

'Right,' I bent down and picked up my cleaning caddy as she held the front door open for me, 'I'll see you tomorrow then, Percy. What time would you like me here?'

She put a thoughtful finger to her lips. 'Well, the invitation was from seven thirty, so could you get here at half past six, darling? That will give us plenty of time to set out the canapés and also have a little glass of something together to get us into the party spirit.'

'Sounds lovely,' I smiled. 'Can't wait.' And then, having received an unexpected kiss on my cheek, I waved goodbye, opened the main front door and made my way down the steps towards the tall garden gate. I had just opened it and stepped out onto the pavement when I heard my name.

'Grace?'

I turned and was dismayed to see James Brooke standing with his hand on the latch of his own gate. It was the first time I had seen him since the day of the box file incident and I felt almost as uncomfortable now as I had then. 'Oh, hi,' I said. 'I've just been cleaning for Percy.'

'I thought maybe you had,' he said, gesturing at the tabard over my arm and the crate of cleaning products I was toting.

I forced a smile, despite there being no hint of one from him.

'But I wasn't entirely sure, as you seem to be lacking the...' he paused before completing the sentence, 'hat.'

I sighed through my clenched grin before attempting a light laugh. 'Ah well, I'm a lot less formal with Percy.'

His only reaction was a slightly quizzical twitch of his eyebrows.

Taking advantage of his silence, and keen to be gone, I said, 'Well, enjoy your weekend away, and maybe I'll see you next week,' before beginning to walk towards my car. 'I have to dash, because I have a package being delivered.'

'But I'll see you tomorrow.'

I stopped and turned back to face him. 'You will?'

'At Percy's,' he explained. 'Emily said you were going.'

'Oh, I see.' I stifled another sigh, disappointed at the thought of now having to serve Dick Dastardly drinks, in addition to cleaning his toilets. 'Sorry, I thought you were going away.'

He shook his head. 'So I'll see you there.' And with that, he opened the gate and walked away up the path and steps which led to his front door.

I stared miserably after him, watching him disappear into the house and aware of a sense of cold dread slowly but surely beginning to displace my happy acceptance of helping out at Percy's party. I tried to rally my mood by reminding myself that, on the upside, Emily would now be there, so that would be at least one friendly face in the crowd. But as my mind turned to Emily, and I continued to gaze unblinkingly at 3 Bennett Park, I began to toy with the idea of knocking on the door, on the off chance she was in, and asking if she could help Percy at the party after all. It would be easy enough to come up with an excuse as to why I could no longer make it, and I had no doubt Emily would step uncomplainingly into the breach, especially as she was going to be there anyway. I had gone so far as to take a couple of steps towards the house when my better self suddenly spoke up and told me to abandon the plan as cowardly, uncharitable and selfish. I took a step back and was beginning what might have been quite a protracted wrestle with my conscience over the matter, when I was distracted by a movement at a second-floor window.

I blinked and focused to discover James looking directly at me, his head tilted at a slight angle, clearly intrigued as to why his cleaning lady was staring so dejectedly at him whilst apparently doing the hokey cokey, a good three or four minutes after she had given the distinct impression of needing to get home in a hurry. I hesitated for a moment, unsure whether to acknowledge him or not, before hastily plumping for *not*. Instead, I raised my gaze little by little to the sky before tracking gradually left, as if following a particularly interesting and extremely slow-moving bird. And then, not daring to look back at him to assess the success or otherwise of this charade, I lowered my eyes, continued to pivot slowly left and, as soon as I was pointing in the right direction, made my way hurriedly to the car.

Chapter 14

'So…' gasped Simone, bent double, hands on hips, 'remind me why I thought this would be a good idea again.'

'Because,' I replied breathlessly, 'you wanted an excuse to dump the kids on Guy every Saturday morning, plus you're worried about your thighs and I…' I paused to gulp from my water bottle, 'stupidly mentioned that I needed to find a way to stay toned when I finish my cleaning job. This isn't it, by the way.'

She nodded, her head just inches from the wet grass of the Downs. 'I'm with you on that. I'm knackered and my pelvic floor is on the edge of collapse. But…' she straightened up and looked at me, her cheeks tomato red rather than their usual rosy pink, 'trying to be positive here, we have managed a run. What distance do you think we've covered?'

I turned and looked back across the Downs towards our start point, the Sea Walls. 'A good two hundred metres, I think. Maybe two twenty-five.' And then, despite the intense burning pain in my chest, I started to laugh, in gasping, barely audible bursts. Simone joined in and we stood for a few minutes more, leaning against each other, every ounce of our remaining energy invested in giggling.

'Anyway,' I said eventually, waving a hand and finally regaining control, 'how about we stomp-stroll the rest of the way?'

'Stomp-stroll?'

'It's like a power walk, only slower,' I explained. 'I've just invented it.'

'Sounds good,' she said, tugging at my sleeve as we began to walk. 'But now you've got your breath back, tell me about tonight. What are you wearing?'

'Haven't really thought about it,' I shrugged.

'Well, what about your navy-blue floaty dress? The one with the wavy hem. Ooh, or that lovely black dress you wore last weekend?' she added, warming to her subject. 'You look great in anything but you looked *amazing* in that.'

I rolled my eyes. 'You do realise, Simone, that I'm waitressing at a party, not participating in a group dating event. There is a difference.'

'No harm in looking nice,' she winked. 'You never know who might turn up.'

'I do, actually,' I said. 'I know absolutely *everyone* who is going to turn up because Percy went through the entire guest list with me yesterday while I was cleaning – or at least it felt like the entire guest list. I was shown child-hood, university and wedding photos of everyone who's attending, and let's just say that most of them were sepia tint.'

'Oh come off it,' she tutted. 'They can't be that old.'

'Well, they all seemed to have survived the Blitz in some amazing way or another. It was a recurring theme.'

Simone laughed. 'Percy sounds great.'

'She is,' I smiled. 'I really enjoy her company. I hope I'm still as excited by and interested in life when I'm her age.'

'You will be,' said Simone. 'I can't see you ever stopping being interested.'

'That's just a polite way of saying I'm nosy, isn't it?'

'It is.'

'Thought so.'

She smiled. 'And with that in mind, Guy asks if you're still snooping?'

'Snooping?'

'At work,' she explained. 'I told him about the box file. I hope it was OK to mention the job to him? He knows he's not to talk about it to anyone else.'

'It's fine,' I said. 'And you can tell him that I'm working my way through every cupboard and drawer in the house in search of diaries. And once I've found those, I have high hopes of my next two books writing themselves.'

'I'll be sure to pass that on,' she laughed. 'It sounds like you could write three books on Percy alone.'

'I could,' I agreed. 'I'd love to write her family history.'

'Have you told her about your books, then?'

I shook my head. 'The topic hasn't come up and I'm not in any hurry to raise it – especially when I'm trying to take a break from it all. You know me, I'd much rather write than talk about writing at the best of times. In any case, I'd want to speak to Rose before I said anything. Maybe I'll chat to Percy in January about getting some of her stories down on paper. She has so many great ones, Sim.'

'Such as?'

'I'll tell you the one about her sister when we get to the café,' I teased. 'It's so interesting and it'll give you something to push towards – other than cake.'

'I love that your job is making you want to tell stories again,' said Simone.

I looked at her and smiled. 'Me too.'

'What about Emily?' she asked. 'Is there a story there?'

'She's just as interesting as Percy. Although in a very different way,' I added, smiling at the thought of seeing her that evening at the party, before the sudden recollection that she would be on James's arm caused my face to drop.

'Is everything OK there?' asked Simone, sounding concerned. 'You look worried.'

'I was just thinking about Emily and James,' I sighed. 'I really don't know what she's doing with him.'

'Does she seem unhappy?'

'No,' I admitted, 'but that's what confuses me. They seem so unsuited. She's open, warm and welcoming and he's the exact opposite – the kind of person who sees no need to put anyone at their ease. I've told you how he looks at me – with a sort of mildly offended fascination, as if I smell odd, or have a bit of something hanging from my nose.'

'He sounds like a really great guy,' laughed Simone. 'But as far as his relationship with Emily goes, I know better than most that it takes all sorts. I'm sure ninety-nine per cent of people can't understand why Guy married me – or why I haven't murdered him yet.'

'That's different,' I smiled. 'You are mismatched perfection. Like when you can't understand why one wildly patterned cushion looks good next to another wildly patterned cushion, but it just does.'

'I wish Guy was a cushion so that I could legally punch him whenever I wanted,' she said grumpily.

'Shut up. You love him,' I laughed.

'For my sins.' She paused and took a deep breath. 'But anyway, maybe that's what James and Emily are,' she suggested. 'Two wildly patterned cushions. You haven't seen them together yet, have you?'

I shook my head.

'Well, perhaps their relationship will become more understandable when you do.'

'Perhaps,' I said doubtfully. 'They're both coming to the party tomorrow now, actually.'

'Really? I thought you said all the guests were over a hundred.'

'They're the exception. Not sure why the change of plan, but I ran into James yesterday,' my mood dropped at the thought, 'and he said they'd be there.'

'OK, well maybe seeing them as a pair will change your opinion of him – and of their relationship,' she said brightly.

'Maybe it will,' I said, not even attempting to sound convinced.

'Just keep an open mind,' said Simone, her tone now motherly.

I turned towards her and smiled. 'I promise to try. I just hate the thought of someone like Emily heading blindly for a fall.'

She nodded. 'That's because you're a woman's woman, Grace Waterhouse.'

I put my arm around her and gave her a squeeze. 'And coming from the ultimate woman's woman, I take that as a huge compliment,' I said.

She returned the hug and then turned and pointed to the café in the near distance. 'Are we close enough for you to start telling me the tale of Percy's sister?' she asked. 'I don't think I can wait much longer. Is it a good one?'

'Your jaw will drop, Sim,' I smiled. 'Your jaw will drop.'

Chapter 15

Percy and I spent the first five minutes after my arrival at her flat the following evening setting out trays of canapés in the long reception room which ran the full length of the back of the house. It was, by day, two rooms – a large lounge and a similarly sized separate dining room, identical to those I cleaned twice weekly for her neighbours. But this evening, a pair of large wooden dividing doors had been pulled back to create a single space, perfect for mingling.

'This is such a lovely room, Percy,' I said, looking at the heavily framed oils and antique furniture, the provenance of which I now knew in such detail.

She smiled and nodded. 'When the architect came to chop up the house, I insisted that this part was left untouched,' she said. 'It's where I spend most of my time and I wanted it to stay exactly the same. Now,' she looked at the six platters we had placed on various surfaces around the room, 'I think that's all the hard work done. I'll show you where everything is in the kitchen, darling, and then would you like some champagne? And can I just say how beautiful you look?'

I laughed. 'You can. But you have already told me that twice, you know,' I said, looking down at my black dress and heels.

'I know I have,' she smiled. 'The problem is that you never quite look like you believe me, dear.'

–

Percy and I were halfway down our second glass of champagne when the doorbell rang for the first time. On that occasion, she came with me to answer it, but, after that, I was on my own. The stream of arrivals was pretty constant, and for the next hour I was kept happily busy running to the door and pouring drinks in between the summons of the bell. But by 9 p.m., the arrivals had slowed and I was just debating whether to circulate with canapés when the doorbell went for what would prove to be the final time that evening. I went out into the entrance hall and opened the door. It was James.

'Hello!' I said with genuine enthusiasm, leaning to the right in an attempt to see past him to Emily. 'It hadn't occurred to me that the two of you weren't here yet. Percy's got quite a crowd in there.'

'She always does.' James stepped inside, closely followed by a tall, dark-haired woman wearing a perfectly fitted grey wool coat. She walked past me as if I was invisible, before turning to James.

'It looks like people are leaving their coats here.' She gestured at the hatstands and small wooden clothes rail which Percy's electrician had brought downstairs for her that morning. She removed her coat and held it out to me, whilst looking towards the open door of Percy's flat. 'Thanks so much,' she said.

I peered out of the front door and into the night and then turned to James. 'No Emily?' I asked, closing the door.

'Not tonight,' he replied, taking the coat the woman still held outstretched. 'Heather, this is Grace Waterhouse. Grace, this is Heather Gorman.'

Heather turned to me, her face suddenly breaking into a smile. 'Oh, I'm so sorry, Grace.' She looked up at James and laughed. 'I thought she was staff!'

'I am staff,' I smiled. 'But apparently I still get to have a name.' She didn't appear to hear me and I took the coat from James without making eye contact. 'Here, I'll hang that up for you. I've just poured some fresh glasses of champagne. They're in the kitchen if you'd like to help yourself.' I turned away and reached for a hanger.

'Thanks, Grace. I hope we get to talk later,' he said.

'God, me too,' said Heather, now tuning in. 'Is your partner with you, Grace? James told me he'd be the only man here under seventy.'

I looked over my shoulder at her. 'Are you sure he wasn't talking about his IQ?' I paused before adding a light laugh.

I turned back to the coat rail, aware of the sound of their receding footsteps on the tiled floor and of Heather whispering something about 'odd sense of humour' as they disappeared into Percy's flat. I stood there for a moment, regretting the dig at James and reminding myself once again that my behaviour towards him could have consequences for Rose.

'Oh my darling, you've been working so hard. Here, let's swap.' I turned to find Percy standing behind me holding a large glass of white wine, which she pushed into my hand as she relieved me of the coat and hung it up. Then, without saying anything further, she threaded her arm through mine and led me back into the flat and through to the small kitchen, into which, in true party fashion, a dozen people had squashed themselves. 'You must try one of these chorizo and spicy pepper rolls,' she beamed, pulling me towards yet another tray of canapés resting on top of the hob.

I smiled and sipped my wine. 'Oh go on then,' I said, taking one. 'I've just seen James with a woman named Heather. Do you know her, Percy?'

'Oh, is James here?' Percy craned her neck towards the open kitchen door. 'I'm afraid I don't know who he's with, darling.' She looked up at me and winked. 'I shall investigate later and report back.'

I had just popped the canapé into my mouth and now hurriedly chewed and swallowed it. 'Oh no, no, it doesn't matter,' I said, fearing that Percy's digging on my behalf might be less than subtle. 'I just wondered. And I was sad not to see Emily here.'

Percy sighed. 'Yes. But I'm sure she's having fun wherever she is.'

It crossed my mind to ask Percy for her take on Emily and James's relationship. But aware that I had perhaps already showed too much of an interest in him, I decided to change the subject. 'Right,' I said, sipping my wine and then placing the glass on the work surface, 'I'll go and circulate with the tray.'

Percy waved a hand. 'No, you've done enough,' she said. 'And I've got lots of people I want to introduce you to.'

I shook my head. 'You mingle. Now the doorbell has stopped, I'm quite capable of introducing myself. Everyone was very friendly as I let them in, and besides, holding a tray of food is quite a draw.'

She looked up at me for a moment and then smiled. 'Well, if that's the way you'd rather do it, so be it.' She rubbed my arm affectionately. 'And I quite understand.' She kissed her hand, pressed it to my cheek, and then I watched her leave, blowing further kisses left and right as she made her way from the kitchen.

Once she'd gone, I took another quick sip of wine, picked up my tray and walked through into the reception room, taking a moment as I did so to look around and assess the demographic of Percy's guests. It had struck me, when welcoming the partygoers into the house, that, as expected, I was most definitely at the very youngest end of the age range, with all the guests, with the exception of James and Heather, appearing to be in their late sixties at least. So it was with some surprise, as I moved around the room being greeted warmly and interrogated gently by each small huddle of pensioners, that I caught sight of a slim, impeccably dressed man with a full head of dark brown hair. He was standing alone with his back to me, but I quickly decided that if his poise, choice of jacket and hair colour were anything to go by, he was definitely in his twenties or thirties. Intrigued, I walked over and held out my tray. 'Canapé?'

'Oh my God, Grace,' he said, turning and spilling his drink in surprise.

'Neil!' I gasped.

'Damn.' He took a handkerchief from his jacket pocket and mopped his trousers.

I began to laugh and after a moment he looked up and joined in. 'I didn't know you knew Percy,' he said. 'She was a friend of my grandmother's.'

'Really?' I smiled. 'She's lovely, isn't she? Oh, but I'm not a guest this evening, I'm staff. I'm waitressing.'

'You're…?' Behind his glasses, his eyes widened briefly before returning to normal size. 'You know, that's fine,' he said with a sigh. 'I'm just going to accept that and be very happy for you.'

'I clean the house next door,' I explained. 'That's how I met Percy and how I got this job.'

His eyes widened once again. 'You mean OCD guy is her *neighbour*?'

'Shh, shh, *shhhhhh*,' I said, looking round. 'He's just over there.' I jerked my head towards the far corner of the room, where James was standing talking to Heather.

Neil looked over my shoulder. 'Dark blonde hair, piercing blue eyes and a strong jawline?' he whispered, clearly impressed.

'Mousy brown hair, psychopathic stare *and a heart of stone*,' I frowned. 'His girlfriend is away and he's brought someone else to the party.'

Neil looked at me with a mixture of pity and disapproval. 'Not all men are the same, Grace,' he said wearily. 'And bringing a friend to a party isn't a prosecutable offence, you know.'

I moved to stand next to him and together we looked across the room at James, just as Heather snaked an arm around his waist before lowering it to his bottom and then, standing on tiptoe, planted a lingering kiss on his cheek. He responded with a kiss to her forehead and an arm around her shoulders.

'Heart of stone,' said Neil.

'He's unbelievable,' I muttered.

Neil smiled and took a chorizo roll from my tray. '*You're* unbelievable. With your canapés and neighbourhood networking. Gavin is going to be so sorry he missed out on this. Especially as your hair is looking very good this evening.' He took a step back and examined me. 'You're looking very good all over actually. Working in service industries clearly agrees with you.'

I looked up at him and smiled a little shyly. I wasn't used to personal compliments from Neil. Personal compliments, and insults, were usually Gavin's domain. 'So where *is* Gavin?' I asked. 'Is he—' I got no further before Neil silenced me with a near-imperceptible shake of his head and a sidelong glance.

'Hi.'

I turned my head at the sound of James's voice to find that he and Heather were now standing beside us. He looked at Neil and then back at me. 'I hope we're not interrupting. Do you two know each other?'

'We do, and you're not interrupting,' said Neil, smiling and holding out a hand. 'Neil Whitfield, literary agent. Grace is one of my…'

I pressed my elbow into his side.

'… cleaners,' he concluded, offering me a smile. 'I have several. But Grace is my favourite.'

I didn't know whether to applaud or punch him. Both crossed my mind.

James nodded. 'James Brooke. Grace and I are still getting to know each other.'

'Ooh, a literary agent,' said Heather, leaning forward and shaking Neil's hand. 'I'm Heather Gorman and I work in boring old recruitment. Do you represent anyone I might have heard of?'

'It depends what kind of books you like reading,' said Neil. 'I represent Tom Bancroft, the thriller writer.' Heather nodded eagerly. 'Or if you prefer beautifully written, escapist romance,' it was his turn to elbow me, 'I represent Elizabeth Canning.'

'Would you like some sausage, Heather?' I asked, holding out my tray.

She smiled at Neil. 'I've never heard of her. But then for some reason I don't tend to be a fan of female authors. I think perhaps I just find men so much more straightforward – both in print and in person.' She offered Neil a pouting smile, whilst stroking James's arm.

I stared at her, realising that the only thing preventing me from straightforwardly smashing her repeatedly over the head with my tray was the fear of making a mess on Percy's carpet.

'Do you think so?' said Neil hurriedly, as if sensing danger. 'I actually think it's possible for an author to disguise their sex very effectively.'

I nodded. 'Yes, there are lots of authors who write very convincingly in both the male and female voice. Gillian Fly—'

Heather turned to me. 'That's *so* interesting, Gail,' she said gently, as if I was a five-year-old and she was my new learning support assistant. 'And I know I'm a pain, but you couldn't get me a refill, could you?' she continued, smiling sweetly and holding out her empty glass to me. 'I feel a bit cheeky trotting into the kitchen and helping myself again so soon.'

I glanced at the chorizo rolls, deciding that they'd probably be quite easy to vacuum out of the carpet.

Neil reached out and took Heather's glass. 'Come on,' he said. 'I need a drink too; because I just spilt most of mine. I'll lead you to the fridge and then we can take our pick of the vintages.'

Heather beamed. 'Great. Let's go.'

Neil smiled and, after giving me a look which I interpreted as *don't hit anyone with the tray*, he walked away, taking Heather with him.

I looked after them and then turned to James. 'I'd better circulate with the canapés.'

'Are you enjoying the party?' he asked.

For some reason, I took the unexpected question as a personal challenge. 'Yes thank you,' I replied, somewhat stiffly. 'I'm enjoying myself very much indeed. Aren't you?'

'I am,' he nodded. 'But I'd be enjoying myself even more if I wasn't getting the distinct impression that you'd like to pelt me with those.' He looked down at the chorizo rolls.

I followed his gaze and then continued to stare mutely at the tray for a moment, completely thrown by his comment and wary of delivering a hasty response which might result in the loss of my cleaning job, and therefore – and much more importantly – the loss of Rose's.

'Here I am, darling, let's swap again,' said Percy, swooping in from nowhere like an elderly nick-of-time superhero in support stockings and pearls. She handed me a glass of wine and took the tray from me. 'You left your wine behind in the kitchen. Oh but how lovely to find you two together, and from over there it looked like you were getting on famously.'

I looked up from the tray, having absently tracked its journey from my hand to Percy's. 'Thank you,' I said, managing a smile. 'We were just saying what a lovely time we're both having.' I kept my eyes fixed determinedly on her.

'Were you?' She turned her head towards James, beaming delightedly. 'I'm so pleased. I always worry that the pace is a little slow for you younger ones. Now, I hope you won't think me rude, my darlings, but I must go and keep an eye on Fiona Saunt. She was hovering near my Italian knick-knacks earlier and I wouldn't put it past her to go home with one. She has a cavernous cleavage and my Meissen ostrich saucer was nowhere to be found after her last visit.'

'That's fine. You go,' I said, despite desperately wanting her to stay.

She seemed to sense my equivocation. 'Now, don't you worry,' she soothed, patting my arm. 'James here will look after you, won't you, James? He's so gallant. And you look so wonderful together. You don't want me spoiling the portrait. Now, where is that dreadful woman?' she said, turning and bustling away.

I forced myself to look at James. 'I expect you're breathing a sigh of relief that she's taken the tray away.'

He nodded. 'I am, actually.' And then he suddenly smiled. Not a token smile, but a genuine one, perhaps the first I had seen. I found myself studying him with a sudden, strange sense of recognition.

'Look, I don't know what I've done, Grace,' he said. 'But if I've made you feel uncomfortable in any way, I'm sorry. Emily often tells me that I'm out touch with my facial features and give the wrong impression. And if that's happened, well, as I say, I'm sorry.'

I continued to stare up at him, now feeling almost certain that I had met him, or seen him, before becoming his cleaner. I also felt my opinion of him unmistakably softening.

He continued to smile. 'So? Are we OK?' he asked, with the directness Rose so admired. 'Or is there a problem?'

I realised that I was now smiling, and I had just opened my mouth with the intention of confirming that there wasn't a problem when I was prevented from doing so by the reappearance of the *huge* problem, which had, for some inexplicable reason, slipped my mind.

'Got my bubbles, James!' said Heather, returning to his side and clinking her champagne flute against his glass of red wine. She tilted her head upwards and he bent down, kissing her briefly on the lips.

I choked on the mouthful of wine I had just taken, prompting a coughing fit.

'Are you OK, Gail? Did something go down the wrong way?' asked Heather, back in teacher mode. 'Oh, and before I forget,' she added slowly, as if fearing I might be incapable of assimilating speech at normal speed, 'Neil would like a word with you in the kitchen. There's someone he wants to introduce you to. He said to tell you there's a cleaning job in it for you. Isn't that great?' She nodded and smiled, looking at me intently, awaiting confirmation that her words had sunk in.

I felt my jaw and fist clench simultaneously but, more grateful for a chance to get away than upset with Neil for the cleaning comment, I took a deep breath and nodded.

'Thanks, Helen,' I said and then, looking up at James, 'Enjoy the rest of your evening.' And with that, I turned and headed for the kitchen.

Chapter 16

I smiled contentedly as I sipped my coffee and then placed it, together with a plate of three mini blueberry muffins, on the dining table next to my open laptop and sat down. I had arrived home that morning from Percy's at 2 a.m., and the 11:30 sugar brunch was my first meal of the day. I picked up a muffin, took an appreciative bite and began to type.

Saturday 19 November: Party poppers and
poopers

Neil was at Percy's party! His expression was priceless when he turned around and saw me. I told him I wished I'd been wearing a headcam and he's promised to get me one for the next time I waitress. It was so great to have him there but, even without him, I wouldn't have been short of people to chat to. Percy's friends are lovely. She surrounds herself with people who delight in life. I even warmed to the infamous Fiona Saunt, but I don't think I'll be sharing that fact with Percy, who spent most of the evening tailing her with all the subtlety of a Keystone Cop. I twice caught her patting the poor woman down on the pretext of 'brushing off crumbs'. Fortunately, Fiona seemed oblivious to Percy's suspicions and actually seemed grateful for the attention. So no harm done.

The only real downer of the evening was the presence of James Brooke, who turned up not with Emily, but with an illiterate, shameless stand-in called Heather something or other, who then proceeded to slobber over him for three hours. God only knows how much saliva she got through, but it was like watching a housefly trying to digest a steak. He, meanwhile, in what I can only assume was a moment of alcohol-assisted lucidity, asked me whether I had a problem with him. I fantasised about replying, 'Not at all, James. Smug, charisma-free, duplicitous gits are my very favourite kind of people.' But I couldn't do that to Rose and, besides, he probably wouldn't have been able to hear me with Heather's tongue halfway down his ear canal.

I stopped typing, distracted by the vibration of my phone in my dressing-gown pocket. I took it out and, my newly formed frown falling away, answered the call.

'Gavin!' I said, now smiling. 'How are you?'

'Not too bad,' he replied, his voice hoarse and barely audible.

'Not too bad?' I exclaimed. 'You sound dreadful.' I stood up and, using my shoulder to keep the phone pressed against my ear, carried my cup of coffee and plate of mini muffins into the lounge.

'I know,' he croaked. 'But I just had to call you. Neil told me a bit about the party, but you know how crap and high-horsey he is about gossip.'

'I know he stayed to help with the clearing up,' I said, placing my muffins on the floor and sitting down on the sofa. 'So I won't hear a bad word said about him for at least twenty-four hours.'

There was a short burst of laughter, followed by a lot of coughing.

'I wish you'd go back to bed – or to a sanatorium,' I said, reaching down for a muffin.

He appeared not to hear. 'Neil said that OCD bloke is beautiful but a bastard,' he rasped.

I nodded pointlessly, whilst eating the muffin whole. 'You should have seen him, Gavin,' I mumbled, spitting crumbs. 'He was brazen. *Brazen.*'

'So who was the woman he was with?' he asked. 'Apparently her bronze bodycon dress was to die for.'

I sneered as much as was possible with a mouthful of muffin. 'Was it? I didn't notice. She said she worked in recruitment, but that was all I got.' I sipped my coffee. 'Ask Neil. He clearly took more of an interest in her than I did.'

'Now don't get all huffy and shut down just because Neil noticed her dress.' He paused for a moment. 'And her shoes. He said they were—'

'I am not getting huffy,' I interrupted. 'It's just that after Neil rescued me, I avoided talking to the pair of them for the rest of the evening. So I don't really have much more to tell. He's a creep. She's an illiterate misogynist. End of.'

'Yeah, I heard she dissed your books,' he giggled wheezily. 'So, anyway, are you going to find out more when you go round to clean tomorrow?' he asked eagerly.

'Emily probably won't be there,' I sighed. 'And to be honest, I'm hoping she's not. She's bound to ask about the party.'

'Perfect… opportunity. It's not your… fault her boyfriend is a… shit,' said Gavin, punctuating the sentences with coughs.

'I know it's not. But I still feel complicit. In any other circumstances I wouldn't hesitate to tell her he spent last night draped all over another woman. But I feel like there's a gagging order on me because of Rose.' I sighed again. 'I wish Percy had said something to him. I don't understand why she's so accepting of his evilness.'

'I know. I thought that. Neil wondered if maybe she hadn't noticed the groping.'

'Maybe,' I said doubtfully. 'But they were hardly furtive about it. Anyway,' I continued, now wanting to move on from what was turning out to be a rather depressing subject, 'are you going to be fit for your holiday? When do you go?'

'On Tuesday. For…' There was a pause while he blew his nose loudly. 'For three and a bit weeks: New York, San Francisco and then a week in LA with Neil's cousin.'

I groaned. 'Everyone is taking such great holidays this year.'

'Well, there was nothing stopping you getting on a plane,' he said, without pity. 'Except maybe that hair of yours blocking the emergency exit.'

'You are such a cheeky—' I began before being interrupted by the buzz of the intercom. 'Gavin, can I call you back in two minutes? Someone's at the door.'

'It's fine,' he said. 'I'm gonna take some Day Nurse and go back to bed. Call me tomorrow, after you've gone to pieces and told Emily everything.'

'You're such a joy to know,' I said.

He embarked upon a second bout of breathless laughter. 'Ah, you know I love you to bits. I'm just sick of being cooped up and need a bit of drama.'

'Well, I'll call you if there are any dramatic developments before you go. But if there aren't, get well and have a great time away,' I said, standing up and making my way hurriedly into the hallway as the buzzer went for a second and then a third time. 'One moment,' I said into the intercom. 'I'm just getting off the phone.'

'Bye then, Grace,' said Gavin. 'And I've booked you in for a shearing as soon as I get back, whether you like it or not: Monday the nineteenth of December at 6 p.m. – just in time to stop you looking like Hair Bear over Christmas.'

I rolled my eyes. 'Thanks so much.'

I heard a final, brief cackle of wheezy laughter and then the dialling tone.

I sighed and pressed the intercom. 'Sorry to keep you,' I said. 'Who's there?'

'It's me. It's Aiden.'

'Aiden,' I echoed in surprise. And then, after only a slight hesitation, I buzzed him in.

–

It was the first time I had seen or heard from him since Simone's dinner party and as I made him a cup of coffee,

Aiden updated me on the events of the intervening seven days – one night of which he had spent in a local hotel after Summer had thrown a jug at him.

'So, it's not been great,' he concluded, as I sat down opposite him at the dining table and handed him a mug. 'She's always been a bit manic, but this past week she's been off the scale at both ends.'

I raised my eyebrows.

He held up a hand. 'I know. And I don't expect any sympathy from you.'

'Good. But if you're not after sympathy, why are you here?'

'To apologise for Saturday,' he said, picking up his coffee. 'And because a week without talking to you seemed like a very long time,' he added quietly.

I drank my own coffee and said nothing, a self-preservatory mechanism instructing me to remain silent.

'I'm sorry to crash your Sunday morning. I did call round on Friday during the day – twice – and again last night, but you were out.' He looked at me questioningly.

I ignored the implied enquiry as to my whereabouts. 'You should have texted,' I said.

He shook his head. 'I didn't know what to say. I still don't. It took me until Thursday to call Guy and Simone, and the apology to you is obviously in a completely different league.'

I took a deep breath. 'Can I ask you something?'

'I'm not having an affair,' he said. 'I'm having a friend-ship – I hope.' He paused and looked up at me. 'You're the reason I'm late home, Grace.' He lowered his eyes to his coffee and fell silent for a moment. 'Do we have a friendship?' he asked eventually.

'I'm not sure what we have,' I said truthfully.

He nodded. 'Well, whatever it is, do you think we can still have it?'

'My side of it is a lot less complicated than yours, Aiden,' I shrugged, trying to sound indifferent and unbothered, while ignoring a nagging doubt regarding the truth of the statement. 'What does Summer have to say about it?'

'I haven't told her,' he said miserably.

'I know you haven't,' I smiled. 'I was just being mean.'

He looked up at me. 'Thanks, because I'm not at all vulnerable right now.'

I sighed. 'Look, I'm sure she'd feel better knowing you're having coffee with your middle-aged ex than she would about the possibility of you having an affair with a...' My voice trailed away as I experienced a crushing echo of the hurt I had felt three years earlier when Aiden had mistakenly sent me a text intended for Summer, and his infidelity had been laid suddenly, agonisingly bare. 'You know, Aiden, I'm not sure I can talk about this. It doesn't make me feel great about you, or myself, and that's a shame, because I had been making great progress on both fronts.'

'God, I know,' he said, leaning forward and placing his head in his hands. 'And I don't want to talk about it either. The problem is that I do want to talk to you about everything else. I need that. I need you. I know you're not mine to have but I can't lose you entirely.' He looked up at me. 'Do you know what an idiot I feel about everything – every single day? I sat next to you on Saturday night and I...' He left the sentence unfinished and instead picked up his coffee. 'I'm sorry, Grace,' he said at last, his voice now calm. 'I'm just so, so sorry.'

I looked at him and tried to remain unmoved, struggling to retain the cynicism and scepticism with which I had regarded his every word and action for the past three years, and keen to write off his regret as an emotion rooted in self-pity and self-interest and nothing more.

But as he returned his coffee to the table and replaced his head in his hands, it was a battle against compassion and forgiveness for which, I realised, I no longer had the heart. And I was surprised to discover that laying down my arms felt, on this particular occasion, like victory, not defeat.

'I believe you, Aiden,' I said quietly, putting down my own mug and briefly resting my hand on his arm. And then, with counterfeit matter-of-factness and pushing the plate of muffins towards him, I added, 'Now here, have one of these. They always made me feel better.'

Chapter 17

I was relieved to find no one at home when I arrived at Bennett Park the next morning. The Sunday-brunch conversation with Aiden was still weighing heavily on my mind and the idea of having an awkward encounter with Emily on top of that didn't appeal at all.

Aiden had, by the time he left, agreed to be open with Summer about our coffees and occasional drinks. He argued that telling her retrospectively about previous meetings was pointless and counterproductive, but he did accept that being truthful in the future was essential for me, and preferable for him to having crockery thrown at his head for a non-existent affair.

Meanwhile, my own thoughts and feelings were confused to say the least. I had been enjoying his company increasingly and had to admit that I was pleased that he wanted our friendship, for want of a better description, to continue at least as much as I did and, quite possibly, more. But I was less comfortable whenever I allowed myself to think about where I saw this particular friendship going. I tried to tell myself that it was perfectly possible for Aiden and me to continue to enjoy a platonic relationship, built on the best of our past and a determination to behave respectfully towards each other in the future. But I was not completely blind to the problem of his obvious dissatisfaction with his present and his increasing tendency, as Simone had put it, to look back. Even more worryingly, I wasn't entirely sure whether I saw that tendency as a problem or a positive.

Desperate to escape from such troublingly deep thoughts, a morning mopping, vacuuming and polishing, whilst focusing on nothing more controversial than the *Desert Island Discs* podcast, was therefore something I was really looking forward to. In fact, as I carried the vacuum cleaner from the top of the house to the bottom, checking out my firmer upper arms and increasingly pert posterior in a landing mirror as I went, I began to fret again over what alternative fitness regime and emotional therapy could replace my cleaning job when Rose came home from Spain and reassumed control of the Dyson in the new year.

Thankfully, I was rescued from pondering even that minor concern for too long by the sound of a key in the lock and Percy's loud 'Yoohoo!' from the entrance hall. I was at first delighted by her arrival, as it coincided nicely – and, I suspected, deliberately – with my ten-thirty tea break.

'Hello,' I said, smiling as she closed the front door. 'Are you free for a cup of tea, or is this a fleeting visit?'

She smiled, putting down her large black handbag and reaching into it. 'It's a shortbread visit, darling.'

'Lovely,' I nodded, whilst unconsciously checking my fillings with my tongue. 'I'll put the kettle on.'

'Is Emily here yet?' she asked, following me into the kitchen.

I felt my smile drop a little. 'Oh, is she joining us?'

'She is,' said Percy, settling herself at the kitchen table and taking the lid off her Tupperware. 'She popped one of her lovely little notes through my door last night, inviting me for a cup of tea and saying she wanted to hear all about the party.'

With my back now to Percy, my smile fell away completely and, after just a moment's hesitation, I decided there was nothing for it but to confide how uncomfortable I felt. 'Percy,' I said, turning round, 'I wanted to talk to you about the party. In particular about James at the party.'

Percy looked up at me and nodded excitedly. 'That's marvellous because I wanted to talk to you about him too, dear. But let's wait until Emily gets here.'

'Really?' I said. 'Because I think I might find it a little difficult to be honest about it all when she's here. I don't want to hurt her feelings and I don't want to cause trouble between her and James. But at the same time, if she asks me about Heather, I feel I have to be honest in what I say.'

Percy shook her head. 'Oh, there won't be any trouble,' she said. 'Emily has her own misgivings but she would never say anything to James. You mustn't worry about it, darling. Everyone involved is a grown-up.'

I frowned, disappointed by her reaction, and was just about to explain that I didn't see things in quite the same way when we heard the front door open and close. A moment later, Emily bounced into the kitchen.

'Hello, both,' she said, placing a small leather rucksack on a kitchen chair and flopping down on another. She looked up at me. 'You're on kettle duty today then, Grace? Fabulous. I am desperate for a cup of tea, please. Ooh and,' she added, leaning forward and peering into the plastic container sitting on the table, 'shortbread. Fantastic.' She reached into the box, took a square of shortbread and attempted to take a bite. 'You know,' she said after failing to make even a dent in it, 'I might save this to dunk in my tea. Because first things first, how did Saturday go?'

I turned back to the kettle and set about making the tea while Percy chattered about guest numbers, alcohol consumption and Fiona Saunt's kleptomania. It was my faint hope that by the time I placed the three mugs of tea on the table, the conversation might have moved on from Percy's party to Emily's weekend. However, two or three minutes later, when it was clear this wasn't going to be the case, I decided to force the transition.

'And what did *you* get up to this weekend?' I asked, as Emily thanked me for her tea and I sat down.

She shook her head. 'No, no, no,' she laughed, wagging a finger at me and grinning mischievously at Percy. 'Percy knows what I *really* want to talk about. I want to know whether James brought Heather along on Saturday or not. I haven't asked him because I know he'll just clam up.'

My heart sank and Percy patted Emily's hand and winked. 'He did, my darling. In fact, Grace and I were just having a little chat about that before you arrived, weren't we?' She looked at me delightedly before turning back to Emily. 'I was very disappointed not to be able to talk to her at any length. But Grace has formed opinions and I told her to be completely honest with you about them.'

'I actually had only two very brief chats with her,' I said.

'And what did you think?' asked Emily eagerly. She appeared genuinely interested.

'Have you met her?' I asked evasively.

She nodded and sipped her tea. 'Yes, twice. The last time was at a corporate thing James actually let me come along to a few weeks ago.'

'And did you like her?'

She hesitated. 'Well, she was very smiley...' she began. 'It's tricky for me to judge because of my relationship to James. I'm obviously not going to be impartial or objective. But she was certainly very into him and I hate his ego being boosted like that.' She laughed again and looked wholly unperturbed, a reaction which left me upset at her ignorance and even more distressed at the thought of enlightening her.

'Oh, that dear boy doesn't have one ounce of ego,' said Percy.

Emily smiled. 'I know he doesn't. And I also know that I'm very lucky. He takes such good care of me. I couldn't ask for a better—'

'Emily, I'm so sorry to have to tell you this,' I said suddenly, talking rapidly and closing my eyes to avoid being deterred by either her reaction or Percy's, 'but Percy has told me that you already have your doubts over Heather's relationship with James, and I'm afraid that after what I've seen and heard, I think you're absolutely right to be worried. I'm so sorry, because I know first-hand how devastating infidelity is and I really didn't want to have to tell you about Heather. But your own relationship with James, and how much you obviously love him, means that I think you need to know and talk to him about it, and, well,' I concluded breathlessly, slumping in my seat and opening my eyes, 'now I've said it.'

Emily was staring at me, her mouth slightly ajar. 'Infidelity?' she murmured, clearly stunned by the revelation.

She looked at Percy and then back at me. 'Heather?' she asked. 'You're absolutely certain?'

I nodded sadly. 'I wonder if perhaps deep down you already knew,' I said quietly.

She shook her head. 'I thought she wasn't as open as I'd like, but…' She hesitated and heaved a sigh. 'Not this.'

'She's not married, is she?' asked Percy, placing a horrified hand to her chest.

I looked at her and frowned. 'Not as far as I know, Percy,' I said gently. 'But I'm not sure that matters for the moment.' I inclined my head towards Emily.

'Of course,' said Percy, nodding thoughtfully. 'You're quite right, my darling. One does not need to be wearing a ring to be unfaithful.'

'Oh, but this is so sad,' said Emily softly, as if to herself, 'but I think,' she continued, looking up at me hopefully, 'I think perhaps James's relationship with her isn't that serious. He tends to hold back, so maybe…' Her voice trailed away and I reached for her hand, my heart going out to her as she grasped at straws.

Percy offered her an encouraging smile. 'Yes, it's probably nothing more than a little bit of hanky-panky kissing at this stage,' she said brightly. 'Nothing to really touch the heart. Nothing which cannot be undone. He hasn't known her that long, has he?'

Emily shook her head and sighed. 'Still very disappointing and distressing, though,' she said, her shoulders sagging. 'I think, Grace,' she continued, 'it's probably best if I tell James that I found out about Heather myself. I don't think he'll like the idea of you knowing. But I'm afraid I'll need a few more details, in order to sound convincing.'

My frown deepened, and, in addition to my empathy for Emily, I began to experience a certain frustration at her apparent refusal to assign any importance to her own feelings. 'I'm sorry, Emily, but you need to forget about James for a moment and think about yourself. To be blunt, he can take a running jump. It's *you* you should be focusing on.'

Percy and Emily looked at each other, and then at me, Emily's expression now one of complete bewilderment. And I was just beginning to consider the possibility that she and James were in some sort of semi-open relationship, when a light cough from the entrance to the kitchen caused all three of us to turn in our chairs.

'Maybe it would help if I clarified and confirmed a few things, Grace,' said James, leaning against the doorway. His hands were in his pockets and he looked completely at ease as he addressed me directly, his unblinking gaze today seeming particularly penetrating. 'Firstly, yes, Heather and I have engaged in hanky-panky kissing – on more than one occasion, in fact. Secondly, she is not in a relationship with anyone else and, as my relationship with her is the only one in which I am currently engaged, there is no question of betrayal or infidelity. And finally, Emily,' he said, turning towards her and now offering her a smile which exactly matched her own, 'I don't think Grace realises that you're my sister.'

Chapter 18

Once home, I flopped down in the armchair with a chilling sense of déjà vu, as it occurred to me that I hadn't felt this despairing about the job since my first day of cleaning five weeks earlier.

Without thinking, I bent down to retrieve my laptop from under the chair, opened it up and began, as a matter of habit, to update my diary.

> *Monday 21 November: Utter, utter, utter*
> *mortification*
>
>> James is Emily's brother, not her twisted, unfaithful lover. This truth was revealed to me, in front of a live audience, by the man himself. The agonising irony was that I realised it for myself the split second before he said the words 'my sister'. I had never seen them together before, but in each other's company, as he smiled at her from the doorway and she smiled back at him, their relationship and the connection was suddenly, glaringly obvious.

I put a hand to my forehead and cringed for the hundredth time at the thought of James listening in on the kitchen conversation. After setting the record straight, he had stayed long enough only to pick up a piece of tooth-cracking shortbread, which he then took upstairs, presumably to suck on at his leisure in the study. Emily and Percy had both immediately made light of the misunderstanding, obviously finding it genuinely funny. When my face perhaps gave away the fact that I wasn't quite so entertained by the situation, they had then spent the next five minutes offering me reassurance upon reassurance, until I told them, untruthfully, that I could now see the funny side of it all and that it was time for me to get back to work. After that, the only positive in a morning of relentless negatives had been that I had seen nothing more of James.

I stared at the laptop screen for just a moment longer and then, realising that, just as on my first day of work, my diary wasn't on this occasion quite up to the task of lifting spirits which had sunk to subterranean levels, I decided to call Gavin. The phone was answered within a couple of rings.

'Hi, Grace, it's Neil,' he whispered. 'Gavin's asleep and I don't want to wake him. Can I help?'

'Oh, sorry,' I said. 'I was just phoning to see how he was.'

'Hang on.' There was a pause, followed by a few grunts, before he spoke again. 'I was halfway downstairs with a suitcase. I'm down now. He's a bit better. How are you? Having a good day?'

'Yes, great.' I bit my lip.

'What's gone wrong?' he asked.

'Nothing. Why?'

'Just tell me what's happened,' he said.

I frowned into the phone, cursing his unfailing ability to read my mood but deciding to share my misery just the same. 'OK, well, do you remember that at Percy's party I thought that James, who I clean for, was two-timing Emily, who he lives with?'

'Yes, I do remember *all* that,' he said wearily, 'on account of not being senile. James was with Heather and they were moderately tactile.'

'That's right. Well, it turns out he's not two-timing anyone because he's her brother.'

There was a pause. 'Heather is his *sister*?' he said after a moment. 'My God, that's horrific.'

'No, no. *Emily* is his sister.'

'Oh, I see,' he said, sounding relieved. 'But how is that a bad thing? Or do you prefer your men with a heart of stone?'

'It's a bad thing because...' I took a deep breath. 'Because he overheard me telling Emily this morning that he was two-timing her with Heather.'

Another pause. 'Now that *is* a bad thing.'

'You want to laugh, don't you?'

'Actually, I don't,' he said. 'Because I feel really sad for you.'

'I think I'd have preferred you to laugh.'

'If it's any comfort, I'm sure Gavin will wet himself when I tell him.'

I frowned at the phone. 'Thanks.'

'James wasn't angry, was he?'

'I don't think so. He just told me he was Emily's brother and then disappeared into his study. But I feel like such an idiot. What an assumption to make.'

I heard Neil sigh and imagined him taking off his glasses and pinching the bridge of his nose, as he usually did at some point during our conversations. 'Well,' he said, 'it seems to me you've got two choices. The first is to forget about it, assume that he couldn't care less and just get on with doing the job he is paying you to do.'

'And the other?'

'Talk to him. Or just send him a text. That'd be enough.'

'What would you do?'

'Well *obviously*,' he said, 'I would forget about it and get on with my job, because I am a pragmatist and ruthlessly commercial. But I think you should text him. Because I know if you don't address this you'll torture yourself and, more importantly, everyone else with it for weeks.'

I leaned back in the armchair, knowing he was right. 'OK,' I said quietly.

'Look, it's not that bad. People have done worse.'

'You really think so?'

'I do. Just don't press me for examples.'

I managed a smile. 'Have a great holiday. Give my love to Gavin.'

'I'm sure he'll send you a postcard or twelve. Bye, Grace. You're a lovely person; don't let a minor misunderstanding spoil things, because you were definitely on the up.'

'OK. Bye.'

'Bye.'

I hung up and, deciding to get it over with, immediately texted James.

> Hello – this is Grace. Rose gave me your number before she left and I hope you don't

mind me texting you. I just wanted to apologise for the misunderstanding over your
relationship with Heather. Emily was very
lovely about the whole thing this morning
and I hope you're not offended either. Rose
speaks so highly of you that I don't know
how I could have jumped to such an awful
conclusion and I feel terrible for doing so.
Sorry again. Best wishes, Grace

I pressed send and then, simply for something to do, rather
than because I felt remotely hungry, went into the kitchen
to make some lunch. I had got as far as eating a KitKat and
putting the kettle on the hob when my phone pinged. I
took it from the pocket of the tabard I was still wearing
and was surprised to see that it was a text from James.
I paused for a moment, wondering whether its contents
would make me feel better or worse. But I could read
the first line without opening it, and after deciding that
the introductory phrase *Hi Grace, thanks for your text* was
unlikely to be followed by *Nevertheless you're fired, you
twisted snoop*, I plucked up the courage to tap it and read
the rest.

Hi Grace, thanks for your text. I thought
the misunderstanding was funny and I wasn't
offended. It did occur to me, though, that
the whole thing might have skewed our relationship a little, which is a shame, and I think
a conversation might be a good idea – to
clear the air and make a fresh start. I'm free
tomorrow evening between seven and eight.

Or another time if you're busy. Just let me
know. James

I reread the text a number of times before deciding that
I had very little choice in the matter but to agree to a
conversation with my employer. I therefore replied that I
was free to talk the following evening and then, still unsure
whether his text had made me feel better or worse, I began
a search for something more substantial than a KitKat.

Chapter 19

When James had suggested a conversation, I had assumed he meant a telephone call. So it came as an unwelcome surprise when he proposed Racked, a wine bar on the waterfront, as a place to meet. He explained that he was going out later that evening and that Racked was convenient for both his office and his date, if it was good for me too. I dreaded the prospect of a face-to-face discussion and wished that Gavin was around to meet me afterwards to give me something frivolous to look forward to. I considered calling Simone, and was pretty sure she would have agreed to come out, but at the same time I knew that impromptu drinks were often a logistical struggle for her with the children. So in the end I decided to see if Aiden was free. I told him only that I had a work-related meeting until eight in Racked and asked if he was free for a drink closer to home after that. It was the first time the suggestion to meet had come from me, and I wondered if, for reasons similar to Simone, or the threat of flying crockery, it might prove impossible for him to make it. As it was, he texted back within half an hour to say he could meet me at eight-thirty and added that Summer was fine with it all.

I arrived at Racked just before seven to find James already there. He was standing at the bar with his back to me and, as I walked towards him, I took a deep breath and reminded myself that, come January, I was unlikely to see him ever again.

'Hello, James,' I said upon reaching him.

He turned and looked at me expressionlessly for a moment before his smile suddenly kicked in. 'Grace,' he said. 'What can I get you?'

'Oh… thank you.' I hesitated for a moment as the barman slid a pint towards him. 'White wine, please. Small. Not fussy which… anything dry – house is fine,' I added as the barman looked at me questioningly.

James nodded. 'OK. Why don't you get a seat and I'll bring the drinks over?'

'Great.' I smiled and then walked over to a table by the large floor-to-ceiling windows, down which heavy, late-November rain was now streaming, and sat down, taking out my phone and checking for messages, in order to distract myself from what was actually happening. Finding nothing new, I pointlessly reread the text Aiden had sent me twenty minutes earlier suggesting a seven-thirty meet if I was running early. I'd replied saying I thought that unlikely, but as I sat at the table waiting for James, I kept my fingers crossed that he might be in a hurry to get away, or, alternatively, that someone might start a small fire; just big enough to force an evacuation of the premises without causing extensive damage.

'Do you have plans after this?'

I started slightly and hurriedly put away my phone as James placed a glass of wine on the table and sat down opposite me.

'I'm meeting my ex-husband,' I said, before immediately wondering why I'd felt it necessary to identify Aiden as anything other than a friend.

James looked as if he was about to say something, but instead picked up his pint and took a sip.

'We still see each other socially from time to time,' I explained. 'We've been divorced quite a while. And he has a new partner – and a new baby actually. So it's—' I stopped abruptly, clueless as to where on earth I was going with the speech and deciding to put it out of its misery. 'How about you? What are you doing later?' I asked.

'I'm meeting Heather,' he said.

I nodded, the mention of Heather making me even more uncomfortable than I already was. 'She seemed very nice… at the party.' I picked up my glass. 'Smiled a lot,' I added uncertainly, racking my brain for compliments.

He looked at me for a moment but said nothing. It was a pause for either thought or scrutiny, which I was beginning to accept as a recurring, and highly unsettling, trait.

'Oh and her dress was lovely. Neil really liked it,' I added.

He nodded. 'And she really liked Neil.'

'He's great,' I said, looking down at my wine. 'His partner, Gavin, is a hairdresser and cuts my hair. All three of us are friends. They're very supportive – apart from when Gavin has a go at me about my hair and my underwear. They've just gone on holiday actually and I miss them whenever they're away. They're in the States for almost a month.' I fell silent, aware that I was starting to ramble in the face of James's conversational self-control – or reticence. Feeling particularly disappointed with myself for the underwear reference, I looked up to discover that he had, at some point, started to smile.

I heaved a sigh and, smiling in return, felt a sudden urge to get things over with. 'I'm so sorry about the mix-up over Heather.'

He shook his head. 'It's honestly not a problem. I'm just disappointed we got off on the wrong foot.'

I nodded. 'I'm sure Rose must have told me that Emily was your sister. I can only think that I was so focused on the details of the job that I missed that crucial fact. So when I saw you with Heather, I thought...' I sipped my wine. 'I just got the wrong end of the stick.' I looked out of the window and, not for the first time, despaired at my own stupidity.

'So, what do you do when you're not cleaning?'

I turned to find that he had addressed the question to his pint, looking up only when I failed to come up with an immediate response.

'Well... I read a lot. And I enjoy walking, listening to music, going to the theatre and I've recently learnt how to...' I began, before hesitating, suddenly aware that I was about to complete a perfect description of my late grandmother, 'how to knit,' I concluded quietly.

James nodded.

'How about you?' I asked.

'Much the same,' he said. 'Except without the knitting.'

'Right.'

'I prefer macramé,' he said solemnly.

I laughed and felt myself relax a little. 'I also like to write,' I said, surprising myself with the confession.

He picked up his beer again. 'Really? What do you write?'

'Non-fiction.' I smiled and again looked out of the window, distracted for a moment by a woman in a long black mac, hood up, running through the rain towards the bar at impressive speed, despite wearing spiked heels. 'It helps me to relax,' I added absently.

'And what does Neil think of what you write?'

'He's very—' I stopped and turned towards him. He looked at me questioningly. 'I don't want to bore you,' I said.

'I don't think you could do that.' He looked at me unblinkingly and inscrutably across the table. 'Is everything OK?' he asked. 'You're frowning.'

'No, it's just that…'

'What?' he asked, leaning back in his chair. 'If we're going to clear the air, we might as well do it properly.'

I hesitated for just a moment before deciding that he was right. 'Do you remember telling me that Emily thinks your face unnerves people?' I began.

It was his turn to frown. 'I'm not sure I remember putting it quite like that.'

'Well, it unnerves me,' I said. 'You don't blink much and you pause before you speak…'

'It's called thinking.'

'… and it makes me feel like I'm being assessed… judged,' I continued, strangely undeterred.

'I'm sorry,' he said, before very deliberately closing and reopening his eyes and then smiling. It was a sequence which rather suited him. 'Better?' he asked.

'Yes.' I smiled back at him. 'Much.'

'I'm afraid I'll have to continue to think before I speak,' he said, 'unless you'd like to give me some tips on kicking that particular habit. But I promise to work on blinking and appearing non-judgemental.'

I nodded. 'OK, and I'll work on not setting off burglar alarms, not wearing shoe covers on my head and not assuming you're dating blood relatives.'

'I'd appreciate two of the three,' he said. 'But I didn't actually have a problem with the shoe cover. You wore it well. I said so to Emily.' He looked at me over the top of his glass and blinked twice, very slowly.

I laughed, aware that I was now actually enjoying the conversation. He held out his glass to me. 'To a fresh start,' he said.

I raised my wine glass. 'To a fresh—'

'Hello, you.' Heather pulled down her hood, bent down and hooked her head in front of James's to kiss him on the lips.

'Hi,' he said, smiling but clearly taken aback. 'I didn't expect to see you here.'

'No.' She took off her long black mac and shook it. 'But it was raining and I was passing, so,' she turned to me and smiled, 'I thought I might as well swing in, dry off and say hi to Gail.'

'You mean Grace,' said James.

She sighed and stroked his hair whilst still smiling at me. 'Of course I do. Sorry, Grace. It must be so annoying for you that I can't remember your name.' She slapped a hand to her forehead. 'Mental block. Can I have a red wine please, James?'

'Sure.' He looked at me. 'Would you like another?'

I shook my head. 'No, I'm fine with this. Thank you.'

He nodded and then stood up and walked to the bar.

Heather sat down in his vacated chair and flicked her long, dark and slightly damp hair over her shoulders. 'So how are you, *Grace*?' she asked with emphasis and a smile. 'Have you been cleaning today?'

'No.' I shook my head. 'I only clean on a—'

'I've had an absolutely terrible day,' she said. 'That's why it's great James called and suggested taking me to dinner. He's *so* good at relaxing me.' She winked and reached across the table to place a hand on my arm. 'If you know what I mean.'

I tried not to tense. 'So, why was your day—'

'Do you have a partner?' she interrupted, now slowly winding and unwinding a lock of hair around her right forefinger. 'I wondered if you and Neil had a little thing going there. Or one of the other men you clean for? Perk of the job, maybe.' She laughed and winked again. 'I'm teasing, of course.'

I drank my wine to prevent my upper lip from curling. 'Neil's a very good friend,' I said.

'Really?' She looked towards James as he paid for her drink and then made his way back from the bar. 'I asked him a little bit about you at the party but he didn't seem to know anything.' She turned back to me and smiled, resting her chin on her hand. 'Maybe he just hasn't been listening. Men, eh?'

She looked up at James and blew him a kiss as he placed a glass of red wine on the table and sat down next to her. 'Thank you, darling. I've just been asking *Grace* about all the hunks she cleans for. So many men, so little time.'

I said nothing, deciding that raising an objection to effectively being labelled a floozy with a floor mop might sound like I was lacking a sense of humour or, worse still, protesting too much.

James looked at me. 'Who else do you clean for?' he asked. 'Other than Neil.'

'Actually, I—'

'Hey, you,' said Heather, laughing and punching him lightly on the arm, 'stop being so nosy. Grace doesn't want you prying into all her relationships. We girls have to have our secrets. Isn't that right, Grace?'

'Yes, that's right,' I said quickly, suddenly realising that, actually, Heather was the small fire I had been praying for. I pushed back my chair and stood up.

To my surprise, James did the same. 'Thanks so much for the drink,' I said, looking up at him across the table. 'I'm going to head off now and leave you two to your evening.'

'You don't have to go,' he said.

'I've had a text to say that my...' I looked down at Heather, who, though still smiling, was now looking at me through narrowed eyes, 'my friend is early and waiting for me.'

'There we go,' she giggled. 'What did I say, James? So many men, so little time. Grace here is a *very* busy lady.'

James looked at me steadily. 'Thank you for coming,' he said.

I thought about shaking his hand, but hesitated, uncertain of the professional etiquette between employers and their recently appointed cleaners. I tried to remember how I used to bid goodnight to my old property company boss on the few occasions we went out for drinks after work. I seemed to recall it was a hug. But that was after knowing each other for quite some time. Perhaps in the current situation, a mini wave would be best.

The consequence of all this social doubt and second-guessing was that I simply stood, staring at James, saying nothing.

'I'll blink if you will,' he said after a moment.

I laughed. 'Sorry.'

'Bye, Grace!' said Heather, suddenly standing up and pulling me towards her for a brief hug. I felt a slight, but unmistakable, push as she let me go.

I picked up my coat and bag. 'Bye.' And then, as James raised a hand and sat back down, I headed towards the door, slipping on my coat in defence of the rain.

I had just exited the bar and was cursing my lack of a hood when I spotted a man walking towards me, waving with one hand, whilst carrying a large corporate golfing umbrella in the other.

'Care to share?' asked Aiden as soon as he was within calling distance.

I smiled up at him and as he reached me, I placed my arms around his neck and hugged him. 'I've never been more pleased to see you,' I said.

'It's the umbrella, isn't it?' he replied, his cheek pressed against mine.

'It's ninety per cent the umbrella,' I said.

'Ten per cent genuinely pleased to see me, eh? Not bad.'

We stood, hugging in silence for a moment longer until I pulled away and asked, 'But what are you doing here?'

'Well, it was so wet. And I was passing. So I thought I'd...' He ground to a halt. 'I was being nosy,' he admitted.

I laughed and took his arm as he held it out for me to link. 'Don't feel bad,' I said, as we started to walk. 'There's a lot of it about.'

Chapter 20

'Are you *honestly* trying to tell me that this is preferable to a Saturday morning with Guy and the kids?' I pulled my bobble hat down as far as was possible without covering my eyes completely and shivered.

'You don't know you're born,' said Simone bitterly, looking down at her mud-caked trainers and leaning against the railings which lined the top of the Avon Gorge. We had met at the Henleaze end of the Downs and had been torso-running (our latest innovation, in which we relaxed our upper bodies, allowing them to bounce and sway in a running-like motion, whilst our legs were, in fact, walking) for almost thirty minutes. 'This is a walk in the park compared to what I'd be doing if I was at home right now. In fact, all we're lacking is a slide and a couple of swings and it would, quite literally, be a walk in the park.'

I nodded. 'Yes, I suppose we should at least attempt to run, shouldn't we? But I wonder if I should invest in a proper running hat first.' I patted my bobble. 'I think maybe this is weighing me down.'

'Could be,' she said. 'And I think maybe *this* is weighing *me* down,' she added, patting her bottom.

'You're so self-critical.'

'I'm just a realist,' she said, taking my hand and pulling me with her as she started to walk. 'Now come on, tell me about your evening out with the boss while we torso-run back to the café.'

I tutted. 'There's nothing more to tell. I was with him for twenty minutes, if that.'

'It was still kind of him to take the time to sort things out with you like that,' she said. 'I don't think many people would have done that for a temp.'

'Guess not,' I agreed.

'Did you pop all the details in your diary afterwards?' she asked.

I sighed. 'There honestly weren't that many details, but yes, I updated my diary.'

'OK, so just tell me what you wrote. I bet it was more than a single sentence,' she pressed, nudging me. 'He's obviously very sensitive and thoughtful. Did you write that down? And you said he was good-looking, too.'

I shook my head. 'No, Simone. *Neil* said he was good-looking – I said he was unnerving.'

'Same thing in my experience.'

I rolled my eyes.

'Oh come on, Grace,' she wheedled. 'Don't you find him even a tiny bit attractive?'

I sighed at the question but gave it some thought nevertheless. Now that Simone mentioned it, I realised that I had thought little, and written even less, about James's physical appearance. With the exception of the occasional mention of his creepy stare, my diary references to him to date had been restricted to his assumed dodgy character, and there was no doubt that prejudice had clouded my assessment of everything else. But with that prejudice removed, and his preference for monogamy now revealed, it was impossible to deny that he was, personally and physically, a rather attractive man. In particular, I mused, picturing his face as I had tried and failed to say goodnight to him in Racked, he had a very nice smile – once it had completed the long, slow journey from his brain to his face.

'What are you thinking?' asked Simone, suddenly poking me in the ribs.

I jumped. 'God, you're shrill sometimes,' I frowned.

'Well, you'd drifted off,' she said.

'I was just wondering whether to have a Danish or a muffin at the café,' I said, surprising myself with the decision not to share my thoughts about James's smile.

'Hmm… you were looking ever so dreamy about it,' she said, sounding sceptical. 'But anyway, to get back to your evening with Mr Brooke…'

'You mean my twenty minutes with Mr Brooke *and his girlfriend, Heather*?' I offered her a pained expression. 'Please don't add him to your list of possible men for me, Sim. He's not even single.'

She looked appalled. 'A list of possible men for you? What an offensive idea.'

'Guy told me.'

She tutted. 'He's so hopeless.'

'He's artless,' I smiled. 'And I love him for that.'

'Me too,' she conceded. 'I just wish he'd keep his mouth shut sometimes. But anyway, if you're not going to tell me anything else about your newly attractive boss,' she continued, sounding disappointed, 'at least tell me what you got up to afterwards.'

'I… went straight home, flopped in front of the TV and then caught up on my diary.' I hesitated only momentarily over the lie.

She looked at me out of the corner of her eye but said nothing. We walked on for a minute in what I believed to be companionable silence before I remembered the tipsy text I had sent her the night before. 'I told you I met up with Aiden, didn't I?' I said.

'You did.' The response was unmistakably clipped.

'Don't look so serious.' I attempted to keep my own tone light. 'It's nothing to worry about.'

'I wasn't worried at all until you just lied about it.'

I bit my lip. 'Sorry.' She looked at me, her concern obvious. 'I just don't want to overthink things and I'm pretty sure that talking about it could make me do that. But I do know there's nothing for you, or anyone else, to worry about.'

'He doesn't deserve you,' she said quietly. 'He never did.'

I stopped walking and took hold of her arm. 'Thank you,' I said and gave her a hug. She hugged me back and I felt her sigh. 'But Aiden and I are getting along again,' I said, 'and it feels so good to be free of the bitterness which went with us *not* getting along.'

'OK.' She patted me on the back and then released me. 'And I don't know whether it's that loss of bitterness, or the cleaning job, or your new hair, but something certainly agrees with you,' she smiled. 'You seem so much happier and you look great.'

'You always tell me I look great,' I pointed out.

'Yes, but this time I'm not lying to make you feel better. This time I'm being honest and feeling jealous.'

I laughed. 'Well, I'll take a jealous friend over a sensitive one any day.'

She smiled a little sadly. 'You will be careful, won't you, Grace?' she asked gently.

I tutted. 'Have you been talking to Neil and Gavin? Because you're sounding an awful lot like them.'

'Yes, well, they love you very much too, don't they?'

I looked at her and smiled. 'I'm very grateful for them and for you. But come on,' I tugged at her sleeve, 'race you to the café.'

Her expression remained serious and, for a moment, I feared the lecture might continue. But instead, she suddenly grinned. 'You're on,' she said. 'Winner picks up the tab.' And with that, we torso-ran slowly in the direction of cake.

Chapter 21

Over a week went by without me bumping into either Percy or Emily following my revelation about James's 'affair' with Heather. On the one hand, I was grateful not to have seen them; it gave my sense of embarrassment an opportunity to fade and also, I hoped, lessened the chances of the subject being referred to again.

On the other hand, I missed being able to talk to them about other things, including, I admitted to myself, James. Immediately following my morning un-run with Simone, I had gone home and continued my cleaning diary, spending most of Saturday glued to my laptop. But I had been frustrated to realise that while I now knew a great deal about Percy, and could paint a relatively clear picture of Emily, I could not claim the same about James, either personally or professionally. And as my early opinion of him had been proved so dramatically wide of the mark, following his unmasking as a kind and well-meaning individual, I now found myself eager to discover more about the real James Brooke, as opposed to the villainous, two-timing construct of my own muddled imagination, about whom I had been writing since first picking up his photograph in early October.

So I was rather pleased when, early one Wednesday evening, I received a text from Emily, passing on an invitation from Percy to pop in for lunch after work the following day. Emily told me that she would be there too and that she really hoped I could make it. I replied, without hesitation, that I would love to come, and the next day, after a quick, and failed, attempt to remove a domestic spillage of some sort from my jeans in the guest bathroom of number 3 Bennett Park, I dumped my tabard and cleaning caddy in the boot of my car and went next door to number 5.

'Come in, come in, my darling,' Percy gushed, as she opened the door to me and immediately enfolded me in a crushing hug. 'I feel like I haven't seen you in months! How are you? Take a seat in the lounge whilst I finish preparing lunch. We are having my special winter warmer soup and freshly baked bread rolls!'

'I can smell them from here,' I said, smiling appreciatively as I followed her into her flat.

'Yes, well, they haven't risen quite as I would have wished, but James is testing one for me this very minute and assures me that they're quite delicious.'

'James?' I queried uncertainly, suddenly aware that my eagerness to find out more about the man fell short of wanting to bump into him before I'd had a chance to check my reflection and conceal any residual whiff of Toilet Duck or Mr Muscle with a squirt of perfume.

'Yes, James,' said Percy, taking my hand and leading me into the living room. 'Here he is.'

She gestured across the room to where he was sitting in one of her enormous winged chintz armchairs. He looked completely at home and was immaculately but approachably professional in dark grey trousers and a pale blue shirt, open at the neck. In his right hand he held a delicate floral teacup, and in his left, a smallish bread roll.

He stood up as I entered, looking at me blankly for a moment before his expression was transformed by an eventual smile. His eyes flickered momentarily to the top of my head and I began to wonder exactly where my hair might be sitting on the roadkill scale today.

'Hi,' I said.

'Hello.' He looked quizzically at Percy and then back at me. 'I didn't realise you were coming for lunch. I thought it was just Emily.'

'Is that what you thought, my darling?' said Percy brightly. 'That's so interesting. You are always so fascinating. Now, I'm just going to go and make Grace a cup of tea and leave you two to chat. I hope you don't mind.' And with that, she was gone.

I sat down on the sofa and looked at James. 'You're having lunch with us too?'

He settled himself back into the armchair and shook his head. 'Percy asked me to come and move her kitchen table and chairs,' he explained. 'And then to move them back to where they were originally.' He smiled again and I remembered my conversation with Simone on the Downs. There was no doubt that monogamy suited him, and I tried desperately not to depress myself by contrasting his current physical and sartorial perfection with my own dishevelled, post-cleaning state.

'Percy's bread smells great,' I said, nodding towards the roll in his hand.

He looked down at it. 'Second only to her shortbread,' he said quietly.

I nodded and smiled. 'My teeth are grateful to you for that heads-up,' I whispered.

He laughed, then after a moment said, 'So how are you? Did you enjoy Tuesday evening?'

'Oh, well…' I hesitated, taken aback by the directness of the question. But accepting that he clearly wanted to maintain the sense of honesty and openness established during our Racked conversation, I decided to provide him with an equally frank response.

'I did, actually,' I said, looking down and rubbing absently at the stain on my jeans. 'And that came as a huge surprise, because I wasn't looking forward to meeting you for a drink at all. In fact, I was dreading it because I had already made a complete idiot of myself and I knew that, under pressure, there was every chance I'd make an idiot of myself all over again. I'm *really* bad at talking off the cuff when it matters. I'm so much better on paper. That lets me tweak and amend and think things through. So when you suggested a one-to-one, I actually felt a bit sick.' I gazed thoughtfully at the floor. 'But you were right – the mix-up had skewed things and the opportunity to begin again, having set things straight, was great. So thank you for suggesting a drink, and, as I say,' I smiled, at last looking up at him, 'against all odds, I did enjoy myself.' I concluded my speech, aware that Gavin would have labelled it arty-farty-rambly, but pleased that I had made it nevertheless. I had respected, and matched, James's directness, and I felt rather proud, and not a little surprised, at how articulately I had expressed my feelings.

He looked at me, nodding slowly, clearly giving his response some thought. 'OK,' he said eventually, 'but I was actually asking whether you had enjoyed your evening with your ex-husband – not with me.'

I stared at him for a moment while his words hit home. 'Ohh, I see…' I murmured. 'And that actually makes a lot more sense. Because asking someone whether they enjoy your company is actually quite Aspergersy, isn't it?'

He nodded. 'It's veering that way.'

I sighed wearily and sank back into the sofa. 'You see, this is exactly what I was talking about when I said I was so much better on paper than in person. I really need that opportunity to review and edit all my thought-processing – or lack of it,' I added quietly, drawing on the only positive, namely that I had just very neatly illustrated my own point.

He laughed and shook his head. 'You're just fine in person.'

It was a throwaway comment, but one which cheered me up considerably whilst at the same time making me feel a little self-conscious. I realised that I was grateful he had addressed it to the carpet and didn't pause for a response.

'And I'm pleased you felt that our part of Tuesday was worthwhile,' he continued, looking up, 'because so did I. I was just sorry you felt you had to leave.'

'It wasn't like that,' I said. 'I just had someone waiting for me and I knew that you and Heather had an evening planned.'

He leaned forward, placing the bread roll with a disturbingly heavy clunk onto a side plate on the coffee table in front of him. 'We actually gave dinner a miss,' he said. 'We were both too tired in the end.'

'That's a shame.'

'It was,' he agreed. 'We needed to talk.'

'Maybe you'll be less tired this week,' I offered. 'You're working from home today?'

'I am,' he nodded. 'And tomorrow as well, in fact.'

'I'm so rubbish at working from home,' I sighed. 'Way too many distractions.'

He smiled. 'You prefer cleaning other people's homes to your own?'

I frowned, confused by the question before remembering that of course he knew nothing about my writing. It was a situation which, in the light of our new-found openness with one another, now felt a little awkward.

I considered for a moment telling him that what I actually meant was that I found it difficult to write books at home and often decamped to the Central Library. But for that to make sense, I would have to share the backstory, and I very much doubted I would be able to explain my break from work, my offer to stand in for Rose and her acceptance of me as a replacement cleaner before Percy returned with the tea and James needed to get back to work. There was, I decided, no rush to burden him with either my troubled history or my CV, and leaving it to another time would also give me a chance to mention it to Rose first.

'Are my facial expressions not on point today?' he asked. 'You look confused.'

I laughed and shook my head. 'Sorry. My mind had wandered. And yes, I'd much rather clean other people's homes than my own. They're far more interesting.'

He smiled again and I congratulated myself on this time opting for a simple response, in preference to an arty-farty-rambly one. I smiled back at him, as he looked past me towards the door and I turned to see Percy re-entering the room carrying a tray on which was a single cup of tea and a small plate of biscuits. As she reached the sofa, James stood up and took the tray from her, placing it on the coffee table.

'Thank you, darling,' said Percy, sitting down next to me. 'There is your tea, Grace, and I've brought you some custard creams to go with your bread, James.'

'Thank you,' I said, leaning forward to take my tea, while James smiled his thanks and settled himself back into the armchair.

'Well, I'm so happy that your paths crossed today,' said Percy. 'And how lovely that you enjoyed your evening together last week and managed to clear the air. But I'm sorry you didn't have dinner with Heather, James. Especially as you needed to talk.' She reached out and patted his knee sympathetically.

I glanced across at James, who, I noticed, was now frowning slightly. I wondered if he was, like me, rapidly reviewing and vetting the content of our conversation.

The doorbell rang, making me jump, as Percy stood up and bustled off excitedly to answer it. I looked at James and pulled a face. 'I'm trying to remember what we said about the bread roll,' I whispered. He nodded and picked up the largely untouched roll, breaking off a small piece and replacing it on the plate whilst popping the remainder into the pocket of his jacket, which lay across the arm of the chair.

I was still smiling at his thoughtfulness when Percy returned with Emily in tow.

'Hello, you two,' smiled Emily, walking over and kissing us each in turn. 'Oh, are you off, James?' she added as he stood up.

'I am,' he said, retrieving and putting on his jacket.

'That's a shame. You can't spare us half an hour? Percy was just saying how she would love you to stay.'

'I was, dear,' said Percy, resting her hand on his arm and peering up at him. 'How lovely that would be. And then you and Grace could carry on talking about working from home and your strange facial expressions and so on.'

I sighed. Both her hearing and her recall were clearly excellent.

James offered me the briefest of sidelong smiles. 'I'd love to stay, Percy,' he said, 'but I must get back to work. Besides, your bread roll has nicely taken the edge off my appetite for now.' He patted his stomach.

Percy looked at the almost empty plate and clapped her hands in delight. 'Oh my goodness, you gobbled that up so quickly. Well before you go, you must come into the kitchen with me, darling,' she said, taking his hand, 'and I'll pop another half-dozen into a bag for you.'

–

Ten minutes later, James had been packed off with double the promised number of bread rolls, plus a fair quantity of shortbread, and Emily and I were sitting at Percy's small circular kitchen table while our hostess busied herself at the hob. Emily smiled at me and sighed. 'It's lovely to see you,' she said.

'You too,' I replied. 'You seem to be at home less.'

She nodded. 'I'm temping and there's a big project on the go, so they've given me extra hours. It's great because I can give James more money.'

'He doesn't want your money, darling,' said Percy, ladling two generous portions of soup into bowls and placing them in front of us on the table.

Emily looked up at her. 'I know, Percy, but I insist. There's a standing order to his account but I also slip extra into his wallet when he leaves it lying around.' She pointed at the soup. 'Yum.'

'Is he very busy?' I asked, taking advantage of this early reference to James to dig a little about his job. 'What does he do? Rose didn't say.'

Emily smiled. 'Probably because he tends not to talk about it. He's a lawyer, specialising in employment law. But because he works in the media sector, he comes into contact with some very well-known people. Discretion is his middle name. Even I don't know who he's working for, or what he's up to, most of the time.'

'He has so much integrity. I trust him with all my deepest, darkest secrets,' said Percy with an air of mystery, as she brought her own bowl of soup to the table and sat down. She looked at me over her specs. 'Silent as the grave when he needs to be.'

I nodded approvingly, whilst feeling a little disappointed at the effective dead-ending of the topic.

'Do tuck in!' Percy pushed a plate of bread rolls in my direction. 'This batch are still warm from the oven.'

'Ooh, thank you,' I said, picking up a roll which was deceptively heavy for its size. I smiled uncertainly and was just wondering whether I could defer attempting to bite into it by extending the conversation about James further, without my interest appearing unhealthy, when Emily stepped in and did it for me.

'But it's not just professional details he's guarded over,' she said with a sigh. 'He changes the subject whenever I try to talk to him about personal things too. He always turns everything around to ask about me. But that's my fault,' she added quietly. 'He's been like that ever since I crumbled.'

I looked up at her and frowned. 'Crumbled?'

She looked surprised. 'Sorry, Grace. I don't know why, but I assumed Rose might have filled you in on that.' She tutted and shook her head. 'But of course she wouldn't. She's too kind. Not that I'd have minded you knowing.' She paused, took a deep breath, and looked at Percy. 'I fell apart last year, didn't I, Percy?' she said, smiling sadly as Percy reached out and took her hand. 'I've had wobbles before, but this was different. I met a man, fell in love, then found out he wasn't quite what I thought, and I crumbled completely. And when it was all over, James swept up the crumbs and put me back together.' She looked at me uncertainly.

I smiled reassuringly, touched that she had felt able to confide something so personal. 'Don't worry. I think most people crumble at some point. I certainly have.'

'Really?'

'Really. And I'm flattered that you look so surprised.'

'What was the cause of your crumble, dear?' asked Percy. 'Unless you'd rather not say,' she added gently.

I waved a dismissive hand. 'I'm happy to talk about it. It was my divorce, or rather what led up to it. Outwardly I carried on just as before: working, socialising... But inside,' I tapped my chest, 'dust. My perspective changed completely, and not at all for the better. I allowed my relationship with one person to cloud everything.'

'Well your perspective seems just fine now,' said Emily.

I smiled. 'It took a lot of quiet moral support and patience from a lot of people – plus one or two good shakes – to get me to this point. Oh and this job has helped enormously. I had made the mistake of dwelling, not doing. I focused on the rubble rather than the reconstruction.'

'Dwelling, doing, rubble, reconstruction!' laughed Percy. 'You know, dear, you do have such a way with words. Have you ever thought of writing?'

I opened my mouth to reply that, actually, I loved writing and, what was more, I would that very afternoon go home and eagerly update the increasingly upbeat diary I had been keeping, in which she and Emily featured so heavily and shone so brightly.

But Percy didn't pause for breath. So instead, I smiled back at her, enjoying the brief literary digression as she shared details of her favourite book of the moment. And while she talked with relish of murders and mortuaries in Victorian London, I decided that I would make a priority of mentioning to Rose my plan to share details of my writing, both fact and fiction, with Percy and Emily. They had been so open with me that I didn't want to keep something as straightforward as my profession from them.

'And you are *so* right about the importance of friends,' continued Percy, having now returned to the original topic of conversation and clasping her hands under her chin. 'I simply do not know what would have become of me after I lost my Patrick if it hadn't been for my friends. And that includes you and your darling brother.' She patted Emily's hand.

Emily smiled. 'Perhaps James more than me,' she sighed. 'I just wish he'd think about himself a bit more and let others support him the way he has supported us, Percy.'

'I'm sure he does feel supported,' I said. 'You are both very positive forces day to day. And maybe he doesn't share concerns because he doesn't have any,' I offered.

'Perhaps,' said Emily. 'It just seems he's either immersed in work or focusing on the needs of others – on my needs mainly. And I think that stops him investing in his own interests and relationships. He's been that way ever since we lost Mum and Dad, but even more so over the past year. He needs to focus on himself – get away from work and relax.'

'He did seem to have been working very hard when we spoke earlier,' I said. 'But he's got Heather,' I added. 'She's a distraction from work and he's relaxed when he's with her.'

Emily's expression brightened. 'Yes, I know you thought they were very at ease with each other at Percy's party.'

Percy lowered the soup spoon she had just raised to her lips and began to giggle. She nudged me mischievously and tried to say something, but 'hanky' and 'panky' were the only words I could make out between the sniggers.

Emily laughed and I put a hand to my mouth. 'God, what was I thinking?' I said, smiling. 'And here I am claiming to have an improved perspective!'

'You know, I think it's great that you told me your concerns about his relationship with Heather,' Emily assured me. 'That says a lot about you.'

Now recovered, Percy nodded. 'A level of integrity on a par with James himself.'

I looked from one to the other and smiled again. 'That's a very kind spin to put on it.'

Emily shook her head and was about to say more, but at that moment our conversation was interrupted by a loud beeping from the hallway. Percy rose from her seat. 'Oh, I'm so sorry to be rude, my darlings, but I am expecting a call,' she said, scurrying out, only to return moments later, slightly flushed and mid conversation. 'No, no, Arthur, you mustn't worry yourself. I thought you looked absolutely dreadful at ballroom on Saturday. I said so to Geraldo. I know you put that stumble down to the fact that you were wearing your slippers, but I knew better.' She paused, placing an anxious hand to her mouth while she listened to the voice on the other end of the line. 'Well you must get yourself to bed, darling,' she said after a moment. 'If Annie is with you this evening, I shall get a taxi and pop round tomorrow morning and again after Maud's celebration. Take a Lemsip and see if you can get some sleep. Lots of love, my darling. And get well soon.' She hung up, sighed heavily and placed the phone on the table.

Emily threw me a worried glance and then turned to Percy. 'Problem?' she asked.

'I'm afraid so,' said Percy, sitting down. 'Arthur is poorly, so he's unable to come to our dear friend Maud's party tea in Abbots Leigh tomorrow. He was to pick me up at lunchtime and we were going to arrive together.'

'Oh that's a shame,' I said and then, realising that Percy actually looked rather close to tears, I added, 'Is he very unwell, Percy?'

She shook her head. 'No, no. Just a heavy cold, he says. He's forever going out in his slippers, so it's hardly a surprise.'

Emily frowned. 'Are you worried about going to the party alone, Percy? Is there another friend you could take along?'

Percy sniffed and forced a smile. 'I'm afraid not. Everyone I could possibly invite will already be there.'

I attempted positivity. 'So you'll know lots of people, then?'

She nodded. 'Almost everybody.'

I looked at Emily, who offered me the slightest of bemused shrugs.

'If you're at all worried about getting there, I can take you and bring you home afterwards,' I offered. 'I have a completely free afternoon tomorrow.'

Percy's face lit up. 'Really, darling? Are you sure?'

'Of course,' I said. 'What time shall I collect you?'

But Percy didn't seem to hear. 'That has so cheered me up, you can't imagine,' she said, clasping her hands delightedly. 'It wasn't something I wanted to make my way to on my own, and I know Maud would be devastated to think of an empty chair at tea. "No empty seats!" she said. "No empty seats!"' She picked up her spoon and scooped up a mouthful of soup.

I looked at Emily, wondering if maybe I had misunderstood. Percy wasn't really expecting me to *stay* at Maud's party, was she? Emily bit her lip, and her expression of anxious pity for me was enough to confirm my fears.

172

Percy spotted the lip-biting too. 'Oh Emily, my darling,' she said, lowering her spoon, 'don't be upset. I shall make a call and arrange for you *both* to come. It would be no problem. Maud would say the more the merrier.'

Emily smiled and shook her head. 'I'm afraid I'm working, Percy.'

'Ah, and you're disappointed,' said Percy. 'Now I understand. I'm so sorry.'

Emily nodded and then, changing the subject, asked for the soup recipe. Percy chatted away, detailing the exact quantities of milk and salt she had added to the ready-made soup she had purchased at Tesco Metro that morning. And while she did so, I retraced the few conversational steps which had led to me spending tomorrow afternoon at a party with Percy and her octogenarian friends. But eventually realising, with a sort of detached fascination, that there was absolutely nothing I could do about it without causing considerable hurt, I shrugged internally and accepted the situation, deciding that it could only add colour to both my day and my diary.

'I wonder what will be on the menu tomorrow,' I said, as Percy finished telling Emily how long one needed to heat the soup. 'Mind you, it'd have to go some way to beat this.'

Percy looked up at me and smiled. 'Well, whatever it is, I know I shall enjoy it all the more with you sitting next to me.'

'Ditto,' I said, returning the smile. And as Emily collected our bowls and Percy began to talk of dessert, I realised that I meant it.

Chapter 22

I started the engine and then groaned as the petrol warning light appeared on the dashboard. I had meant to fill up the evening before, but the matter had been pushed from my mind by a lengthy phone call from Aiden, who wanted me to review some marketing material for him.

I looked at the car clock and relaxed a little, deciding that there was still just enough time to collect Percy and then swing into the petrol station on the way to Eastleigh Hall, the imposing nineteenth-century manor house on the outskirts of Bristol which was to be the venue for Maud's party. And in any case, I couldn't risk making the first leg of the journey on the fumes I had left in the tank only to find myself traipsing back from the party with a petrol can in one hand and my navy high heels in the other.

I arrived in Bennett Park twenty minutes later, the traffic along the Downs having been much heavier than expected, thanks to a burst water main. Now very conscious of time, I hurriedly parked the car and ran as fast as my shoes would allow up Percy's front path and steps. I rang the doorbell and waited, listening impatiently for any sign of movement. When there was none, I rang the bell again and at last heard the door to her flat creak open and the sound of unhurried footsteps across the entrance hall.

I had already started my apologetic speech about the petrol situation before the door was even fully open. And I had got as far as 'I've been so stupid, Percy. I forgot to fill the—' when I realised that it wasn't Percy standing in front of me but James. He looked as surprised to see me as I was him. 'Oh hi,' I said. 'You're here… again. Is, er… is Percy ready? Only we're running late. My fault entirely.'

'I'm not sure what she's supposed to be ready for.' He looked me up and down and offered me a late-as-ever smile. 'A formal event of some sort, I'm guessing.'

I nodded. 'Yes, we're going to her friend's party. It's an afternoon tea. Is everything OK?'

'Percy's not very well,' he said, taking a step back and beckoning me inside. 'You'd better come in.'

I followed him into Percy's flat and heard her before I saw her. 'I know who that is,' she croaked. 'It's darling Grace, isn't it?'

'It is,' said James, standing aside to let me lead the way into the living room, where Percy was stretched out full length on the sofa, propped up by cushions and with a green velvet throw covering her legs.

'Oh Grace,' she said, dabbing at her nose with a white cotton handkerchief. 'I've got Arthur's cold. Whatever am I to do?'

I sat down on the edge of the sofa. 'You'll just have to get well, Percy,' I smiled. 'How are you feeling? Do you have paracetamol?'

She looked up at James, who was standing behind me. 'I do now,' she said, managing a weak smile. 'I telephoned Emily, because I had nothing but Rennie and iodine in my bathroom cabinet and felt too poorly to go to the shops. And although she was out, James was working from home and came straight round. Isn't he lovely?' Her lower lip wobbled and her eyes brimmed. 'And has made me a cup of tea and tidied up around me. But I do hate being such a bother.'

'It was no problem at all,' said James. 'I needed a break from the screen.'

'And I should have called you, Grace, because now you've made the journey for nothing.' She reached forward and patted my knee. 'And you look so beautiful for Maud.' At this, the floodgates finally opened and she began to sob quietly. I turned to look up at James, in response to which he pulled up an armchair and sat down next to us.

'Tell us what we can do to help,' he said gently to Percy.

'I'm not sure you can do anything else, my darling. I'm just so terribly upset at letting Maud down,' she sniffed. 'She so wanted a full house.'

'Oh, but she'll understand,' I said. 'You can't help being unwell.'

Percy nodded. 'I know. I just wish I could have apologised.'

'Well, is there someone we can call?' asked James.

'I'm afraid not,' said Percy, 'I don't have her daughter's number and she's arranging everything. And my other friends are all too deaf or too addled for mobile phones.'

I pursed my lips at this in an attempt to prevent an inappropriate smile, and noticed James's hand go to his mouth as he nodded understandingly.

'Why don't I just pop along and pass on your apologies?' I suggested.

Percy looked up at me. 'Oh Grace, I can't ask you to do that.'

'It's no problem. Would that make you feel better?'

She blew her nose and brightened a little. 'My goodness, it would. But are you sure you wouldn't mind?'

'It's no bother at all,' I said. 'As I told you yesterday, I am totally free this afternoon.'

Percy smiled. 'You're a darling,' she said. 'But what time is it?'

James looked at his watch. 'One forty-five.'

I stood up. 'Right. It's about a fifteen-minute drive. I've got to get some petrol en route, but that will be OK, won't it, Percy? They're not sitting down bang on two, are they?'

Her face fell again. 'I fear it will all start rather on the dot. I'm not sure you'll get there in time.' She took a deep breath. 'But thank you so much for offering, dear. It was a lovely thought.'

James stood up. 'Come on,' he said. 'We'll take my car and if we set off now, we'll make it.'

'Oh James…' began Percy, but he was already on his way to the front door.

'I'll text Emily and she'll come to see you as soon as she's home,' he called. 'That'll be in about an hour.'

I looked down at Percy. We were both, I think, a little in shock. 'I'd better go,' I said, bending down to kiss her forehead, 'or he'll leave without me. And he hasn't actually asked where we're going.'

Chapter 23

We swung into the gravel car park of Eastleigh Hall with two minutes to spare, James having shown an impressive knowledge of back roads and an occasional and convenient disregard for speed limits. The doors of the house stood wide open, and while there was no sign of any other partygoers, the number of parked cars and the huge banner strung between two pillars – which read *Party on, Maud!* – assured us that we were at least in the right place on the right day.

I looked at James as he turned off the engine. 'I'll pop in. There's no need for you to come if you'd rather not.'

He undid his seat belt and opened the driver's door. 'No, it's OK, I'll come. I might recognise one or two of Percy's friends.'

I smiled, actually very glad of his moral support, and together we made our way across the car park and up the sweeping sandstone steps. Just inside the doorway we were greeted by a middle-aged couple. The woman, I thought, looked worryingly downcast. The man, short and balding, wore, in marked contrast, the kind of expression which made him appear perpetually on the verge of laughter. He reached for my hand and, once it was in his grasp, pumped it vigorously up and down before moving on to James. 'So pleased you could both come,' he said. 'Penny,' he turned to the woman, 'had just mentioned that there were still a couple of spare chairs, hadn't you, Pen?' Penny nodded and attempted a smile. He put his arm around her and squeezed. 'See, I told you, love. Not a single empty seat. Just as she wanted.'

She nodded. 'You were right, Tim,' she said quietly.

I looked up at James to find him staring at Penny. I wished he would smile.

I cleared my throat. 'Well actually,' I began, 'I'm here...' I looked again at James. 'I'm Grace and this is James and *we're* here to extend apologies on behalf of Maud's friends, Percy and Arthur. I'm afraid they are both unwell and so unable to be here today. They are devastated to be missing her party.'

Tim smiled a little sadly. 'These things happen,' he said as Penny's head dropped. 'But thank you so much for making the trip today.'

'I wonder,' said James, still looking at Penny, and now at last smiling, 'whether we might be able to meet Maud?'

'Meet her?' Penny's head lifted and she looked uncertainly first at James and then at me.

'Oh yes,' I said, nodding eagerly. 'It would be lovely to introduce ourselves and say a quick hello. So long as that wouldn't delay things too much.'

'Say hello,' echoed Penny, sounding slightly dazed. I began to wonder if maybe she had hit the fizz a little early.

'If there's time,' I said brightly. 'If that's OK.' I looked at Tim.

He blinked at me for a moment and then turned to Penny. 'If they want to, love,' he said quietly. 'And who cares if we're a few minutes late starting. Maud's certainly not going to fuss, is she?'

Penny rolled her eyes at him and, with what seemed like enormous effort, managed a smile. 'Come on then,' she said, gently taking my hand. 'She's in here.'

With James and Tim following, she led me across the large marble-tiled entrance hall and past a set of open doors to our left, through which I saw a dining room festooned with balloons and with circular tables laid for, I guessed, eighty or so guests. We walked on before stopping outside a door at the very back of the hall. 'Here we are,' Penny whispered, opening the door and placing her hand on my back to guide me gently inside.

I took two steps forward and stood for a moment, taking in the rows of chairs and the crowd of faces to my right, before turning my head slowly to see several more chairs and a pale wooden lectern at the top end of the room.

The coffin – the open coffin – was the last thing I noticed.

I was aware of my mouth forming the words 'Oh no' but of no sound being emitted. I felt a hand on my elbow and glanced up to see that James was now at my side. He looked down at me, his expression as impassive as ever, but I was aware of a slight, yet unmistakably supportive, squeeze. 'Maud is *dead*,' I mouthed in horror. 'This is a *funeral*.'

He shook his head. 'This is a *celebration*,' he said quietly, the corners of his mouth twitching slightly.

'That's right,' said Tim brightly, as Penny nodded along emotionally. 'That's exactly what it is, James. Now, if you two would just like to say hello to Maud, then we'll begin.'

I swallowed. 'Yes, of course,' I said hoarsely.

James and I walked the dozen or so paces to the dark wooden casket, coming to a stop either side of it. I looked across at him and then we wordlessly and simultaneously looked down at Maud.

Braced for what I might see, I was relieved to find myself looking at a woman who appeared to have fallen asleep whilst enjoying a particularly good joke. And it was, I thought, immediately obvious why today was a celebration; Maud had definitely been a party person. If her expression hadn't given it away, then the sparkling purple ball gown, matching evening gloves and pink diamanté tiara she was wearing as she lay, so peacefully, on cushioned pink velvet certainly would have. I didn't know whether to laugh or cry.

I looked up at James, who offered me a smile which somehow fitted the bizarre situation perfectly, before returning my gaze to Maud. 'Hello, Maud,' I began in a whisper, 'I'm Grace and this is James and we're here to… to tell you that Percy is so, so sorry not to be with you today. She didn't want to miss this for the world. Arthur very much wanted to be here too, but they've both got dreadful colds. But what's clear to us is that they both loved you – still love you… very much.' I looked up at James a second time. He smiled again, walked round to join me, and then together we turned to make our way towards the exit – just as the celebrant entered the room, closed the door with a quiet click and walked to the lectern. 'Good afternoon, friends and family of Maud Gibb,' he said with a smile.

'I'm afraid your seats are right at the back,' said Tim quietly, now approaching and extending an arm to corral us towards the rear of the room.

James nodded and turned to me. 'That's fine, isn't it, Grace?'

'Of course,' I replied. And then we made our way to our seats and sat down.

Chapter 24

As soon as the celebrant concluded proceedings, James and I were amiably accosted by Penny and Tim and invited to stay for afternoon tea. I tried, by means of raised eyebrows and narrowed eyes, to convey to James that I didn't at all mind if he wanted to leave and get back to work. However, either he misinterpreted my twitches, or he had nothing better to do all afternoon than scoff scones and sip tea. So we sat in the places intended for Percy and Arthur and chatted with each other and with our tablemates. The latter turned out to be very friendly, but frighteningly inquisitive, and it was with some relief, after a particularly intense fifteen-minute interrogation into my personal circumstances by Phyllis of Ipswich, that I felt James tap my arm and was able to say, 'Oh, excuse me, Phyllis. I think James wants a word.'

'More tea?' he asked, picking up the pot which sat between us on the table as I turned gratefully towards him.

'Oh God, yes please,' I said, as Phyllis immediately began to press her other neighbour, Norman, for a detailed explanation of his limp.

James smiled as he poured the tea. 'Bearing up?'

'Phyllis seems to be some kind of Mary Berry/Jeremy Paxman hybrid,' I murmured, 'lulling me into a false sense of security with fairy-cake recipes before going for the jugular. How about you?'

'Similar,' he said quietly. 'So far I've been forced to reveal my height, weight, marmalade preferences and sexuality.'

I laughed and then widened my eyes questioningly. 'And?'

'And what?' he asked, before adding, 'Oh, I see. Six foot-ish, twelve and a half stone, chunky cut and heterosexual, despite never having been married. That last response was greeted with undisguised scepticism, by the way.' He put down the teapot. 'And to what have you confessed?'

I counted the points on my fingers. 'A very happy childhood, an inability to cook and the long-term lack of a man.' I picked up my tea and took a sip. 'I'm pretending to be offended,' I said, 'but I'm actually loving it.'

He nodded. 'I agree. The company is great.'

I smiled, wondering whether he was including me in the compliment, and I found myself hoping that he was. It was a hope which took me a little by surprise. 'Thank you…' I began, adjusting my napkin, 'for driving me here, I mean.'

'I wanted to,' he said.

Unable to tell from his intonation whether this was a complete sentence or merely the beginning of one, I looked up at him. He took a breath, as if he was about to say more, but at that moment his attention was again demanded by one of the ladies to his right and our conversation was at an end.

The tea of sandwiches, scones and cakes lasted for another hour or so, and was interspersed with ramblingly reminiscent, highly entertaining speeches from Maud's friends – plus a five-minute turn by a very elderly, hugely unskilled magician, who seemed to consider his main trick to be a proud ability to pick up the cards he repeatedly dropped.

By eavesdropping on James's continued exchanges with his uninhibited interrogators, I discovered that he had lost both his parents in quick succession five years earlier, preferred rugby to football and enjoyed holidaying in the Lake District. I also heard him refer to me repeatedly as his friend, making no mention of my employee status. And as I listened to him chatting amiably with Joan and her husband Bobby from St Albans, I came to the conclusion that James Brooke was as charming, patient and kind as both Rose and Percy had always declared him to be. In fact, my only regret of the afternoon was that the more I got to know him, the more miserable I felt about having so badly misjudged him.

–

It was six-thirty, and I was preoccupied with mentally reviewing the feelings and events of the day in preparation for adding them to my cleaning diary, when James suddenly broke the comfortable silence of the drive home.

'Everything OK?' he asked as we approached the suspension bridge.

I turned towards him. 'Yes, why?'

'You've been very quiet since we left Abbots Leigh,' he said.

'Oh.' I shrugged. 'I was just thinking… I do do that occasionally.'

'I never doubted it.'

I smiled, looking out of the window and along the winding length of the gorge as he brought the car to a halt, wound down the window and paid the toll to cross the bridge.

'Actually, I was thinking too,' he said as we pulled away again. 'I was wondering whether it'd be acceptable to report back that I had really enjoyed the funeral.'

'I think so,' I said. 'But maybe stop short of saying it's something you'd like to turn into a hobby, or you're keen to do again soon. I suppose you could say you wouldn't mind doing something *similar* again – minus the death element.'

He smiled and then nodded.

'Are you going to see Percy this evening, then?' I asked.

'Yes. I think she'll be waiting to hear how it went.' He glanced at me before returning his attention to the road. 'Do you have time to come with me?'

'Actually,' I said, checking the time on my phone and noticing two missed calls from Aiden, 'I was going to be cheeky and ask if you could do a slight detour and drop me home; my flat is in Henleaze, just off the Downs. I'm running with a friend tomorrow morning and I thought I might pick up the car and see Percy then.'

'No problem,' he said, taking a left turn. 'Emily texted to say that Percy slept most of the afternoon and was feeling better when she woke up.'

'Good,' I said. 'It upset me to see her so unhappy this afternoon. She's such a kind woman.'

'She says much the same about you.'

I turned and smiled across at him. 'That's nice to hear.'

'She said you refused payment for helping her at the party.'

'Oh…' Taken by surprise, I felt myself blush. 'Well, it didn't feel like work. I enjoyed myself.'

'Really?' He raised an eyebrow. 'Because you didn't seem to be enjoying yourself at all whenever I spoke to you.'

'Hmm… well.' I looked down at my lap. 'Maybe if I'd known…'

'That I wasn't cheating on my sister?'

I sighed. 'The fact that you might be related just hadn't entered my head. But what's interesting is that when we chatted at Percy's party and you smiled, I felt a sense of recognition. I realise now that I was obviously thinking about Emily – making a connection. And then the moment I saw you together…' I heaved a second sigh. 'I still feel so stupid about the whole thing.'

'Don't worry,' he said, focusing on the road ahead. 'Everyone says our smile is about the only thing we have in common, in terms of either looks or personality. Emily is a carbon copy of our mother, whilst I'm definitely all Brooke.'

I looked across at him, taking in the unequivocally masculine jawline and broad shoulders so admired by Neil, and contrasting these with Emily's elfin features and stature. The genetic outcome had certainly been a happy one.

'I'm a fifty-fifty mix of my parents,' I said. 'My mother gave me her ski-jump nose and my father kindly donated his mad-professor hair.' I put a hand to my head and attempted to re-pin some escapee curls into my far-from-perfect updo. 'Although he always had the sense to keep it short.'

He smiled. 'I think the chaos of it suits you,' he said, before adding, 'That was meant to be a compliment, by the way. Chaos was probably the wrong word.'

'Not at all. Percy described it as mayhem when she first met me,' I laughed.

'Beautiful mayhem,' he said.

'That's right! She's so kind. Did Emily tell you?' I asked, before suddenly realising that I was almost home. 'Oh, we need to turn right here,' I said hurriedly, 'then my road is first left after the mini roundabout and my flat is about halfway down.'

He indicated right, and a few minutes later we pulled up outside my flat. 'Thanks so much for the lift,' I said, unbuckling and turning away to open the door, 'both home and to the funer—' I paused and corrected myself. 'To the *celebration*.'

'My pleasure,' he said. 'Genuinely.'

I smiled, aware that I had begun, at some point in the day, to scrutinise his conversation for a subtext – and was now very pleased by any indication, no matter how slight, that he thought of me as something more than an employee. 'That magician was something else, wasn't he?' I said.

'Something else other than a magician, you mean?'

'I thought he was great,' I laughed, and then, turning back towards him, 'Oh, you're not…'

'Blinking,' he said, nodding slowly, his expression blank as he stared straight ahead. 'It's because I'm thinking relatively deeply about something,' he added, still apparently transfixed by the lamp-lit street scene. 'After you mentioned the lack of blinking, I asked a work colleague about it and he said he'd noticed it too – as had everyone

188

else in the office. It's whenever I'm deep in thought, apparently. I'm seemingly incapable of doing the two things simultaneously – blinking and thinking.'

'Well, I wouldn't worry,' I shrugged. 'I'm sure it works to your advantage when negotiating a tough deal. And Neil says I'm incapable of simultaneous intelligent thought and speech under pressure, which is a much worse handicap. Apparently I'm fine with thinking and talking rubbish, though,' I added. 'So that's something, I guess.'

He blinked suddenly. 'You've stopped thinking,' I said, smiling.

'It turns out it isn't always helpful.'

He at last turned towards me and something in his expression made me suddenly conscious of the very small physical distance between us. I guessed it to be about thirty centimetres and wondered what that might be in inches.

I looked up at him. 'Isn't it?'

He shook his head. 'Not in this case,' he said quietly.

'Right.' I nodded, and racked my brains for something else to say. Ending the conversation was not, I realised, something that I was now at all keen to do. In fact, getting out of his car and waving goodbye to James Brooke was at that moment hovering somewhere between being guillotined and having my eyes pecked out by crows on my mid-life wish list.

And as he smiled across at me, I felt precariously close not only to asking him what thirty centimetres was in inches, but also to inviting him into my home for a coffee so that he could share his thoughts – with or without blinking, I really wasn't fussy – on whatever subject he chose.

However, before my brain was able to convert these intellectual meanderings into speech, all hope of our evening together continuing was brought to an abrupt end by a sharp knock on the window behind me. I turned with a start, and then a rapidly sinking heart, to see Aiden bending down and waving in at us – or more accurately, at James.

'Hi!' he said, beaming through the closed window. 'I thought it was your car, James. How are you?' He continued to smile as his gaze transferred to me, at which point the smile fell away and was replaced by a look of utter confusion. 'Gra—' he began, but that was as far as he got. He stepped back from the car door as I opened it and climbed out.

'Aiden,' said James, also getting out of the car and walking round to the pavement, where Aiden stood next to me, now silently looking back and forth between James and myself. James held out his hand. 'How are you?'

'I'm great,' said Aiden, recovering and taking his hand. 'But how do you two know each other?'

James looked at me. 'You know Aiden?'

Aiden laughed and put an arm around my shoulders. 'She does,' he said. 'We've known each other for a *very* long time.'

I looked up at James. 'Aiden is my ex-husband,' I said, aware of a sudden, almost overwhelming, weariness.

'I see,' said James and then smiled at Aiden. 'Small world.'

'I met James when we divided his neighbour's house into flats,' explained Aiden. I nodded dumbly. 'But how do you two know each other?' he asked again.

I took a deep breath, deciding not to worry about the questions and explanations which would inevitably follow when I revealed to Aiden that I was James's cleaner.

'We were at the same funeral today,' said James. 'I gave Grace a lift home.'

'Oh dear,' said Aiden, his face falling. 'No one I know, was it, Grace?'

I shook my head. 'No, no. A friend of a friend. An elderly lady.'

'I'd better be going,' said James suddenly.

'Why don't you stay?' asked Aiden. 'I need to talk to Grace about a little bit of work. Did you get my message?' He looked at me briefly but didn't wait for an answer before turning back to James. 'I'm sure we have time for a drink, if you're not rushing off. You haven't got anything planned, have you, Grace?'

He smiled down at me, his arm still around me, his hand rubbing my shoulder gently. I hesitated. 'Well...'

'That would have been great,' said James, 'but I need to check in with a friend.'

Aiden grinned. 'That wouldn't be the beautiful woman you were with when I bumped into you at the Old Vic, would it? Heather, wasn't it?'

Heather. I felt my shoulders sag. I had forgotten all about her during the course of my afternoon with James, but she now crashed back into my consciousness, about as welcome as a cat at Crufts.

James walked back around the car and reached for the door. 'No, it's not Heather, but yes...' he glanced at me and then smiled at Aiden, 'we are still together.'

'Good to hear,' said Aiden, as James climbed back into the car. 'Heather is great, Grace. The pair of you would get on like a house on fire.'

I enjoyed picturing Heather in a house on fire for a moment, and then gazed miserably down at my shoes in preference to risking eye contact with anyone.

'I'm pleased that's going well for you, James,' continued Aiden. 'It's a wise man who knows when he's onto a good thing. Unfortunately, I'm an idiot.' He addressed the final sentence of his speech to no one in particular, James having already closed the car door and started the engine. I watched as he pulled away without a wave. 'A complete idiot,' repeated Aiden quietly.

I looked up to find him now staring into the distance, apparently lost in thought. I said nothing and eventually he looked down at me. 'What?' he asked, his eyes questioningly serious.

I shook my head. 'I didn't say anything. And if you're waiting for me to contradict you over the idiot assessment, you may as well pull up a chair and pour yourself a drink, because you're in for a long, *long* wait.'

He laughed and rested his chin gently on the top of my head. 'I'll wait if you'll let me,' he murmured. I closed my eyes and, for my own sake as much as his, pretended not to hear.

'So what's this work thing you need to see me about then?' I asked after a moment, pulling away and poking him in the ribs.

He looked surprised. 'What? Oh, that. Yes. Marketing material, remember? I was hoping you'd take a look at it.' He smiled and held up the laptop case he had been carrying under his arm. 'It's all on here.'

I looked up at him questioningly. 'Why on earth didn't you just email it to me? That's what you said you were going to do.'

'Because I know you work best under pressure and because I…' He looked at me for a moment and then shrugged. 'Because I'm a complete idiot,' he said.

'Still not disagreeing with you,' I smiled. 'But come on in and I'll get reading.'

Chapter 25

Following another Saturday-morning cake fest in the Downs Café with Simone, for which we both pointlessly wore running gear, I decided I should attempt some form of actual exercise by, at the very least, speed-walking the mile or so from the Downs to Percy's house.

In fact, the speed-walk was to prove a lot less exhausting than the grilling I had received at the hands of Simone as we worked our way through a plate of mini Danish pastries. Early on in the conversation I had made the significant mistake of mentioning that I had seen Aiden the night before. And as Simone was aware that Summer was out of town, this led to a line of questioning with which I wasn't particularly comfortable – not least because she asked me all the questions I had already asked myself following Aiden's departure at 11 p.m. the night before, and to which I honestly, as yet, had no answers.

The truth was, I seemed unable, or unwilling, to pinpoint my feelings towards Aiden with any degree of accuracy. By midnight, I had got as far as allowing myself to acknowledge that I was once again enjoying his company, but beyond that, perhaps with some uncon-scious sense of preserving my mental health, I was unable to go. And when I tried to guess at *his* feelings, I repeatedly ran up against the fact that during our marriage I hadn't been able to guess them at all. So even though it seemed increasingly clear to me that his affection for me was growing, or resurfacing, I couldn't allow myself to accept this as an undeniable truth.

Simone drove her remarkably similar concerns home, for the most part, indirectly and with a smile, but that didn't make them any easier to sit through. She wondered 'just a tiny little bit' about the new direction my friendship with Aiden was taking, and although she was 'not at all worried' that I would do anything stupid, she was slightly concerned that I might find myself caught up in 'a little bit of bother' if the mother of Aiden's child interpreted his current preoccupation with me as anything other than friendly and professional. She said all this with an unmistakable this-isn't-going-to-end-well glint in her eye, and although I tried to sound casual whilst reassuring her as best I could, she was clearly unconvinced.

I was therefore rather relieved when she looked at her phone in horror and announced that she was ten minutes late for picking up Harry from his guitar lesson. She had then departed in a whirl and I had headed off to Percy's, with a determination not to waste any more worry-time on Aiden when there were so many unknown factors and feelings in play. I would instead tread carefully and deal with each new situation as it arose. A little voice somewhere deep inside asked me whether this approach might not be worryingly similar to burying my head in the sand; however, the exertion of the speed-walk served to quash any and all concerns, other than whether I might imminently die of a heart attack. Consequently, by the time I staggered up Percy's steps, I was feeling relatively at peace, if incredibly knackered.

The door was opened, before I had an opportunity to ring the bell, by a smiling elderly lady whom I recognised from my evening of waitressing for Percy. She reintroduced herself as Caroline and explained that she was just leaving and that Percy was much better, having been buoyed by a steady stream of concerned visitors.

Twenty minutes later, as Percy and I sat in armchairs and chatted over the cups of tea I had made for us, I was pleased to see for myself that, although still a little pale and coughing intermittently, she was, as Caroline had said, undoubtedly on the mend.

'And James thoroughly enjoyed Maud's party too,' she said, looking at me over the top of her teacup. 'And who knew he had such a fascination with death?' she added brightly. 'Penny phoned me this morning to say he had insisted absolutely upon viewing the corpse. And that you both then had a lovely little chat with it.'

'Well you see, we—' I began, but got no further before Percy was off again.

'And I understand I missed Ronald doing his magic tricks. Phyllis said they were even more shambolic than at Molly Reynolds' memorial service in the cathedral. No one asks him to do them, you know,' she said, her lips pursing disapprovingly. 'He just turns up everywhere with a pack of cards and those dreadful rainbow handkerchiefs of his and away he goes. His daughter is forever ringing round apologising, poor dear. She blames herself for buying him a David Blaine DVD two Christmases ago. Mind you, as I said to Arthur this morning, if it means Ronald keeps his trousers on for more than ten minutes at a time, it's all to the good. Oh, and my darling,' she said, finally taking a breath, putting down her tea and leaning forward to place a hand on my knee, 'would it be asking too much of you to come in and clean for me next week? It's just that with being under the weather, I don't want things to get out of hand.' She patted her hair. 'I could really do with a trip to the salon too, but that's impossible at the moment. My wonderful hairdresser is away and I wouldn't dream of going elsewhere.'

'Of course I'll clean for you,' I said, looking round the room. 'I'd offer to start right now, but everywhere is immaculate!'

She picked up her teacup. 'Ah, that's because James did it all last night, you see.'

'He did?'

'Yes. He vacuumed in here, despite my protests. Then he made me a Lemsip and disappeared into the bathroom. He was quite some time and I thought maybe he had had an off sandwich at Maud's. But when I went to bed, I realised he had been cleaning in there. And in the kitchen too.'

'That was thoughtful.'

She nodded. 'Yes, he's a very thoughtful man.'

I sipped my tea. 'Doesn't let a lot slip.'

'Ah, well that's a two-way street, my darling.'

I looked up at her, slightly taken aback and not quite knowing how to respond. But, as was so often the case with Percy, the need to reply was snatched away by her ongoing chatter. 'So after Penny said goodbye, I spoke to Arthur,' she said, beaming. 'He sounded much better and said it was down to two days of wearing wrapping paper next to his skin. I asked if he meant brown paper, but he said no, it was some of the rainbow wrap he had saved from his birthday.' She sighed and shook her head. 'I'm assuming he put a shirt on over it, but I honestly wouldn't put anything past him.'

—

Percy and I chatted for well over an hour, and it was almost one o'clock by the time I finally settled down in my favourite armchair, after a shower, to catch up on emails. The first to catch my eye, as I picked up my cup of coffee and opened my laptop, was from Rose. I had had a postcard from her earlier that week, confirming that she was having a great time and looking forward to Tony joining her very soon, but other than that, I had heard nothing. So it was with genuine eagerness that I opened and read the email, which she had sent just an hour earlier.

From: rosefortune1947@hotmail.com
To: gbwaterhouse@blueyonder.co.uk
10 December 2016
Re: Hola!

Hola Gracie!
  Just thought I'd drop you a little line to see how you're diddling and to say thanks again for making my break in the sunshine possible. I would have been in touch sooner but I'm hopeless with computers. Reg, Vi's husband, keeps trying to sort me out but I've already gone wrong twice this week trying to send you a message and I don't like to keep bothering him. I still prefer paper and pen really. I've sent you a postcard by the way, although I expect I'll see you before that does.

Tony has been here for almost two weeks now and loving it. He flies home the day after tomorrow and had a long chat last night to Reg about the cost of villas. Not that we could ever afford to buy one and keep the house in Bristol. I think Tony was just having a little daydream about moving here but I can't see us doing that. Sounds funny, but I think I'd miss the grey. You need the grey to really appreciate the sunshine, don't you?

I hope you're well and not too puffed out doing all that hoovering for me! Are you doing some writing too? Not too many more weeks now and then your dusting days will be over! Give my love to Emily and Percy. And send my best to James if you bump into him. Are you getting to know him at all?

Thanks again, Gracie. I couldn't be more grateful, you know. Going to go and get Reg to press the right button to send this now. Taking no more chances.

Rose xx

I smiled my way through the email, lingering a little over Rose's final question, touching as it did on a subject with which I was now increasingly preoccupied.

Was I getting to know James?

I closed her email and opened my cleaning diary, scrolling down and scanning the pages for any mention of him. And I was surprised at just how frequently he featured, popping up in almost every entry; first as a humourless, controlling, cold-hearted chauvinist, before metamorphosing into an attractive, intelligent, kind-hearted brother and friend. A man quick to forgive the hasty, highly unflattering assumptions of a new employee, and also, I now knew, one who thought nothing of taking time out of a busy working day to clean his elderly neighbour's loo.

I smiled and leaned back in the armchair, preparing to bring my diary up to date and remembering the afternoon spent with James at the funeral: his refusal to let me go in alone, his quiet support and the gentle pressure of his elbow against mine as we drank cups of tea from the finest bone china and watched Ronald, the non-magician, pull a long string of slightly grubby silk handkerchiefs from his unzipped flies.

It had, somewhat bizarrely, been one of my happiest afternoons in a long time, clouded only by my disappointment at Aiden's unexpected arrival and interruption of our evening. My mood dipped slightly at the thought, and I was aware that I had felt a similar sense of disappointment only an hour or so earlier, when a vague hope of running into James when I left Percy's flat had come to nothing. I had wanted to talk to him about Aiden. I wasn't exactly sure why, or even what I wanted to say. Maybe simply 'Isn't it funny that you know Aiden?' would be enough. But what I did know was that having said nothing at all made the matter feel like unfinished business between us, and that bothered me.

I reopened and reread Rose's email and felt no doubt; I was getting to know James, but I wanted to get to know him more. And I wanted to let him get to know me too. Percy was right: openness was a two-way street.

I began to type.

From: gbwaterhouse@blueyonder.co.uk
To: rosefortune1947@hotmail.com
10 December 2016
Re: Hola!

Hola, Rose!

Great to hear from you. So pleased that Tony is loving Spain as much as you are. I'd like to say I know what you mean about missing the grey skies of Bristol, but as I look out on a dank December day, I'm not sure that I do.

Now, after all your thank-yous, I have one of my own. Thank you for entrusting me with your job. It has cheered me up, toned my biceps and tightened my glutes no end. I've seen quite a bit of Emily and Percy. In fact, I'll be cleaning for Percy over the next week or so, and I even waitressed at one of her parties! I've got to know James too. I have to say I found him rather hard to read when we first met, but now that he's explained to me that he has difficulty thinking and blinking at the same time, I'm much more relaxed in his company.

And yes, I'm writing. And enjoying it. My cleaning diary is coming along nicely. It's just observations and anecdotes (mainly courtesy of Percy). Nothing I'd ever use, of course, but it's outward-looking and, Neil will be delighted to learn, increasingly upbeat. It's a start.

Talking of writing, I was thinking of telling Percy, Emily and James a little bit more about myself. In particular, I'd really like to talk to them about my writing and how I came to be filling in for you. Emily has been so frank about her past problems that I'd like to be more open with her about mine. Of course, I'd emphasise that your choice of me to do your job was based a hundred per cent on my cleaning experience and expertise. I just want to give everyone a bit more Grace.

Anyway, I'm rambling now. In short: all good here. Very good, in fact. Thank you again for trusting me. I couldn't be more grateful.

Grace xx

Pressing send, I decided to leave all the other, less interesting emails until later. Instead, I clicked once again on my diary and began a remarkably cheery account of a funeral.

Chapter 26

The irony was that having decided that I wanted to give everyone a bit more Grace, there was suddenly no one around to give her to. Despite usually sharing at least one, and often both, of my Monday and Thursday tea breaks with Emily or Percy, I didn't see either of them all week. Neither did I, despite Simone's worries about his growing preoccupation with me, see or even hear anything from Aiden. And with Gavin and Neil out of the country, the upshot was that things seemed much quieter than usual. I had text-chats and phone calls with friends, but face-to-face interaction with anyone other than neighbours and the window cleaner was nil, and I blamed this for my strangely flattened mood.

I considered calling Simone to arrange a drink, but as I was already due to see her for a cake run on Saturday, and because I couldn't quite face another possible lecture about Aiden, I discounted that idea. Texting Aiden also crossed my mind, especially as his total silence was, these days, very out of character, but I couldn't bring myself to make the call. I knew deep down that Simone was right to be concerned about the situation, and although I found that I was missing his company, I told myself that a little breathing space, if that was what he was seeking, would benefit us both.

So instead of resorting to coffees and cocktails, I filled my working week with my usual cleaning duties, my writing and the much-needed redecoration of the guest bedroom. It was the only room of my flat which I had left untouched since moving in, and although overnight guests frequently commented favourably on the oak bedside cabinet and pretty bedlinen, they remained notably silent on the subject of the eye-wateringly floral wallpaper and swirling mud-brown carpet. Gavin was, of course, the exception to this politeness and had long referred to the bedroom as Room 101, and to any weekend visitors as Winstons.

Percy's total and unusual absence from my week had been explained in a note which I found waiting for me, along with the keys to her home, on the kitchen table of 3 Bennett Park when I had arrived to clean on Monday morning. In a beautifully cursive hand, she advised that she had gone to stay with Arthur in Long Ashton. They were both on the mend and planned to complete their convalescence together, watching *Countdown*, playing knockout whist and eating sugared almonds. She wouldn't be home again until Saturday lunchtime and asked if I could clean before then, if it wasn't too much bother.

By Friday afternoon, I had very nearly completed the redecoration of my spare room, in inoffensive creams, and had chosen a carpet to be fitted in between Christmas and New Year. Proud of my progress, and keen to finish the job before the weekend, I was still touching up woodwork at six-thirty, when I suddenly remembered that I had yet to clean Percy's flat. Quickly downing my brush, I grabbed my tabard, cleaning caddy and Percy's keys and headed off.

By seven-thirty, I was doing well, having mopped the tiled floor of the communal entrance hall and cleaned the kitchen. However, things came to a frustratingly sudden halt when I switched on Percy's ancient vacuum cleaner and realised that it was merely relocating dust rather than sucking it up, leaving me no choice but to attempt to replace the bag.

After a lengthy and fruitless search for a new bag, I decided to empty and reuse the old one. And when I eventually managed to remove the top of the Hoover, it was pretty clear that reusing, rather than replacing, the bag had been Percy's approach for some considerable time. It appeared to be just about as old as the Hoover, and not only was it worryingly fragile, it also looked disturbingly full. Kneeling down and leaning forward to peer into the mechanism of the cleaner, I delicately, with the care and concentration of a surgeon, set about removing the bulging bag, all the time wishing that I had thought to ask Percy for a tutorial. After less than a minute of precision fiddling and pulling, the bag came away suddenly in my hand, tearing with a sad inevitability and throwing up a cloud of dust into my face in the process.

After sneezing three times in quick succession, I opened my eyes and looked in dismay at the even layer of dark grey dust now coating a largish patch of living-room carpet around me. I touched it lightly with my hand and, staring at my blackened fingertips, wondered if Percy had perhaps taken to vacuuming the patio. But whatever the constituent parts of the dust, I knew there was nothing for it but to drive home, pick up my own vacuum cleaner, and then come back and attempt to clear up the mess. I hurried into the kitchen, took a bin bag from under the sink and then, placing the remnants of the Hoover bag, and whatever dust it still contained, inside it, I went outside and down the steps to pop the lot into Percy's wheelie bin.

I spotted James just as he locked his car and began to walk briskly towards his garden gate. Delighted to see him, I closed the lid of the wheelie bin and, climbing a couple of steps to make myself more visible, I raised my arm and waved enthusiastically. 'Hi, James!' I called.

His head turned and, presumably because he initially failed to recognise me in the darkness, he hesitated before replying. 'Oh, hi, Grace,' he said after a moment, glancing up uncertainly at his own house before turning and walking slowly towards Percy's. He pushed open the gate, walked up the garden path and came to a halt a few feet away from the bottom step. I smiled down at him.

'I've been cleaning for Percy,' I explained. 'She's back tomorrow. Just had a bit of bother with her Hoover.'

He nodded but didn't return my smile, instead staring at me as if I was a particularly quirky exhibit in the Tate Modern. I put a self-conscious hand to my hair, experiencing an unexpected and uncomfortable flashback to my first meeting with him. 'Is there dust in my hair?' I asked, laughing uncertainly. 'There was quite a cloud.'

He nodded again. 'A little,' he said.

'There's probably some paint in there too,' I sighed. 'I've been decorating all week. Haven't had a moment to think really.'

He didn't reply, now apparently transfixed by my hair. 'So, how has your week been?' I asked in an attempt to distract him. 'It doesn't seem like seven days since Maud's, does it?'

At that, he transferred his attention back to my face and managed a smile, but it was definitely a polite one, and again my mind returned to his study, to my hand on the box file, to Grace the cleaner and James the employer. 'No, it doesn't,' he said, and then, 'Sorry, I should let you get on. Have a great weekend.'

'Thanks,' I said. 'You too.' I turned and walked up the remaining steps, pausing as I reached the front door and adding impulsively over my shoulder, 'Isn't it funny that you know Aiden?'

He was still standing at the bottom of the steps, looking up at me and now frowning slightly at the question. 'Small world.'

'Yes, you said that at the time.'

We continued to look at each other for a moment longer and I was just wondering whether to say more about Aiden when he spoke. 'I'd better go,' he said, inclining his head towards his house. 'Heather's here. I only came out to get this from the car.' He held up a phone.

'Oh yes, Heather.' I smiled, but it was an effort. 'Well, you two have a lovely evening. As soon as I've finished here, I'm going out for dinner with a friend.' I maintained a cheery smile, despite feeling immediately disappointed with myself over the undeniably needy lie.

'Sounds good,' he said, walking away. 'Enjoy.'

'Thank you, I will,' I called after him, hearing my voice crack a little. Then, angry with myself for such a complete misreading of our relationship, and feeling about as deflated and unattractive as Percy's old Hoover bag, I pushed open the door and trudged back inside.

Chapter 27

It was late by the time I finished polishing Percy's bathroom taps and stood back with a sense of satisfaction at a
job well done. It was a small but uplifting sense of achievement which, hot on the heels of disappointment and a
rather crushing blow to my ego, came as an unexpected
but very welcome surprise, and brought with it a renewed
appreciation of the therapeutic aspects of my cleaning job.

I hadn't hurried back to Percy's after my trip home
to collect my vacuum cleaner. One glance in my hallway
mirror was enough to confirm that a significant degree of
personal deep-cleaning was required. I had, fortunately,
instinctively screwed my eyes tight shut when the Hoover
bag popped just inches from my face. But the downside
was that I had been left with a flesh-coloured ring around
each eye, making me look not unlike Dick Van Dyke's
chimney sweep in *Mary Poppins*. If I hadn't felt so miserable, I would have found it funny. I might even have taken
a selfie to send to Gavin. But as it was, I had simply stared
at my blackened reflection whilst allowing tears of hurt
pride to trickle down my grimy face. I had then headed
off, full of self-pity, for a tearful shower, before dragging
myself back to Percy's, damp-haired and Dyson in hand,
to fulfil my obligation to clean her flat.

However, as I closed and deadlocked Percy's front door behind me a little after 10 p.m., I realised that my increased levels of positivity at completing the set task, although small, were ongoing, and there was no doubt I was feeling much better than I had two and a half hours earlier. I had just reached the car and was still pondering the emotional and psychological benefits of mopping, when I was startled by the sound of heavy, fast-approaching footsteps close behind me. I whirled around, lifting and preparing to swing my Dyson.

'It's me!' said James. He held up a hand in an apparent mixture of greeting and self-defence. 'Sorry, I didn't mean to frighten you.'

'Oh.' I attempted a smile, and then, feeling relieved but flustered, opened the boot and placed the vacuum cleaner inside. 'I was miles away. I thought you were a mugger,' I said, slamming shut the boot and looking up at him, 'trying to snatch my Small Ball.' I pointed at the cleaner. 'That's what this model is called,' I added, in case he thought I was being smutty. 'It's a Dyson Small Ball.'

'Really? I didn't know that.' He smiled, raising his shoulders towards his ears in a slight shiver. It struck me that he wasn't wearing a jacket, or even a jumper, just a white shirt, unbuttoned at the collar. My eyes travelled down his dark trousers to his feet and I noticed that his brown brogues were unlaced.

'Have you just popped out for something again?' I asked, looking up at him. 'It's freezing, isn't it?'

'I came out to see you actually,' he said hurriedly, slightly crashing my observation on the weather.

'Oh?'

'Yes, I wanted to talk to you earlier, but it wasn't the best time.' His smile was now slightly less relaxed and his manner more businesslike.

I nodded. 'I didn't quite appreciate what a state I was in. That black stuff was on Percy's carpet, you know. But I think I got it all up with my...' I sighed at the inanity of my conversation as I gestured again towards the boot of the car, 'with my Small Ball. But sorry, I'm rambling and you must want to get back inside to Heather. What did you want to talk to me about?'

He put his hands in his pockets and cleared his throat. It was the first time I had seen him looking even vaguely uncomfortable or uncertain, and as he stared at me unblinkingly and his frown lines deepened, I was in no doubt that he had something significant to say. But what? Had he found mould in the fridge? Was my vacuuming not up to scratch? Or, worst of all, had he perhaps spotted that I was now a little more intrigued by him than a cleaner should be by her employer? I held my breath in anticipation of the possible annihilation of my self-esteem, whilst at the same time resolving to keep my head and plead for Rose's job, even if I couldn't keep my own.

At last, James blinked. 'This is strangely difficult,' he said quietly.

I looked up at him resignedly. 'It's fine,' I said. 'I'm ready.'

He took a breath. 'OK, well, I realise our relationship is a professional one...'

'Yes, absolutely,' I said, nodding rapidly. 'Completely professional. I'm a cleaner and you're my employer. I'm not at all intrigued by you.'

He frowned. 'That's… good to know,' he said hesitantly. 'But I hope that doesn't mean you don't enjoy my company, because I really enjoy yours.'

'Oh, I see.' I continued to nod, despite now having no clue where the conversation was going.

'I really enjoyed the funeral in particular,' he continued. 'And I thought perhaps we could do something similar again. Minus the death element. And possibly the magician.' He suddenly smiled and I continued to stare up at him, my mouth hanging open, as I rapidly binned my speech about Rose and tried to make sense of the current situation. Was he asking me out on a date?

Still smiling, his eyes narrowed slightly and he tilted his head questioningly. He had never looked more attractive. 'Dinner maybe? Tomorrow night?'

Yes, he was asking me out on a date – despite the fact that his current girlfriend was sitting not forty feet away. I looked up at the house. Did he plan to run inside and give her the old heave-ho if I said yes? Or maybe he'd let us overlap for a week or two, just to be really sure he'd made the right decision. How very prudent. I continued to gaze up at the house, feeling a huge sense of disappointment and resentment towards him, and an equally enormous sense of regret over the inevitable loss of my job. Then, turning and addressing his unlaced shoes, I began the only reply possible in the circumstances. 'I really can't believe you actually—'

He placed a hand briefly on my arm, causing me to look up, and then touched a finger to his lips in a gentle request for silence. 'Sorry to interrupt, but if that looming rejection of my invitation is based upon the fact that you are reverting to your favourite theory, namely that I am an amoral, two-timing bastard, then I'd just like to get in an early defence: I ended my relationship with Heather a week ago. She was here briefly this evening to collect a few things and then she went home.'

I stared up at him and said nothing, as my thought processes were forced to execute yet another handbrake turn. His smile fell a little. 'However, if the looming rejection was based upon something else… or someone else,' he said, 'then of course I understand and I'm sorry to have put you in an awkward position. None of this will impact upon the tenure or terms of your employment in any way.'

I shook my head and laughed.

'What?' he asked. 'What does that mean?'

I smiled. 'It means you sound like a lawyer.'

His expression remained serious for a moment longer and then his smile returned. 'I just wanted to be sure you didn't feel under any pressure.'

I shook my head a second time. 'I don't have a something or a someone else, and I'd love to come to dinner.'

His smile broadened. 'Great.'

I continued to look up at him, feeling a pleasant awkwardness I hadn't felt for years and wondering what to do next. I thought about complimenting him on his shirt, or telling him a bit more about my Small Ball but just in time, a quiet internal voice, which sounded an awful lot like Neil, recommended that I skip any attempt at small talk, or conversation of any kind, and go home before my inability to think and speak intelligently under even the slightest pressure spoiled what was actually a very lovely moment.

'I think I'd better go home,' I said.

He looked thoughtful and then nodded. 'And I should probably go inside and catch up on my blinking. I've been doing a lot of thinking this week and my eyes are on fire.' He smiled. 'Shall I text you?'

'Yes please,' I said, and then, raising a slightly shaky hand in farewell, I climbed into the car and headed home, feeling pretty great.

Chapter 28

'I knew it!' exclaimed Simone as we sat down with our order in the Downs café. We had met there ten minutes earlier, both, as usual, wearing running gear and both, as usual, having little or no intention of actually running anywhere at all. 'I blinking knew it! The moment you said he was thoughtful and good-looking...'

'*You* said he was thoughtful and *Neil* said he was good-looking,' I corrected.

'... I knew there was potential,' she continued, not listening, staring off into the middle distance. 'As soon as I got home, I added him to the list. Just wait till I tell Guy. That'll be the last time he disses the list.' She picked up her Danish pastry and took an alarmingly aggressive bite.

'This list...' I said, dipping a teaspoon into my cappuccino. 'Who exactly is on it?'

She hesitated for a moment and then grinned. 'Oh well, I suppose there's no harm in telling you, seeing as you're now going on a date.' She reached across the table and squeezed my hand. 'Actually going on a date!' she repeated.

I sighed. 'The list?'

She put down her Danish. 'OK, well, my brother was the most recent addition, before James.' She looked at me uncertainly. 'Is that an insult?'

'No!' I exclaimed. 'I told you I thought he was nice.'

'Phew,' she said, looking relieved. 'And just before him there was Joe, your electrician.'

'What?'

'You said loads of nice things about him,' she said. 'Including that he was quite hunky.'

'I also said he was happily married with two small children!' I protested.

'Yes,' she rolled her eyes exasperatedly, 'and that's precisely why I put him in the "Unlikely But You Never Know" section – along with Gahmummnee...' She mumbled the conclusion of the sentence into her mug of tea.

'I'm sorry,' I frowned, 'I didn't quite catch who else was in that section. Could you repeat that?'

She put down her tea. 'Gavin and Neil.'

I lowered the muffin I was just about to eat and stared at her open-mouthed. 'And you wonder why Guy disses your list?'

'Oh who cares?' She smiled triumphantly. 'The point is, I was right about James and that's the bit I'll rub Guy's nose in.'

'Actually,' I began hesitantly, 'not wanting to rain on your smug parade or anything, but could you delay telling Guy about James for a little while? At least until we see how tonight goes.'

Her face fell. 'Why?'

'It's just that, as I told you last week, James knows Aiden. It's only a loose connection, but...'

Simone smiled sadly. 'But you're worried that Guy will let something slip, and before you know it, Aiden will find out.'

I pulled an awkward face and she shook her head. 'Don't worry. You're quite right,' she sighed. 'Guy wouldn't mean to muck things up, but he's such a chump.'

'I just think he might not appreciate the possible repercussions.'

'I'm certain he wouldn't.'

'Have you told him anything much about James?' I asked, trying not to sound anxious.

'No, you're quite safe,' she smiled. 'All he knows is what I told him when you first started work, so he probably still thinks James is a bit of a bastard actually – if he thinks anything at all. He certainly won't be expecting you to be having dinner with him. All Guy's really focused on is that you're feeling better.' She shrugged. 'You know him. He's quite basic really. He's just happy that you're happy.'

'He's lovely,' I said. 'And you can definitely tell him all about it if things go OK. I'd just like to feel in total control of what Aiden does and doesn't know about me right now.'

'Absolutely. Very sensible,' she said, her face now serious. 'And how is...' She hesitated.

'Not heard from him in over a week,' I said matter-of-factly.

She raised her eyebrows, in either surprise or disbelief, I wasn't sure which.

'Well from that reaction, I take it you had no hand in that,' I said.

'No hand in what?' she frowned. 'You mean in Aiden not being in touch?'

I nodded.

'I wouldn't interfere like that,' she said, sounding mildly offended.

I said nothing and instead picked up my muffin again.

'OK,' she sighed, 'so it might have crossed my mind to give him a call.'

I sighed and bit into the cake.

'But I didn't,' she said emphatically. 'So his silence is nothing at all to do with me. Let's hope it's more to do with him putting other people's feelings before his own.' She sipped at her mug of tea before adding in a mutter, 'And I don't mean Summer's.'

I tutted and then said, 'Thank you for being such a lovely friend, Sim.'

She looked up at me and smiled. 'I hope everything goes brilliantly tonight. Are you going to tell him about your books?'

'Absolutely,' I said. 'I feel like I know more about him than he does about me at the moment and it's only fair to level the playing field.'

'Agreed. And what are you going to wear?'

'Damn.' I put a hand to my mouth. 'I haven't got a clue. And that's quite important, isn't it?'

She shook her head and put down her cup. 'Don't panic. We can head to your flat now and go through your wardrobe. I can be an objective eye.'

She stood up and took my arm, hauling me up with her as I grabbed in vain for the remains of my muffin. 'Right now?' I asked. 'But what about our run?'

'You're not serious, are you?' she asked, looking appalled.

I laughed. 'Of course not.'

'Thank goodness for that,' she said, placing a relieved hand to her chest. 'You had me really worried for a moment.'

Chapter 29

I had arranged to meet James at seven-thirty at No Man's Grace, an appropriately named smallish wine bar and restaurant, conveniently located an equal distance from each of our homes and, it turned out, a favourite of both of ours. But despite the familiar location and my initial excitement at being invited out by James, as I made my way to meet him, I felt sick with nerves.

I arrived at the restaurant fifteen minutes early, and as there was, unsurprisingly, no sign of him, I ordered what I hoped would be a calming spritzer from the bar and took my seat at the table he had booked for us. I then decided to try to allay my fears with a little rationality. This was, I told myself, just a meeting with a man, and I met and interacted with lots of those on a daily basis without any kind of awkwardness or anxiety whatsoever. OK, so it was true that most of those men were either gay, my friends' partners, the postman or my ex-husband, but they were still men and so they still counted.

I picked up my drink, took a large gulp and, not for the first time during the past three weeks, wished that Neil and Gavin were in Bristol, rather than in Los Angeles, five thousand three hundred and sixty miles away. It was a distance I had googled earlier in the day, along with Pacific Daylight Time, when I had considered ringing

Gavin's mobile. In the end, I had decided it might be best not to interrupt their pre-flight sleep with my insecurities and opted instead for a neurotic text to Gavin and then a state of complete denial. The denial held for a while but ended abruptly the moment I slipped into the not-trying-too-hard jeans, black top and boots approved by Simone, and proceeded to apply eyeliner and mascara with an undeniably shaky hand.

The truth was that I liked James. A lot. He was kind, clever, funny, honourable and, as I had always known, far, far from ugly. And although I didn't want to set myself up for devastating disappointment, I couldn't quell the hope, or even expectation, that this evening might prove to be the beginning of a significant new positive in my life. I had been surprised and delighted by his invitation to dinner and was desperate not to screw things up. Unfortunately, that desperation and weight of expectation, together with a complete absence of any recent dating experience, had combined to turn me into an absolute nervous wreck.

I looked around the restaurant in search of a distraction, whilst consciously slowing my breathing, deciding that if I couldn't calm down mentally, I could at least attempt to lower my heart rate. There were no interesting conversations on which to eavesdrop. A largely mute, extremely bored-looking couple were, apart from small groups arriving for a private party in the basement, the only other diners in the restaurant this early in the evening. So instead I studied the pictures on the walls, read the wine list and cocktail menu twice and was just about to begin counting the Christmas baubles balanced on each of the shelves behind the bar, when James walked in.

He looked calmly around the restaurant, unwrapping a grey scarf from his neck and taking off a black coat as he did so. When he spotted me, he stared analytically for a moment, giving no indication of ever having met me before, then smiled and raised a hand. It was a delayed facial reaction I had come to expect, but that initial unsmiling gaze, no matter how familiar and fleeting, did absolutely nothing to help my nerves and I felt myself hit a previously never experienced level of panic. I watched as he said something to the waiter, pointed in my direction and handed over his coat. Then he walked over to the table and sat down opposite me.

'Hello,' he said, checking his watch. 'You're early. I was sure I'd be here before you.'

'Were you?' I asked, my voice a little hoarse. I picked up my spritzer and took a sip.

'Yes,' he smiled.

My mind a blank and searching for a topic of conversation, I played for time. 'Were you really?'

He looked at me for a moment. 'Yes,' he repeated, nodding thoughtfully, as if second-guessing himself, 'I really was.'

'Maybe I set off earlier than you did, or maybe I just walked more quickly,' I said hurriedly, keen to avoid any kind of gap in the conversation.

'Either is a possibility,' he agreed, still smiling.

'But I can't really imagine I walked more quickly than you because I'm wearing heels and I'm a disaster in heels at the best of times, and the pavements are a little bit icy this evening, aren't they?'

'They are.'

'So maybe I misread the time on the kitchen clock before I left. It's a very easy clock to misread because it's the kind that doesn't have any numbers on it. It just has four little lines. A line like this for the twelve,' I turned slightly in my chair and described a short vertical line in the air, 'another one like this,' I drew a horizontal line, 'for the three. And then there's another like this for the six, and then a line over here for the nine. And the other problem is that the hands are really short. The minute hand is about this long,' I said, developing my mid-air diagram. 'But the hour hand is so ridiculously short – like this – that it's impossible to tell which number it's pointing at.' I dotted my finger around the invisible clock. 'Which *imaginary* number it's pointing at, I mean, because as I say, there... are... no... numbers.' My voice trailed away to a whisper and I paused, staring at my still-raised hand, before slowly lowering it, and my eyes, to the table. 'I'm sorry,' I said, miserably aware that I had just thrown years of Neil's thinking/speaking advice out of the window. 'I know I'm talking rubbish.'

There was a slight pause before James spoke. 'Not at all,' he said. 'I was gripped by your wall-clock anecdote. And, as it happens, I've got an interesting story about the clock on my oven. It's digital and, from certain angles, all the numbers look like eights.'

I looked up at him. He clearly wanted to laugh.

'I'm just very nervous,' I said apologetically. 'I was quite nervous before you walked in, and then you arrived and did your unnerving face...' I gestured at his head, making a circling motion with my index finger, 'and that moved me up several notches to very nervous. On top of that, I haven't been on a date for years, which adds to the anxiety because I didn't know what to wear, quite obviously don't know what to say and honestly can't even remember what makes a date a date. This morning, my friend said, "You're going on a date, Grace!" And I thought, why can't it just be coffee, dinner or a walk? Why does it need the date label? It just places an enormous weight of expectation on everyone, doesn't it? But an expectation of what? And now,' I leaned forward, resting my elbows on the table and placing my head in my hands, 'I feel like I might actually throw up.'

'Would it help to pretend we're at a funeral?' he asked.

I sighed and leaned back in my chair. 'Don't tell me you've got a set of coloured hankies down your trousers.'

He laughed and leaned towards me, lowering his voice. 'Look, Grace, I'm sorry about the…' he hesitated and pointed to his face, 'about this. But whatever you think my face is saying, you have to know that there's nothing negative going on up here.' He tapped the side of his head. 'Far from it,' he added. 'And it may be cold comfort, but I'm not one hundred per cent relaxed myself. Inviting you to dinner was one of the most unexpectedly challenging things I've done in a long time.' He glanced up as a waiter brought a bottle of mineral water to our table, pouring us each a glass. 'Thank you,' said James, waiting for the waiter to leave before returning his attention to me. 'I had actually wanted to suggest lunch on the first day I met you, because things had gone so badly that morning.' He smiled and picked up his glass. 'At least I told myself that was why I wanted to suggest lunch. I considered asking you a number of times, but your vacuuming action made you strangely intimidating.'

'Intimidating?' I frowned. 'With a plastic bag on each foot and another on my head?'

He nodded. 'I think the bags actually enhanced the fear factor for me. That and the way you said my name as you left the study – as if I was something you had stepped in and couldn't wait to scrape off.'

'I never think of myself as remotely intimidating.' I shook my head at the thought.

'No?' he said, his eyebrows raised in surprise. 'Well maybe you should take a look at yourself in the mirror the next time you're toting a tray of canapés.' He took a sip of his water. 'Or a Dyson Small Ball,' he added in a murmur, picking up a menu and passing it to me before beginning to study his own.

I stared unseeingly at the menu whilst recalling one of Neil's more recent lectures on the subject of not assuming that I had a monopoly on self-doubt. It was simply, he had said, that most people managed to set such negative emotions to one side, instead of focusing on them in the manner of a small child trying to set fire to dry grass using only a magnifying glass and the power of the sun.

I lowered the menu. 'Thank you for inviting me to dinner – despite being intimidated,' I said.

James looked up. 'And thank you for coming to dinner,' he replied solemnly, 'despite wanting to throw up.'

I smiled and, as he looked at me unblinkingly in a way I suddenly didn't mind at all, I felt my nerves begin to give way to the same pleasant uncertainty I had experienced the evening before. 'That's OK,' I said. 'And the good news is, I've just started to feel a little bit like I'm at a funeral.'

'Me too,' he said, returning my smile with one which made me wonder exactly how many centimetres apart we were this evening. 'And should either of us feel the need to chat to a corpse, I think there are a couple sitting at that table by the window.'

Chapter 30

Three courses and one bottle of wine later and my nerves were a dim and distant memory. The restaurant was now heaving, with every table occupied and a sizeable crowd, most wearing party hats, standing with drinks around the small bar. The evening had pleasurably flown. James had been funny, charming, interesting and attentive, and his reduced capacity for blinking now seemed a smouldering plus rather than an unnerving negative. Consequently, I was thoroughly enjoying myself and, as I checked my watch and saw that it was approaching 10 p.m., I was also increasingly aware of a growing hope that the fifty-centimetre distance between us would, at some point that evening, be reduced to zero.

We had, over the course of the meal, covered an impressive range of topics, including family, friends, favourite holiday destinations and friction-powered carpet sweepers. Our professional lives, though, was one subject that had not been even vaguely touched upon. I wasn't surprised by this, already aware of James's famed reluctance to discuss work, but I was determined that the evening shouldn't end without me talking to him about my main occupation. However, as our waiter brought coffee to the table, we had returned to the topic of family, and as James began to talk with obvious concern and affection about Emily, it wasn't a subject I wanted to crash or rush.

'The past year or so has been very difficult for her,' he said with a frown, picking up his coffee cup. 'I know she told you about it.'

'She mentioned needing your support,' I said.

He shook his head sadly. 'I didn't offer the right kind initially. My instinct was to view the situation from a professional and legal point of view. As her boss, his behaviour effectively ended her career, and that was my focus. It distracted me from the emotional impact on her and, of course, the toll on her mental health.'

I hesitated before answering, uncomfortably aware that he thought I knew more about the extent and circumstances of Emily's problems than I actually did. I was about to make that clear when he spoke again. 'I think if I'd woken up to what was really important sooner, things wouldn't have deteriorated as they did.'

'Oh no,' I said hurriedly. 'Emily doesn't blame you in any way. She is so grateful to you.'

'She doesn't blame me,' he agreed, 'but I did fail her at that moment. On a positive note, it was a wake-up call for me. I won't lose sight of the important things again. *And*,' he smiled into his coffee cup before looking up, 'she's much better now and the flat will be ready in time for her to move into after Christmas.'

'The flat?'

'Didn't Percy tell you?' he said, appearing surprised. 'One of her flats is for Emily. Oh, but she doesn't know yet – Emily, I mean.'

'That's such a great idea,' I smiled. 'She'll be delighted.'

'I hope so. But if she has any qualms, she can stay put.' He looked up at me and, after a moment, returned my smile. 'Are you free tomorrow?' he asked quietly.

I blinked enough for both of us and nodded. 'Yes.'

'Perhaps we could go for a walk, or a coffee,' he said. 'Or you could teach me to knit.'

I laughed. 'I'm a bit rubbish, I'm afraid. I've made Neil a scarf for Christmas but I can't cast off, so I'm going to glue the final row to the needle as a feature.'

'I like the sound of that,' he said, 'but only because it's not for me.'

I smiled across the table at him, my mind now turning to the walk home. To my flat or to his house? And then a taxi for one of us. But not before I had kissed him goodnight. I took a deep breath, experiencing a strange rush of both self-confidence and nerves. It had been a very long time since kissing a man goodnight had been top of my to-do list.

I dragged myself back to the moment and, aware that it was my turn to speak, said, 'Knitting is very low down on my skill set. There are things I'm much, much better at.' There was a pause, during which he smiled, and I realised that I sounded like a poor man's Mae West. 'I didn't mean sex,' I added hastily. 'I meant non-sexual skills.'

He nodded slowly. 'Thank you for clarifying that. But actually,' he continued, looking at me over the top of his coffee cup, 'I already know you have considerable non-sexual talents. I've been given a copy of one of your books. It has come highly recommended, but apparently I might not be your target market.'

I stared at him and felt my face redden, the sudden change of subject, as well as the subject itself, taking me by surprise – and not in a good way. I wasn't sure why his announcement made me feel quite so uncomfortable, but it undoubtedly did.

James laughed. 'Percy told me this morning. She's very adept with Google and, as it happens, quite a fan of yours.' He paused, his amusement now tinged with mild concern. 'What's wrong? It's hardly a skeleton in your closet,' he said reassuringly.

I smiled uncertainly and shook my head. 'I know. It's fine.'

He put down his cup and leaned back in his chair. 'What I'm curious about is why you never mentioned it. You had more than one opportunity. I'm assuming Neil is your agent?' He raised an eyebrow questioningly and smiled.

And there was the rub, the cause of my discomfort. Instead of my writing being an interesting personal fact to share with James, it was now a closeted skeleton. Instead of being able to happily confide, I had been cornered into a catch-up confession. And instead of my profession being James's primary interest, he was now more intrigued by the secrecy in which I had swathed it. And why wouldn't he be? It must have seemed to him such a strange thing to keep to myself – especially in comparison to the things he, Percy and Emily had shared with me. I looked across at him. He was still smiling, so at least, I thought with some relief, he was entertained by the situation. I began my explanation.

'When I first offered to fill in for Rose, it seemed best to focus on my cleaning credentials. Also, I needed a complete break from—'

'Graaaaaaaace!' The cry rang out from my right and, along with James and most of our fellow diners, I turned towards the group at the bar, amongst whom I spotted Guy. He was holding a glass of red wine high above his head in salute to me, whilst with his other hand he attempted to straighten the conical gold party hat, held on by a length of thin elastic, that currently sat slightly askew on his head.

I blinked in surprise and then, always pleased to see him, smiled and held up a hand. 'Hello, Guy,' I mouthed, watching as he said something to the group he was with and made his way across the restaurant towards us. The route he took was tipsily indirect, and I thought it more than likely that Simone would send him straight to the spare room on his arrival home.

'Grace!' he repeated on reaching us. 'Grace, Grace, Grace. You're looking magnificent.' He bent down to kiss my cheek. 'And this is?' He turned towards James and held out his hand.

'Guy, this is James. James, this is Guy; husband to my very good friend Simone.'

'And a friend of yours in my very own right, I hope!' exclaimed Guy good-naturedly as he shook James's hand.

'Oh go on then,' I laughed.

He beamed at me, his hat again beginning to slide slowly down the side of his head and his cheeks rosy with the warmth of the busy restaurant and, I guessed, the far greater than usual amount of alcohol he had consumed. 'So, are the pair of you having a good evening? This is my last hurrah,' he said, pointing to his wine glass. 'It was the company Christmas party this evening. We've been downstairs for absolutely *hours*!' He stared intently at the floor, as if attempting to see through it, and swayed slightly.

'Yes, we're having a lovely time,' I said. 'The food was great.'

Guy smiled to himself and nodded absently as he continued his study of the floor. When it became apparent that he wasn't going to continue the conversation without a prompt, I repeated, more loudly this time, 'The food was great, Guy.'

'What?' He looked up with a start. 'Oh yes, yes, that's marvellous.' He looked back and forth between James and myself for a moment, as if gathering his thoughts, then cleared his throat. 'Well, I'll leave you two in peace. Great to meet you, Jeremy,' he said, turning to James and holding out his hand for a second shake. 'So sorry if I'm a little uncommunative... uncommunitacative... uncommunta...' He paused and took a deep breath. 'Sorry not to be more chatty but, truth of it is, I'm a bit the worse for wear this evening. Not a big drinker, and I've had several big drinks.' He bit his lower lip in an endearingly guilty fashion.

James shook his hand and smiled. 'Not a problem, Guy. 'Tis the season, after all.'

'You couldn't come home with me and tell my wife that, could you?' said Guy, laughing loudly and then turning to me and wagging a finger. 'No dobbing me in to her, Grace.'

I rolled my eyes. 'I think she might just notice.'

He laughed again, held up a hand and began to totter away, before suddenly whirling round and returning to the table.

'So sorry. It's me. Guy. Back again,' he said, looking at me. 'Very rude of me not to ask. How are you? How's the cleaning job?'

I glanced at James, who smiled across at me.

'Damn,' said Guy, looking stricken. 'Does Jeremy know about the cleaning job?' He jerked his thumb questioningly towards James.

I laughed. 'Yes, you're fine. *James*,' I said with emphasis, 'knows all about that.'

Guy put a hand to his chest and looked at James. 'Thank God for that. I'm always putting my foot in it, James. And the new job was a bit of secret, wasn't it, Grace?' He lowered his voice to a stage whisper and made a zipping gesture across his lips. 'I remember that now,' he added in a mumble, his lips pursed.

'Well done,' I smiled, 'but you're OK. As I say, James is as fully in the picture as it is possible for anyone to be.'

'And it's going well? After that shaky start?' Guy closed his eyes in concentration. 'If I remember rightly, on your very first day the bloke with the creepy stare caught you in the study just about to rifle through his files.'

My smile became a little fixed. 'Er, I don't—'

'And then, according to Simone...' Guy paused, laughing to himself, 'you spent the next two weeks casing the joint for CCTV.' He opened his eyes and looked towards the bar in response to a shout from one of his friends. 'With you in just one moment, chaps and chapesses!' he called. 'Yeeees... don't think Grace has sniffed out any diaries yet, James. But she still reckons she's got enough plot material for the next book or two.' He winked at James, while the latter studied him with a benign expression, apparently significantly less perturbed by Guy's account of my employment to date than I was. 'Isn't that right, Grace?' laughed Guy loudly, turning to me and tapping the side of his nose, as the nausea I had experienced earlier in the evening began to make an unmistakable and unwelcome return.

'Oh Guy.' I laughed nervously, determined not to give any indication of taking the revelations seriously. 'Just how many big drinks have you had?' I stretched my mouth into a smile, whilst widening my eyes in a discreet attempt to get him to shut up. Unfortunately, this proved way too discreet in the circumstances, and I realised just a few seconds later that what I should have actually done was hit him with a chair.

'Yes, you've certainly uncovered some great characters, haven't you?' he continued happily, now apparently bored of the floor and addressing the ceiling instead. 'The unpleasant autistic chappy with the weird eyes, that poor unfortunate girl we all feel sorry for, the man-eater who was after Neil – hiding to nothing there, of course... And did Simone tell me there was a funny little old lady with an arsonist in the family?' He frowned, lowering his gaze to look at me before his expression suddenly brightened. 'Hey, but great to see you looking so happy,' he said, bending down to bestow a second kiss, blissfully oblivious to the fact that I was now just about as far from happy as it was humanly possible to be. 'Ta-ta then, both,' he said, his own bonhomie fully intact. 'Best be off!' And with that, he hurried away to catch up with his friends, who were now energetically beckoning to him as they exited the restaurant.

I gazed after him, not wanting to face James, either literally or figuratively, until I absolutely had to. In the end, he forced the situation.

'I'll get the bill,' he said.

I turned towards him to find his hand raised as he attempted to catch the attention of our waiter. A few seconds later, mission accomplished, he lowered his hand and we finally made eye contact. He looked at me expressionlessly and I counted to three, waiting for the delayed smile as his face caught up with his feelings.

Three seconds came and went.

Another five passed.

James said nothing, and his expression remained unchanged.

'So, what are your plans for Christmas?' I asked, in a pitiable attempt to convince myself, and him, that the exchange with Guy was a figment of both our imaginations. 'I usually dot around to see aunts and cousins, but this year I'm spending Christmas Eve to Boxing Day with Gavin and Neil because they've… been…' My voice faded, leaving the sentence unfinished, as James continued to look at me impassively across the table. He moved only when the waiter placed the bill between us.

'Thank you,' he said, looking up. 'And can you call a cab for Henleaze, please?'

'Of course,' said the waiter and walked away.

James picked up the bill and then shifted in his chair, reaching into his trouser pocket and taking out his wallet.

'It wasn't as it sounds,' I said quietly, surprised at the calmness of my voice, which belied an internal disintegration. I wondered if it was the tone of the prisoner at the gallows; the tone of despairing resignation.

'Really?' said James casually, carefully selecting and removing ten- and twenty-pound notes from his wallet. 'Because it sounded like a timely explanation of all the secrecy.' He looked up at me. 'Or was he lying?'

'Lying?' I felt myself bristle at the question. 'Guy is a man of huge integrity and enormous warmth, and certainly not a liar,' I said, stung on his behalf. 'He just…'

I ground to a halt, feeling it utterly pointless to waste any further effort on the sentence. What could I say? Label Guy a confused drunk who just happened, by pure coincidence, to describe five people who closely resembled James, Emily, Heather, Percy and the latter's twisted fire-starter sister? Not to mention his recounting of the box file incident. The problem was that he had pretty much repeated word-for-word everything I had told Simone, including my early, bitter descriptions of James and my fear of hidden cameras. I couldn't easily explain away, or deny having said, any of it. Guy had been, for the most part, surprisingly on the ball with his facts, just woefully behind the times with my feelings.

'He just?' James prompted. He was looking at me with no hint of emotion save for a slightly furrowed brow. Puzzlement? Impatience? Anger? Odds on the latter, I decided, and I couldn't blame him. In fact, a significant part of me applauded his righteous indignation towards me, a woman who, it would seem, had entered his home disguised as a cleaner and proceeded to pump his vulnerable sister and elderly neighbour for personal information, with the sole purpose of creating a money-making work of semi-fiction.

I shook my head. 'Guy is a lovely man,' I said quietly.

At this point, the conversation was interrupted by the return of the waiter, suddenly at James's side with a card reader. 'I'll pay cash,' said James, handing over the notes.

'Wait,' I said, reaching down for my bag. 'I'm paying half.'

The waiter looked uncertainly between us. 'It's OK,' said James, glancing up at him. 'You take that and we'll finalise the split. We're just waiting for that taxi now.'

The waiter nodded, apparently picking up on the fact that the atmosphere at our table was now marginally more icy than the street outside, and walked quickly away after offering us only the briefest of smiles.

James checked his watch.

'There's no need for you to wait.' I replaced my bag on the floor and turned to look out of the restaurant window.

'I don't want to leave you sitting here on your own,' he said after a moment.

'I'd actually prefer that.'

I didn't turn to note his reaction, and there was a pause before I heard his chair scrape back as he stood up. I was aware of him turning and walking away from the table.

I continued to stare impassively out into the street, returning my attention to the room only when I judged that I risked seeing him walk past the window. Then I picked up my bag, collected my coat and, telling the barman that I had decided to walk home after all, I left the restaurant and began to cry.

Chapter 31

My pace on the walk home was in marked contrast to the unconscious energy with which I had sped towards James several hours earlier. Consequently, the return journey took almost twice as long as the outgoing one. To my credit, I had outwardly managed to pull myself together relatively quickly, conquering all visible signs of distress, silent weeping included, within the first few minutes of my dejected amble. Internally, however, the misery was ongoing, and for a full fifteen minutes or so I watched and rewatched, without intermission, a mental showreel of the most ridiculous and heartbreaking moments of my evening out with James.

I was just reliving Guy's cheery exit from the restaurant, with his party hat sticking out at an uber-jaunty right-angle from the side of his head, when I turned the corner of my road and spotted a tall male figure under the Victorian streetlight, a short distance from my front door. He was wearing a long dark coat and was standing, hunched and unmoving, with his back to me. The overall effect, on what was now an increasingly foggy evening, was undeniably sinister. Feeling immediately wary, I quietly cleared my throat, ready to scream if necessary, and reached into my pocket for my keys, feeding them one by one between the fingers of my clenched right fist to create an improvised knuckleduster. Behind me, I was aware of the sound of a car turning into the road. Glancing over my shoulder, I saw a Bristol blue taxi moving at slow speed, the driver clearly looking for an address. My heart pounding, I considered stepping into the road, flagging him down and asking him to wait while I went into my flat. But fearful of overreacting, I instead turned away from the taxi and continued to walk.

I was approximately five metres from the figure, and about the same distance again from my front door, when the sound of my heels on the pavement finally caused him to turn.

I stopped dead as Aiden's tired eyes widened in surprise. 'I thought you must be away,' he said quietly.

I shook my head dumbly.

'But I stayed here anyway.' His voice was hoarse and barely audible. 'Obviously.'

I stared at him for just a moment longer and then, walking quickly towards him, I reached up to place my arms around his neck and pulled him towards me. I felt his arms enfold me and his head lower to rest gently on the top of my head, as I leaned against his chest.

'I miss you so much, Grace,' he breathed. 'Every single day, I miss you. I miss *us*.'

I closed my eyes tightly, trying not to think about an alternate life with Aiden. A life in which he had never left; or, more dangerously, a life in which he returned.

I felt the comforting warmth and strength of his body and I imagined myself lifting my head and kissing him. Just a forty-five-degree upward tilt of my face was all that would be needed for my miserable winter evening of rejection to be transformed into the triumphant defeat of Summer.

'Tell me what you're thinking,' he said, his voice heavy with emotion.

'I think…' I paused, breathing him in, holding him tightly, not wanting to let him go and feeling more connected to him than I had in years, perhaps ever. 'I *know*,' I began again quietly, 'that you should go home and be faithful to her, Aiden.'

I felt his frame tense for a moment and then relax, his hands moving slowly up my body to my head and stroking my hair. 'I love you so, so much,' he murmured. 'I always loved you but I never deserved you.' He kissed my forehead softly. 'I could never deserve you. You'll always be too good for me, Grace.'

I didn't reply, and I felt him gently brushing away my tears before I even knew I was crying. 'I want those tears to be for us,' he said. 'But I suspect they're not.'

I looked up and saw that he was now smiling sadly.

'Some of them are for us,' I said.

He stroked my cheek and looked towards the flat. 'Much as I'd like to, I don't think I should come inside,' he said. 'But do you want to tell me about it?'

I pulled away from him slightly and dabbed at my eyes with the sleeve of my coat. 'It's all a bit depressing,' I sniffed. 'Are you sure you don't mind?'

He sighed. 'If you're going to tell me that you have feelings for someone else, then I think listening to you might be one of the hardest, and certainly the most selfless, things I've ever done. But you have more than earned the right, and it's the very least I can do.'

I stood on tiptoe and kissed his cheek. 'Thank you,' I whispered.

He shook his head and then, after walking hand-in-hand the short distance to my flat, we sat down on the freezing doorstep and, pressed against each other for warmth, I told him everything.

Chapter 32

I woke the next morning with a jolt to the sound of what I assumed was my phone ringing. But after finally locating said phone, following several seconds of semi-conscious panic-scrabbling under the bedside table, I realised it was, in fact, the sound of the doorbell. Hanging over the edge of the bed, I squinted in dismay at the phone, wondering who on earth would think it was OK to repeatedly ring my doorbell – or anyone's doorbell – at 8.34 a.m. on a Sunday morning without obtaining prior written permission.

I sighed and hoisted myself back into bed. To say I had slept badly would be an understatement. I had fallen asleep quite quickly following Aiden's departure at just after midnight, feeling calmed by his company and enormously grateful for his listening ear and, quite literal, shoulder to cry on. He hadn't, quite understandably, been able to offer me much hope regarding the resuscitation of my relationship with James, but he hadn't been negative either. He had just listened, nodded and then shared one or two sad facts about his own relationship. These included a confession that, despite his assurances to the contrary, he still hadn't told Summer about our renewed friendship. While I wasn't totally surprised by this, I *was* surprised that the conversation about her, although interesting, didn't touch me personally at all, other than, for the very first time, to make me feel a little sorry for Summer.

But the main thing I took away from my doorstep chat with Aiden was that he and I had shared, with honesty and without ego, our relationship woes. And an additional positive was that when you're feeling low, the company of someone who is feeling equally or even more cursed than yourself can be enormously comforting. Sadly, however, my unlikely sense of calm and well-being had not persisted into sleep, and my night had been filled with dreams of multiple Guys, all sporting party hats, pelting me with paperbacks, whilst an equal number of Emilys sat in various corners quietly sobbing.

Consequently I was in no mood, either physically or psychologically, for an early-morning visitor, and I had just decided to pull the covers back over my head and ignore the bell, when it occurred to me that the ringing was of the persistent kind often associated with some sort of emergency – including buildings being on fire. And so, albeit still with some reluctance, I threw back the duvet and, sniffing the air for smoke as I went, slouched my way to the front door.

'What is it?' I asked grumpily on reaching and pressing the intercom.

There was a silent pause during which I suddenly experienced a tiny spark of optimism that this particular early-morning caller might actually be a very welcome one. 'Hello,' I said more lightly. 'Sorry about that. I've just woken up. Who is it?'

A voice spoke, somewhat hesitantly. 'Hi, Grace. It's me.'

I frowned. 'Simone?'

She laughed nervously. 'I was just passing and I wondered if I could borrow a—'

I pressed the buzzer to let her in. 'I'm not even going to let you finish such a crappy lie,' I sighed, and then, opening my front door and leaving it ajar, I headed back up the hallway towards the kitchen.

–

'You know, I actually thought about divorcing him this morning when he told me what he'd said.' Simone picked up the mug of tea and plate of toast she had made for me and brought them over to the dining table. 'And I'm not joking,' she said, placing her offerings in front of me. 'I just kept my fingers crossed that it hadn't been as bad as it sounded.' She looked at me miserably and sat down.

I sat with my hands in my lap and stared at the tea and toast, not wanting either. 'It's not Guy's fault,' I said.

'I've not come here expecting you to make me feel better about this,' said Simone. 'I'm here to apologise and, if at all possible, to help.' She pushed the plate towards me. 'And the first thing I'm going to do is make sure you eat at least a few bites of that.'

I didn't look up. 'I'm not trying to make you feel better. It's my fault. I told Guy that James knew everything about the cleaning job. The only thing Guy got muddled over was who James actually was and, again, that's my fault for not spelling it out. He didn't say anything that I hadn't said to you, or do anything wrong.'

'OK, so can I just ask you this,' she said, her tone at a controlled simmer. 'If Guy hadn't turned up, or if he had just waved from a safe distance and kept his stupid mouth shut, would your evening with James have been delightful and have ended perfectly?'

I didn't move or speak, but simply raised my eyes to look at her.

'Case closed,' she said and then, without warning, her expression changed from utter rage to complete devastation and she burst into tears. 'God, I'm sorry,' she sobbed. 'It was all going so well for you. We were so happy for you. I blame myself as much as Guy. I should know not to tell him anything which… well, I should just know not to tell him anything at all. I knew, you know,' she began, before pausing, standing up and walking briskly into the kitchen, returning to her chair with a piece of kitchen roll. 'I knew the minute he staggered into the bedroom last night. All he had to say was that he'd bumped into you and I thought, "Shit, I bet he's ruined everything." I couldn't think *how* he could have possibly ruined everything, but I just knew he would have.' She blew her nose on the kitchen roll and looked up at me. 'I'm not going to apologise again, because you'll just keep saying it's OK, and it is not OK. But I'd really like us to think about how this can be put right.'

I leaned back in my chair and sighed. 'I've already thought about it,' I said. 'Guy simply presented the facts to James as I had presented them to you. The closest I can come to a denial is telling him that the bit about scouring his house for diaries, and writing a book about it all, was a joke.'

She offered me a watery smile. 'Well, let's start with that then.'

I shook my head. 'Let's face it, Sim, if James is willing to believe that of me, then, well, it's a bit of a lost cause, isn't it? And besides, he'll just think that I'm trying to save the situation – and my reputation. He's an intensely private man and I've been caught out gossiping about people he is very close to, and of whom he is highly, *highly* protective. Plus, he currently thinks I hid my profession from everyone for the worst of reasons.' I sighed heavily, imagining the length of speech I would have to make, and the amount of back-pedalling I would have to do, in order to even begin to explain things to James. 'It's no good.'

Simone's shoulders sagged. 'I don't believe that. There must be something we can do.' She dabbed her eyes again and then pushed the plate of toast a second time, until it was now precariously close to falling off the table. 'Just one bite.'

I managed a smile and picked up the mug. 'I'll drink the tea.'

'Look,' she said, 'I know I might be one of the last people in the world you want to spend time with today but, for my sake more than yours, will you come for lunch? Guy won't be there,' she added quickly. 'I made him take the kids to Weston on the train.'

I looked out of the window at the threatening black clouds and trees bending in the wind. 'Weston? In this weather?' I asked. 'And with a hangover?'

Her jaw jutted. 'He deserved it and the kids love it all year round. They'll want to go on the wheel. Hopefully that'll make Guy throw up.'

I tutted and smiled.

She laughed tearfully and then leaned towards me. 'It's going to be OK,' she said.

I nodded, knowing that neither of us believed her.

'Please come with me now and stay for lunch,' she said quietly. 'I really don't want to be on my own today. Who knows what I might do to Guy's vinyl collection? Besides, if you don't come, I'll only keep calling you.'

I looked down at the toast and realised that, despite a deep conviction that nothing at all would make me feel better, I didn't want to spend the day alone – again – in my flat.

I picked up a piece of toast, taking a large bite and then chewing and swallowing whilst looking at Simone significantly. 'Thanks,' I said, smiling at her and standing up. 'I'd really like that. I'll just go and shower.'

Chapter 33

I arrived home from Simone's at six-thirty, having set off approximately five minutes after Guy texted her to say he and the boys would be back in half an hour. I was keen to avoid him, not because I was cross with him – I genuinely wasn't – but rather because I knew he would be embarrassingly apologetic, and after a day during which Simone had seemed to apologise for the situation every hour, on the hour, I couldn't take any more self-abasement. Additionally, I didn't trust Simone to keep her temper in check. Her anger towards Guy had shown no signs of abating as the day wore on, and I didn't want to hang around to witness the near-inevitable blowing of several gaskets.

But despite our mutual lack of perkiness, my day with her had gone much better than I'd expected. This was thanks in part to my decision to leave my phone at home – thus preventing myself from worrying about texted repercussions – and also to my impulsive offer to vacuum, in preference to Simone's kind, but unrealistic, suggestion that I 'relax' while she prepared us lunch. When I first made the offer, she hesitated, clearly assuming it to be an early indicator of complete mental breakdown. But when I insisted that cleaning her home would have both physical and emotional benefits for me, she gave in, whilst apologising in advance for the state of her first floor.

'This house is all fur coat and no knickers,' she had said, reaching into a cupboard and dragging out the vacuum cleaner. 'We just about manage to keep the ground floor looking OK, but I'm warning you, upstairs is Armageddon.'

And as I flopped down in my armchair at six-forty that evening, glass of red in one hand and charging iPhone in the other, I reflected on the fact that she hadn't been joking. The family bathroom had looked like it had been put through a blender and the den, with its dismembered cuddly toys and plastic weapons, resembled the kind of place in which the twins from *The Shining* might have enjoyed hanging out. The boys' bedrooms were little better, with so many toys and books covering almost every inch of floor space that I had wondered whether a snow shovel might not be the most efficient initial approach to tidying up. But sorting things out, as much as was possible in the hour or so that Simone was busy in the kitchen, was an excellent workout, as well as a total distraction from my woes. And the look of delighted surprise on Simone's face when she trotted upstairs to tell me lunch was ready provided me with my first burst of genuine pleasure and sense of worth since waking up that morning.

I smiled at the memory and relaxed back into the armchair before the buzz of my phone springing back to life caused every muscle in my body to tense. I sat up and unlocked the phone to discover five texts awaiting my attention: one from Gavin, one from Guy, one from Aiden, one from Emily and one from James. It was a toss-up as to which of the latter two made me feel most sick and this being the case, I decided, with enormous cowardice, to ignore both completely.

Aiden's text was brief and to the point: he hoped I was feeling OK and wanted me to know that he had 'sat down with Summer and told her everything.' I wondered briefly what his definition of 'everything' might be before realising that I didn't hugely care. I was interested, and I cared enough about him to want him to be happy, but I was now well and truly of the opinion that his relationship with Summer was no longer capable of impacting upon me personally.

Guy's text was, as expected, painfully contrite. It had been sent several hours earlier and despite containing no specific references to his location or to the weather, it was heavy with all the despair and gloom of a cold, grey December day spent at the beach with only two hyperactive kids and a hangover for company.

Gavin was, of course, Tigger to Guy's Eeyore, and paradoxically this made his text far more depressing. He was excited about his holiday, excited about seeing me on Monday and, most of all, he was excited about my date with James. His text opened with a request for me to tell him everything and concluded with an announcement that he'd changed his mind and wanted to hear absolutely not one word about it until I saw him the next day, by which time he would be 'insane with anticipation'.

I sighed and scrolled up the screen to reread the text I had sent him a little over twenty-four hours earlier.

> Hi! Going nuts with nerves and missing you and Neil SO MUCH. Guess what? I'm going on a date with James Brooke this evening.

He's the NOT evil guy who ISN'T dating his
sister. I know! Mad, isn't it? But I really, really
like him. Was over the moon when he asked
me last night but now wanting to chuck up.
So tempted to phone you and Neil but will
resist the urge. Keep your fingers crossed for
me. Deep, deep down, beneath the nausea,
I'm starting to feel very good about myself
and I think he's got a lot to do with it.
But won't say anything else. Don't want to
jinx it. Will report back when I see you on
Monday – give you a chance to recover from
the jet lag. Love to you and N. Happy nearly
Christmas!! G x

I stared at the words, miserably fascinated by just how
completely a situation could change in twenty-four hours.
And then, unable to bring myself to type any replies at that
particular moment, I placed my phone on the arm of the
chair and my glass on the table, and bent down to retrieve
my laptop, with the intention of adding my experience
of Simone's fur-coat-no-knickers home to my cleaning
diary. I had scrolled almost to the end of the document
when a slight readjustment of my position caused my
phone to fall from the arm of the chair and down the
side of my seat cushion. After some tutting and delving,
I retrieved it and, with it once again back in my hand,
decided that, as much as I didn't want to, I had to read the
two remaining texts. And so, after a deep breath to steady
my nerves, I plumped for James's first.

Grace, this is to let you know that we
won't be needing a cleaner between now and

Rose's return in the new year. Percy has asked
me to pass on her thanks to you for cleaning
her flat on Friday. She was very pleased with
the result and will arrange payment. James

My immediate response was one of overwhelming relief at
the lack of any recriminations and also that Rose's job was
safe. What was more, it seemed that James had told Percy
nothing of what had gone on between us. On reflection,
none of that surprised me and simply served to underline,
somewhat depressingly, what a thoughtful, measured and
private man he was. And an acute awareness that my
opinion of him was so totally at odds with his opinion of
me only added to my misery. Any initial sense of relief was
therefore quickly smothered by one of enormous regret.

I deleted his text and opened Emily's.

Grace! How are you? I'm just off on a pre-
Christmas tour of the country to hook up
with friends but wanted to drop you a line
because I won't see you this week when you
come to clean and that means I might not
see you till the new year :(I know Rose
is back with us then and while we're really
looking forward to seeing her, Percy and I
are both keen not to lose touch with you, so
I hope you'll find time in your diary for a
cup of tea with us every now and then. I am
certain James would like to stay in touch too
;) You might not think he gives much away,
but there are some things a guy can't hide
from his sister. Hope I haven't embarrassed
you with that, but, as you know, I like to

pass on compliments and there's definitely
one in there somewhere. Much love, Emily
xx Ooh! And Percy says can you pop in after
cleaning on Thursday and stay for a cup of
tea? She has something for you. Can't believe
I nearly forgot to tell you. Happy Christmas!
E xx

I switched off my phone and placed it on the coffee table next to my glass. So he hadn't told Emily either. Not even about the termination of my cleaning contract. My reputation was fully intact with absolutely everyone – except him.

I took a deep breath and, determined not to cry, no matter how much I wanted to, returned my attention to my laptop, smiling sadly at the diary entry for 9 December, entitled 'All the fun of the funeral', which was currently on-screen. I read it and reread it, enjoying the sense of time travel and picturing myself sitting happily next to James, first at Maud's afternoon tea and later in his car outside my house. And then, when I knew it was time to return to my less-than-perfect present, I lingered for just a moment longer over the words 'I wanted very much to narrow the distance between James and myself' before clicking on the document and slowly, but purposefully, dragging it diagonally across the screen and depositing it, together with all hope of any future relationship with James, into 'Trash'.

Chapter 34

If I thought I had been anxious and depressed going to bed on Sunday evening, that was nothing to how I felt the next morning. My alarm woke me at 8:15, as it had every Monday for the previous ten weeks, leaving me plenty of time to shower, breakfast and be at Bennett Park by 9:30. Except, of course, this morning I had absolutely nowhere to be; no one was relying on me and I had nothing to do. I felt completely without purpose.

Worse still, in my initial state of autopilot, the empty reality of the situation didn't hit me until I got all the way to the bathroom and turned on the shower. I had then sat on the bathroom floor, letting the shower run and the room fill with steam, while I wondered what on earth to do with myself in the nine hours and forty minutes between that moment and my salon appointment with Gavin at 6 p.m.

Recent experience, coupled with a determination not to sink back into the inertia and cynicism which had followed my break-up with Aiden, told me that I had to find an occupation; a practical occupation. Sitting and thinking at home was not an option. So, after dismissing the possibility of a walk as too potentially introspective, I decided, despite feeling far from festive, to go and choose a Christmas tree. I had planned to buy and decorate one that afternoon, after cleaning. However, as there was now no cleaning to be done, I decided to use the task to fill a morning which would otherwise have felt depressingly empty.

I walked rather than drove to the nearest garden shop in order to add an extra thirty minutes to the tree purchase process. And once there, I asked the owner, whose ruddy cheeks, beard and large frame gave him the appearance of a forty-something Father Christmas, to talk me through every single height, shape and needle-drop option there was. However, on noticing a dangerously impatient glint in his eye as I asked him to unwrap a fourth tree, I decided I couldn't spin things out any longer and would have to make a choice.

'Erm…' I said, looking round and tapping my lower lip thoughtfully. 'I think I'll take that one.' I pointed to a three-foot specimen in a red, glazed terracotta pot, decorated with a large silver bow.

The owner's bearded jaw jutted. 'So not this one then,' he said, indicating the newly unwrapped seven-foot tree leaning on the wall behind him.

I shook my head. 'I'd love it, but I haven't got the car with me and, in any case, I think it might be a bit big for my living room.'

'Four foot too big,' he said.

'That's right.'

'And you couldn't tell that it was four foot too big before I unwrapped it?'

I smiled awkwardly.

'Or before I unwrapped that one, that one and that one.' He pointed in turn to the other sizeable trees resting against a fence outside the shop.

'Sorry,' I said quietly, blinking rapidly due to the sudden realisation that tears were a very real prospect.

He looked at me for a moment and shook his head. 'Never mind,' he sighed wearily. 'Fortunately, I actually really enjoy unwrapping and rewrapping Christmas trees.'

I felt a little better. 'Do you?'

'*No*,' he said with emphasis.

'Oh.' I took a steadying breath. The purchase of my tree was proving to be unexpectedly emotional.

'That *very small* blue spruce you've chosen will be...' he ran his finger down a list, '£35, including the pot.' I nodded and, determinedly focusing on the practicalities, quickly took out my purse and handed him my debit card. 'It'll be heavier than you think,' he said, 'because of the pot, and also there's a lot of compost in there. So you'd better borrow one of my trolleys to wheel it home, or you'll hurt your back.'

'Thank you,' I said, finding his gruff thoughtfulness just as difficult to handle as his impatience. 'That's so kind. I'm sorry to have taken up so much of your time.'

He tore a receipt from the top of the card reader and handed it to me. 'That's all right. It's not exactly heaving in here, is it? Most families chose their trees last weekend.'

I nodded, his use of the word 'families' increasing my sense of solitude to almost physically painful proportions. I looked at my vertically challenged tree and then back at Father Christmas. He cleared his throat. 'Right then,' he said. 'Let's get it onto that trolley.' He picked it up with a grunt and placed it heavily onto a metre-long wooden board on wheels; a long metal handle was attached to one end for steering. 'Just go careful over the bumps,' he said. 'And if you have to get it up any stairs, make sure you've got someone there to...' He paused and looked a little awkward. 'You'll be fine on your own, so long as you take it slowly and bend your knees.'

I sighed and wondered if maybe the words 'all alone in the world' were etched across my forehead. But, touched by his attempts at sensitivity, which were so clearly against type, I made the effort to smile before hurriedly manoeuvring the trolley out of the shop, across the small fenced forecourt and towards the exit. The length of the trolley made it impossible for me to check whether the way was clear before I began to edge out onto the pavement and, as I emerged fully, I discovered two bag-laden pedestrians and a woman with a pushchair standing patiently, waiting for me to exit.

'Thank you,' I said, focusing on keeping the tree upright whilst turning my trolley through ninety degrees. 'I'm a bit of a long load.'

The bag-carriers murmured their acceptance of the situation and slid past me, whilst the woman with the pushchair continued to wait. Once pointing in the right direction, I moved to the side of the pavement and turned towards her. 'I think there's enough room for you to get past now...' My voice trailed away as we finally made eye contact.

There was a God, I decided. And he hated me. It wasn't enough that I was lying prone and dazed on the canvas of the boxing ring of life; he just couldn't resist giving me another swift kick in the ribs.

Summer and I stared at each other for a few seconds, during which time neither of us was able to rearrange our features into anything even vaguely resembling pleasant surprise. It was of absolutely no comfort, cold or otherwise, that she looked as horrified as I felt and, just when I thought I could feel no worse, I realised that, of course, she wasn't alone. My eyes lowered to the pushchair, its hood up in defence of the cold, hiding her child – *their* child – from me. I stared at the back of the hood and then, feeling that I really couldn't take much more, I looked up at Summer and shrugged. 'I don't know what to say. And I haven't got the energy to come up with anything.'

She nodded.

'I'm going this way,' I said, pointing up the road and looking miserably at the trolley. 'Very slowly.'

'Thank you,' she said, her voice quivering.

'For what?' I turned back towards her and realised she was crying. The tears were of the silent variety, streaming down her face, washing away her foundation and leaving two pale scars of naked skin in their wake.

'Oh my goodness, don't cry,' I said, abandoning the trolley and walking hurriedly around the pushchair to her side. 'Please don't. I'm so close to crying myself, you'll set me off.' I put an arm around her and she rested her head on my shoulder, suddenly heaving a huge hiccoughy sob, as passers-by edged awkwardly past us, pretending not to notice the hysterical young mother having a breakdown the week before Christmas.

'I'm sorry.' She lifted her head and reached into her pocket, taking out a blue muslin square and blowing her nose on it.

'That's OK,' I said, removing my arm from her shoulder and putting my hands into my pockets. 'As I said, I'm not far off tears myself today.'

She blew her nose a second time and looked up. 'I didn't mean sorry for crying. I meant sorry for what I did. For Aiden. And for…' She gestured towards the pushchair and my gaze automatically followed the sweep of her hand. Warren was fast asleep, his face just visible under a tiny blue-and-white-striped hat. Chin down, all I could see was the collar of a navy blue padded jacket before the rest of him was hidden by the winter cover of the pushchair. I unconsciously leaned forward for a better view. As I did so, his mouth formed something like a brief smile before relaxing back into seriousness. I knew it was probably indigestion, but the effect was beautiful nevertheless. I smiled down at him and then looked up at Summer.

'You mustn't apologise for him,' I said.

She looked at me, her exhausted eyes far redder than they would have been had her current tears been the first of the day. 'I love him,' she said.

I nodded, uncertain whether she was talking about Aiden or Warren but realising that it didn't matter. Either was fine with me and, actually, I found myself hoping that she meant both.

'Good,' I smiled.

'Aiden told me you sent him away,' she said quietly. 'Thank you for that. I know he didn't want to come back to me.' She looked down into the pram. 'To us.'

I hesitated, shocked to discover that apparently Aiden really had told her everything, just as he had claimed. 'I'm sure that's not true,' I said, recovering. 'He was just tired and confused.'

She shook her head miserably. 'I don't know how you can be so nice. I wish you weren't. It just makes your pedestal even higher. I know Aiden wants you. He always has. I was just something to make you want him more than he wanted you. He needs that.' She hesitated and looked up at me. 'If you'd asked him to stay back then, years ago, even once, he would have. I knew that was what he hoped for all along. But you didn't ask him. You were too strong. So he stayed with me. I wasn't a choice for him. I was just there. And I wanted him more than he wanted me. That was all I had going for me.'

I stared at her, searching for the triumphant, youthful, super-confident bitch who had stolen away the man I loved. But instead, all I could see was a broken woman, in a broken relationship with someone I wasn't sure could ever love anyone quite as much as he loved himself. I remembered how she clung to him at every social event. I had thought it was a display, to remind me and everyone else that she had won and I had lost; that he was hers and not mine. Now I realised that she had simply been desperately trying to keep hold of him.

I took a deep breath. 'Summer, I don't want Aiden and he doesn't want me. All that is in the past. You and he have Warren now. That's a really important shared focus – exclusive to the two of you and nothing to do with me or anyone else. Warren is who you should be thinking about.' I looked at him a second time. 'He's gorgeous. Don't regret him.'

I turned towards her to find her staring unblinkingly at the pushchair. 'I wish I was you,' she whispered.

For my own sanity, I decided to assume she meant Warren. The alternative interpretation of the statement held far too many tragic implications, past, present and future, for me to cope with in my currently depressed state.

I sighed and put a hand to my forehead. 'Where are you off to now?' I asked.

She didn't look up. 'Nowhere,' she said.

I nodded. 'Know the feeling, but look,' I glanced forlornly at the trolley, 'I've got to get this home and don't know whether I can manage it all in one go. Do you want to come to Costa for a coffee? I can leave the tree outside.'

She raised her head and frowned. 'But what if someone steals it?'

'Win-win,' I shrugged.

She offered me an exhausted smile. 'I am so sorry for what I did. It's a mess for everyone.'

I felt an uncomfortable lump form in my throat. 'Let's not talk about the past any more,' I said quietly.

She didn't say anything in reply but simply nodded her agreement, wiping away the remainder of her tears and returning the muslin square to her coat pocket. And then, with me pushing my tree and Summer pushing her son, we headed for the coffee shop.

Chapter 35

'Bloody hell,' murmured Gavin. 'I thought it was going to be all mulled wine and jingle balls on a rug in front of a log fire.'

We sat slumped on the small white leather sofa in the window of his empty salon. Around us, white fairy lights twinkled, and in front of us two untouched glasses of Prosecco rested on a low glass coffee table. I had arrived approximately twenty minutes earlier and had just finished bringing him up to date with the events of the past few weeks and, more crucially, the past seventy-two hours.

'Afraid not.' I shook my head sadly. 'No wine, no log fire.'

'God, it's such a shame,' he said, staring off into space. 'He sounded really nice. Personality as well as looks. Perfect for someone a bit hysterical, like you.'

'Thank you,' I said.

'And did Simone kill Guy?'

I rolled my eyes. 'What do you think?'

'Poor bugger,' he said. 'Don't know who I feel more sorry for – him or you.'

I turned my head slowly towards him and frowned. He pointed at me. '*You*, obviously,' he said quickly, leaning forward and picking up both drinks, handing one to me. 'But Neil's going to be so upset, you know. He's been really relaxed on holiday and this is going to set him right back, on top of the jet lag.'

'Yes, well, I'm sorry to keep dragging the tragedy of my love life back to *me*, Gavin,' I said tetchily, 'but I don't think Neil's distress is going to be in quite the same league as mine.'

He took a gulp of Prosecco whilst flapping a hand at me. 'Oh don't get your knickers in a twist. He's going to be upset because he *loves* you, you silly cow.' He put an arm around me and rubbed my shoulder. 'We both do,' he added gently.

'I'm sorry,' I sighed quietly, leaning my head against him. 'I'm just a bit fed up about everything.'

'Not surprised,' he said, giving me a squeeze. 'And at Christmas too. I'd be just about ready to top myself if I was you.'

'Helping,' I murmured.

'Oh, I'm winding you up!' he laughed. 'And it's not all gloom and doom, is it? At least you're well and truly over Aiden. And Summer sounds like she's as depressed as hell. Don't tell me that one wasn't top of your Christmas list.'

I sat up and sipped my drink. 'Last year, maybe. Now I just feel sorry for her. I hope they can work things out.'

'Have you gone insane?' He slapped my arm lightly and looked appalled, before breaking into a grin. 'Never been more proud of you,' he said, his eyes becoming dewy. 'And I've been proud of you loads.'

I smiled back at him. 'Thanks, Gavin.'

'Anyway,' he said, clinking his glass against mine, 'I'm sure we can sort this out.'

I shook my head. 'After you've thought about it for a bit, you'll realise it can't be fixed. James clearly thinks the worst of me and I don't want to try and talk him out of that. It is what it is.'

Gavin didn't say anything. Instead he jutted his lower lip in a gesture of pity and squeezed my hand.

'I'm OK,' I reassured him. 'And don't worry, I'm not going to be a Debbie downer over Christmas. I'm really looking forward to it.'

He put down his drink and clapped his hands together. 'Me too. Neil's doing the main and I'm doing starters and pudding. There will be flames!'

I laughed. 'And what would you like me to bring?'

'How about booze, nibbles and chocs?' he said. 'Ooh, but nothing you've made yourself,' he added hastily, patting my knee. 'Like, say, those home-made truffle things you handed round at Easter, for example. Wouldn't want you going to all that trouble again.'

'They did take ages but I've got nothing else to do, so it'd be no bother,' I said. 'Mind you, I wasn't actually that keen on them, you know. I think maybe something I put in them was a bit off.'

He raised an eyebrow. 'You reckon? My Auntie Tina loves you to bits, but she said they tasted like you'd picked them out of a litter tray.'

I laughed again and he pulled me towards him, kissing the top of my head and ruffling my hair. 'Now,' he said, 'what about this mop of yours?'

'I don't mind what you do to it,' I said. 'How about a crop? A complete change – new start.'

'Nope,' he said, standing up and pulling me with him. 'I'm thinking just a light trim and a scattering of foils.

When you walked in here, I thought, "God, she's looking sexy, and with not even a whiff of Bellatrix." And I wouldn't want to ruin that, would I?'

Chapter 36

Despite having confirmed with Percy on Monday afternoon that I would love to drop by for a cup of tea on Thursday, I was far from looking forward to the visit for several reasons.

Firstly, because I suspected she wanted to pay me for cleaning her home and I really didn't want payment.

Secondly, because I still felt pretty low and I wasn't sure I would be able to hide that from her.

And thirdly, and most importantly, because I really didn't want to go anywhere near Bennett Park. It wasn't that I was afraid of running into James. It was more the horrible suspicion that simply the sight of his home might prove a huge setback to my emotional recovery.

But weighed against all that was the simple fact that I didn't want to hurt Percy's feelings. And I knew a refusal to see her would do just that. Besides, after seeing Gavin on Monday evening, I had spent Tuesday and Wednesday largely on my own, with only a handful of brief texts from him, Neil and Simone to distract me.

This had surprised me because, since Sunday evening, Simone had been texting me almost hourly, and at some length, to check on my emotional status. But her check-ups came to an abrupt end late Monday afternoon, and the only texts I received from her after that were to agree a start point and time for our Christmas Eve un-run the following Saturday. Whilst part of me was relieved to be free of her round-the-clock concern, when her apparent lack of interest in my state of mind continued into Tuesday and throughout Wednesday, I began to experience a mixture of anxiety that maybe all was not well, and a tiny bit of hurt that her preoccupation with my well-being seemed to have waned so suddenly and so quickly.

I tried to dismiss any sense of abandonment as ridiculous, unhelpful self-absorption, but the feeling was heightened by the fact that Neil too had been unexpectedly silent on the subject of James, and that there had been only one follow-up communication on the topic from Gavin. I put this down to neither of them wanting me to dwell, and both being extremely busy during the week running up to Christmas. I also reminded myself that I would actually be spending the next weekend with them, so no doubt Neil was waiting until then to talk to me about it all, rather than trying to chat via text or over the phone. And as I would be seeing Simone as usual on Saturday, it occurred to me that I could use the same argument in her case too. Still, the relative lack of communication from all three of them did seem a little odd, and I rebooted my phone more than once on the basis – soon disproved – that technology might be playing a part in the situation.

As the week wore on, then, the prospect of visiting Bennett Park began to lose some of its terror when compared to the possibility of ongoing solitude. And by Thursday morning, having read three novels, eaten four selection packs and polished every tap, table and work surface in my flat to within an inch of its existence, I was very much looking forward to seeing Percy and was in no doubt that the visit would actually do me good.

According to my dashboard clock, it was exactly 2 p.m. as I parked my Mini in a road adjacent to Bennett Park and glanced through the windscreen, delighted that heavy ongoing rain meant I would be able to pull up the large fur-trimmed hood of my parka. The hood not only created tunnel vision, thus preventing me from seeing anything other than what was directly in front of me, but also allowed me to walk the short distance to Percy's house with my face almost completely hidden. I thus arrived at her front door at 2.05 p.m., incognito and untortured by even the slightest glimpse of number 3.

I raised my hand to press the bell but could already see Percy bustling across the hallway towards me. My hand was still mid-air as she opened the door.

'Grace, my darling!' she exclaimed, immediately grabbing my arm and pulling me inside. 'I've been looking out for you. Come in, come in out of this foul weather. Oh, you're soaked!' she said, before adding at increased volume over her shoulder, 'She's soaked through, poor thing!'

I lowered my hood and bent down, giving her a hug. 'I'm fine, honestly,' I protested with a smile, whilst looking anxiously towards the door of Percy's flat, wondering if perhaps Emily was back early from her festive road trip. 'Who else is here, Percy?' I asked.

She put both hands to her mouth and looked up at me mischievously. 'Oh, I'm hopeless, aren't I?' she said, turning and once again shouting towards the flat. 'You might as well come out, dear! I've completely given the game away! Doddery fool that I am.'

She helped me out of my coat and then, hanging it over one arm, took me by the hand, leading me across the hallway and into her flat. I looked around as we entered, but there was no sign of anyone. Percy tutted. 'I expect the poor dear can't hear me,' she murmured, walking towards the low under-stairs cupboard in which she kept the vacuum cleaner. Turning the handle and opening the door, she bent down and stuck her head inside. 'She's here!' she announced excitedly. There followed the sound of muffled excitement, accompanied by grunts and some clattering as the Hoover and several buckets were pushed out into the hallway by the mystery guest. And then, at last, emerging on all fours, looking slightly dishevelled, but giggling and in unmistakably good health, came Rose.

–

'So it was wonderful,' said Rose, 'but there's no place like Brizzle.'

'Even in the drizzle?' I queried, as Percy handed me my second cup of tea.

'Even then,' she smiled.

'Well, I'm so torn,' sighed Percy, sitting back down next to me on the sofa. 'I'm overjoyed to see you, Rose, but quite devastated at the thought of perhaps seeing less of Grace.'

Rose smiled proudly. 'I knew you'd love her, Percy. Just as I do.'

I blinked rapidly, slightly overwhelmed, not for the first time that afternoon, by the protestations of affection from both women.

'Careful,' I said, 'you'll make me weepy. Besides, I have every intention of staying in touch, Percy. Before I leave here today, we'll fix a date for you to come to my flat for tea.'

Percy beamed.

'There,' said Rose happily, 'that's that sorted.'

'And I know Emily would love to see you too,' said Percy, patting my knee gently. 'And, dare I say it,' she added, winking at Rose, 'a certain young man not too far from here might *also* welcome an invitation to tea.'

Rose giggled and I felt myself blush.

'Ooh, now, Percy,' said Rose with concern, 'we're embarrassing her with our teasing. It is only teasing, Gracie, isn't it, Percy?'

'Dear me yes, darling,' said Percy, biting her lip. 'We're just two old biddies excited at the prospect of a little romance. It was just that I know the pair of you had such a lovely time together at the funeral.'

'Funeral?' asked Rose.

'Maud,' said Percy.

Rose nodded sadly.

'James and Grace represented Arthur and me, because we were too unwell to attend,' explained Percy. 'And they had the most marvellous time. It was especially wonderful for James because he has such a fascination with death, you see.'

A slightly bemused expression crossed Rose's face but she chose not to query the statement. 'All teasing aside, James is lovely, though, isn't he, Grace?' she said instead.

I smiled and lowered my eyes to my teacup. 'He is,' I said, as matter-of-factly as I could manage. 'But I'm afraid if you're hoping for romance, you won't find it here. I don't think I'm at all his type.'

I looked up to catch Percy mouthing something at Rose, their expressions uncharacteristically serious. Rose, noticing that I was watching them, cleared her throat and inclined her head slightly towards me.

Percy appeared momentarily confused before turning to look at me and saying, 'Oh yes. I see. So, now, who is for shortbread?'

I nodded, relieved that they were prepared to let the subject of James drop. 'I'd love some shortbread, thank you,' I said, whilst sending up silent prayers for my molars.

'Ooh, me too,' said Rose. 'I've really missed your shortbread, Percy.' I searched her face for any hint of fear or irony but found none.

'And,' said Percy excitedly, 'I have some Christmas crackers for us to pull too!'

I laughed in spite of myself, feeling a renewed gratitude for the warmth and friendship of these two senior citizens. 'I love crackers,' I said. 'And that'll be my first pull of the season.'

'Well, darling,' said Percy, rising to her feet before leaning over and planting a kiss on my forehead, 'I am absolutely certain it won't be your last.'

Chapter 37

It was agreed that Rose's husband Tony would collect both Rose and me from Percy's house. I was unable to drive myself home thanks to Percy offering me a taste of her special-recipe mulled wine just as I had made a move to leave at around four o'clock. My intention had been to have one glass and then walk home. What I hadn't bargained for was Percy's considerable powers of persuasion regarding a second glass, and also the vast quantities of brandy involved in her special recipe, an ingredient she had omitted to mention and which she had cleverly disguised with equally vast quantities of sugar. My first inkling that the drink might be slightly more alcoholic than either Rose or myself had suspected occurred when I experienced mild room spin during a trip to the loo and then, shortly afterwards, when Rose fell asleep mid-sentence.

I had tried insisting that I would walk home, or call a taxi, but Rose, when roused, wouldn't hear of it, despite the fact that my flat represented a considerable detour on her journey home. So at 7 p.m., having been alerted to Tony's arrival outside by a phone call, Rose and I went into the hallway of Percy's flat, slipped on our coats and, after pulling one final cracker, at Percy's insistence, prepared to leave.

'Happy Christmas, Percy. And thank you so much for a lovely afternoon and evening,' I said, bending low both to kiss her and to enable her to place my recently won gold paper crown on my head. 'It was just what I needed.'

She kissed my cheek and then held my face for a moment in her hands. 'You are a wonderful girl, Grace. I consider it a privilege to know you.'

My self-control weakened by alcohol, I felt my smile wobble. 'Likewise, Percy,' I said quietly, straightening up as she released me. She moved on to Rose just as the doorbell rang.

The latter tutted. 'My Tony can be so blooming impatient,' she sighed. 'I told him we had to get our coats on.'

Percy laughed. 'You finish buttoning up,' she said, opening the door of the flat, 'while I go outside and tell him off,' she added, making her way with the cautious gait of slight inebriation across the large entrance hall.

I popped on my boots and began to zip up my parka, looking up only when I heard a delighted gasp from Percy, who had by this time reached and opened the main front door. 'Oh my goodness, it's you!'

There was laughter from the unseen visitor, followed by 'Yes, it's me. Why so surprised? Have you already fixed the curtain rail? Are my services no longer required?'

I turned, appalled, to Rose. 'That's James, isn't it?' I breathed.

Tipsily, and at half-speed, she transferred her gaze from Percy to myself. 'Percy left him a message this morning asking if he could come round after work,' she whispered. 'She just thought it might be nice if you bumped into him. Reckon we'd both forgotten all about it.' She put a hand on my shoulder. 'Is it…' She paused to refocus on my face. 'Is it OK, Gracie?'

I returned my attention to Percy just in time to hear her inviting James in for mulled wine. There was a pause before he answered. 'Well, that would have been great,' he said, 'but if the curtain pole is back up, I'll head home. I have a visitor coming.'

I breathed a sigh of relief.

'A visitor?' said Percy, her voice heavy with disappointment. 'So you can't come in?'

There followed another pause. 'You know what,' said James, 'I've got half an hour, so I guess I could have a glass.'

Percy beamed and seemed to have completely forgotten all about Rose and me until James stepped over the threshold and they both turned towards us. At that point, she let out her second happy gasp of the past two minutes. 'Oh James, yes, Rose is home and we've been having mulled wine with Grace. And we've been pulling crackers too. Doesn't Grace look beautiful in her smart anorak and golden crown?'

She looked at me, her hands clasped under her chin in admiration, whilst I racked my brains for an appropriate facial expression to pull in this situation. However, having no past experience or information upon which to draw, I simply stared blankly and unblinkingly at James. And it was, momentarily, like looking in a mirror, until his eyes at last flickered and he turned to Rose, smiling and striding purposefully towards her, his hands outstretched. 'Welcome home, Rose,' he said, taking her right hand between his and kissing her cheek. 'We have all missed you.'

Percy and Rose laughed simultaneously, and I was relieved that their delight and respective states of inebriation seemed to render them oblivious to the fact that James was completely ignoring me, and that I was immobilised by shock.

'And I've missed you all too,' said Rose. 'I'd love to stay and have a drink with you, but I reckon I may have had too many already and also my Tony is waiting for me and Grace. Ooh, but,' she said suddenly, putting a hand to her mouth, 'I don't seem to have my handbag. Did I leave it in the living room, I wonder?' she murmured.

Percy looked thoughtful. 'I think I saw it in the kitchen, dear. I'll look there whilst you check the living room. And maybe the bathroom.' And away they teetered.

James watched them go, while I gazed up at his profile and said nothing, feeling as utterly lost for words as I was for facial expressions. Instead I examined the face of the man whom less than a week ago I had been expecting to kiss me goodnight. I stood unmoving and silent, vaguely aware of the comments and elderly laughter associated with Percy and Rose's ongoing handbag hunt, while experiencing wave after wave of regret over what might have been. And then, at last, when unable to bear it any longer, I turned and made my way across the entrance hall to the front door. After a moment, I heard footsteps behind me and felt a hand on my arm.

'Grace,' said James quietly.

I stopped and turned. 'What?'

'They'll wonder where you've gone. They'll be anxious.' His tone wasn't angry, but it was far from light. He was exercising, I could tell, enormous self-restraint, as if my sudden decision to exit, and the subsequent need to discuss it, was an irritation he could definitely do without. And I had the distinct impression that if necessary, he would simply drag me back into the flat, if that was what it took to spare Rose and Percy any upset or concern.

He stared down at me, awaiting a response, appearing increasingly on the edge of something and making no attempt to smile. And yet, I thought, as usual, his intentions were perfect, his motives unquestionable. He loved and cared for his family and friends and, as far as he was concerned, I was simply, yet again, showing a total disregard for their feelings.

'Good point.' I nodded, feeling strangely numb. 'Tell them I've gone to let Tony know that we're coming,' I said. 'He must be wondering where we are. I'll see Rose in the car.'

And then, without waiting for a reaction or a reply, I turned, opened the door and walked away down the steps.

Chapter 38

'So, yes,' said Neil happily, as he poured the tea, 'our trip was great. It's just a shame we can't take that kind of break every year. I mean, for me, it's easy – a case of have laptop, will travel – but Gavin gets anxious if he's away from the salon for too long.'

I smiled across at him, leaning back in my chair as I picked up my cup and gazed around the café, admiring the intertwined holly and ivy strung from its beams. We hadn't been back since our tense meeting at the beginning of October and it was good to be here now, under circumstances which were so much more relaxed.

Neil's text inviting me to meet him for afternoon tea had come as an unexpected but very welcome surprise the evening before; unexpected because I would be seeing him the next day anyway, as it was Christmas Eve, and welcome because the offer of his company, and the subsequent jovial texted exchange with both him and Gavin, had saved me from the misery which had threatened to overwhelm me on my return home from Percy's house.

'Does Gavin know you're taking him to Paris for New Year yet?' I asked.

'No.' Neil looked uncharacteristically mischievous as he shook his head. 'And he doesn't know that I'm going to propose either.'

I gasped and pressed my hands to my mouth before leaping up and hurrying round the table to hug him. 'Oh that is *the* most wonderful thing I've heard in… well, maybe a decade,' I laughed, squeezing him tightly.

'Thank you,' he said, somewhat breathlessly. 'Now let's just hope he says yes.'

I stood up and returned to my chair. 'Of course he's going to say yes. The pair of you couldn't be more perfect together. Completely different and totally complementary. I think that every time we go out.'

He smiled whilst straightening his glasses, which I had knocked askew during our embrace and which momentarily gave him the look of a young, impeccably dressed Eric Morecambe. I smiled at the thought as we each picked up and sipped our tea.

I was just about to comment that I only wished I could meet someone as perfect for me as Gavin was for him, when he beat me to it. 'Gavin and I both just want to see you as settled as we are,' he said. I smiled at the coincidence of our thoughts, but on looking up, I saw that for some reason Neil's face had fallen a little, despite an obvious, very valiant attempt to maintain a smile. 'We love you very much,' he added gently.

I frowned and wagged a finger at him. 'Now don't you dare get all wobbly and sentimental on me, Neil,' I warned. 'I can just about cope when Gavin tells me he loves me, but if you do it, I'll start crying and won't be able to stop.'

'I've got some things to tell you, Grace,' he said, clearing his throat, his tone now unmistakably anxious. 'But I want you to remember the whole time I'm talking that Gavin and I only want what's best for you. Promise me you'll hold that thought.'

'OK, so now you're scaring me,' I said, as miserable possibilities, ranging from Christmas being cancelled to Neil no longer wanting to be my agent, began queuing, unbidden, for my consideration. 'But go on. What do you want to tell me?'

'Well,' he began, taking a deep breath, 'the first thing is that two days ago, on Wednesday, I went to see James Brooke at his office.' He paused. 'Are you OK so far?'

'You…' That was as much as I could manage.

'That's right,' Neil nodded. 'After Gavin told me what had happened, I went to see James to assure him of your integrity and sensitivity and that you would never contemplate the inclusion of actual events and real people in any of your works of fiction. And I took the opportunity to explain to him that your fictional characters and situations tend to be…'

'Unrealistic?' I suggested in a stunned, slightly disconnected monotone, whilst staring into my tea.

'I actually used the phrase "outside the realm of most people's day-to-day experiences".'

'Unrealistic,' I repeated, now looking up at him. 'I can't believe you did that, Neil.'

He anxiously adjusted his glasses and his mouth stretched into a worried grimace. 'In a good way or a bad way?' he asked.

'It's just so out of character for you.'

'In a good way or a bad way?' he said again, his expression becoming, if possible, even more pained.

'In a good way,' I murmured absently.

'Thank God for that,' he said, visibly relaxing and beginning to reach for his tea. 'I wasn't sure what you were going to say.'

'I mean,' I said, still in shock but now attempting to order my thoughts, 'if you'd said *Gavin* had rushed round to see him, I think I'd be slightly less surprised, although still very, *very* surprised, obviously. But *you*...'

I paused, realising that Neil had frozen mid-reach, his hand hovering a few inches from his teacup. In addition, the worried grimace had returned. 'Yes, well, talking of Gavin...' he removed his glasses, placing them carefully on the table, then closed his eyes and pinched the bridge of his nose between his right thumb and forefinger, 'that's the other thing I have to tell you.'

'What?' I asked, this time bracing myself. 'What has he done?'

Neil sighed. 'He went to see James Brooke.'

I blinked rapidly. 'But I thought *you* went to see James.'

'I did.'

'So Gavin went with you?'

Neil shook his head. 'I'm afraid not.'

'He went *separately*?'

'Yes.'

'Independently? On his own?'

'Yes. He went yesterday.'

'To tell James exactly the same things you had told him the day before?'

'Well, I think he might have come at it from a slightly more... emotional angle.'

'How emotional?'

'Apparently he cried quite a bit.'

'Oh God.' I leaned both elbows on the table and placed my head in my hands.

'I'm sorry, Grace,' said Neil, his shoulders sagging. 'Of course we didn't intend that both of us should go. It's just that I didn't tell Gavin I was going, because I wasn't entirely sure I should but didn't want to be talked out of it. And he didn't tell me for… well, precisely the same reason. It only came to light yesterday evening when I came home to find Gavin sobbing to his favourite bear and insisted he tell me what on earth was going on.'

I sat back in my chair and stared at the ceiling. 'Oh well,' I said eventually, 'it doesn't really matter, does it?' I sniffed and reached blindly for my napkin as a few tears escaped. 'It's not like you could've made things any worse, and you have made me feel exceptionally loved.' I dabbed at my eyes. 'You bastard.'

He laughed gently and I transferred my gaze from the ceiling to him. 'Seriously, though,' I said, 'I'm very grateful to you both.'

'Can I tell you what he said?' he asked.

I shrugged resignedly. 'OK, but I think I can guess. I saw him briefly at Percy's yesterday evening, and to say the atmosphere wasn't great would be an understatement.'

Neil shook his head. 'It's not a fairy-tale ending, Grace, but he doesn't think badly of you.'

I frowned. 'I find that hard to believe.'

'He said pretty much the same thing to both of us,' said Neil, leaning towards me and taking my hand across the table. 'He said he accepted that you had no intention of using your experiences as a basis for a book…'

I tutted. 'Because he knows that I know he'd sue the pants off me if I tried to.'

Neil shook his head. 'It wasn't like that at all. He was gracious – no hint of threat – and he was kind enough not to embarrass Gavin by telling him that I had been to see him the day before.'

'But if he really believes I have no evil intent, why hasn't he told *me* that? Why did he look at me last night like I was the last person in the world he wanted to walk past in the street, let alone talk to?' I felt Neil's hand tense against mine. 'There was something else, wasn't there? Tell me.'

He frowned. 'It wasn't a lengthy meeting. He didn't pour out his heart to either Gavin or me. The only other thing he said was that although he held you in high regard—'

'High regard?' I snorted. 'Who even says that in the twenty-first century? Apart from politicians – or lawyers, I guess,' I added bitterly.

'Although he held you in high regard,' Neil repeated calmly, 'there were personal circumstances which meant a continued relationship wasn't possible.'

'What?' I exclaimed. 'And did you ask what those circumstances were?'

'Of course I didn't,' said Neil. 'It was perfectly obvious he didn't want to talk about it.'

'But I'm assuming Gavin asked him?'

Neil sighed. 'Naturally.'

'And?'

'He said that as those personal circumstances involved the private lives of others, he was unable to discuss them.'

'In short: he's found someone younger.'

'Now stop it,' said Neil, suddenly stern. 'You've come a hell of a long way in the cynicism stakes since we last sat together in this café, and I do not want you sliding back into the ridiculous state of bitterness and joylessness you were in then. And neither does Gavin. So pull yourself together. Not every man in this world is a bastard, Grace, and I would bet an awful lot of money that James Brooke most certainly isn't. I'm not sure what's going on but I do know that, at the very least, there remains the possibility of friendship between you; even if neither of you realises it yet.' He reached again for his cup of tea, this time completing the move and raising it to his lips with a slightly shaky hand. His brow was deeply furrowed and two telltale crimson stress spots had appeared on his cheeks.

I hung my head, feeling ashamed. 'I'm sorry, Neil,' I said. 'The thing is, I know he's gorgeous and honourable. That's what's making me so miserable. Plus the fact that I also know deep down that the situation is no one's fault but my own. But thanks for trying to mend things.'

I heard him replace his cup on its saucer. 'Gavin and I are confident that everything will work out,' he said quietly.

'I expect that's why Gavin can't stop crying.' I looked up at him and smiled.

He rolled his eyes. 'Look, just stay happy and write me a book, for God's sake. That's the most important thing in all this.'

'Let me come round and clean your house from time to time and it's a deal,' I said.

He looked thoughtful. 'A bit kinky, but OK.' Then he smiled his perfectly white smile, picked up and replaced his glasses and reached for the menu. 'Now, how about we seal that arrangement with some cake?'

Chapter 39

'I can't believe we're *actually* exercising,' I puffed as Simone and I jogged, at what felt like almost negative velocity, up a beautifully frosty but bone-freezingly cold Ladies Mile towards the café.

She waved a hand and shook her head to indicate that speech was impossible. A moment later, she tapped my arm, stopped running and, clutching her side, mouthed the word, 'Stitch.'

I nodded and stood next to her, my hand resting gently on her back as she leaned forward. 'I think,' I gasped, 'we've done really well.' I spoke rapidly, trying to maximise the number of words I could eke out of the impossibly short breaths I was currently able to take. 'And it had to be done... From six o'clock... tonight, I'm going to be... doing nothing but eating, drinking... watching sing-along musicals... and playing Battleships for forty-eight hours.'

At that, Simone either groaned or guffawed, I couldn't tell which. 'Ba... ba... batt?' she panted.

'Yep. Gavin really loves Battleships. Odd, I know.'

She inhaled deeply and noisily through her nose and stood up, before exhaling slowly through her mouth. 'Beyond unfit,' she said, her hands on her hips. 'Shameful.'

I offered her an empathetic smile. 'We're not far from the café now. You OK to walk?'

She nodded, linking my arm as we set off. 'I've got to take this running thing more seriously in the new year,' she said. 'I've actually put on weight, you know.'

'You haven't,' I tutted.

'Have,' she insisted. 'Two kilograms since we started. It's all those Danish pastries. So how come you're looking so svelte? That's what I want to know.'

I shrugged. 'It was the cleaning, wasn't it? You watch, the pounds will pile on now that's all over.'

She said nothing, but squeezed my arm.

'I'm fine,' I said.

'And looking forward to Christmas with Gavin and Neil, I bet,' she smiled, resting her head momentarily on my shoulder. 'What time did you say you're going round tonight?'

'About six, and yes, I am really looking forward to it. But I would have loved to have been with you guys too,' I added, 'if Gavin hadn't already asked me. I was so spoilt for choice this year. I feel very lucky.'

'Well you're bloody lucky not coming to us,' she said bitterly.

'Why? You're not still being mean to Guy, are you?' I frowned disapprovingly.

'No, no, I forgave him,' she sighed. 'Or semi-forgave him. Eventually.'

'Good. Or semi-good.' It was my turn to squeeze her arm. 'But if Guy's not the problem, what is? You've got his mum coming, haven't you? And I seem to remember her being good fun.' Simone rolled her eyes. 'Catheter aside,' I acknowledged.

284

'My brother is coming,' said Simone.

'But Matt's good fun too,' I protested. 'Or are you worried he'll start cracking catheter jokes?'

'Wouldn't put it past him,' she said. 'But the real problem is the new girlfriend he's bringing with him.'

'Another political activist?' I asked, recalling Simone's sad tale of a previous family gathering, ruined after Matt's girlfriend took offence when Guy revealed that he thought Margaret Thatcher had 'kindly eyes'.

'Worse,' said Simone. 'She's a vegan.'

'No!' I exclaimed, appalled. 'Even at Christmas?'

She nodded solemnly. 'Even at Christmas.'

'That's so rude.'

'That's what I said.'

'Not sorry I'm not coming now.'

'Don't blame you. I might sneak round to Neil and Gavin's.'

I laughed. 'They would seriously love that. Ooh, but,' I said, stopping suddenly, 'I haven't told you my shock news about Neil, have I?'

Her eyes widened. 'He's straight, isn't he? I *knew* it!'

I stared at her. 'I'm just going to pretend you didn't say that and tell you the *actual* shock news, Simone.'

'Oh, OK,' she said, looking deflated.

'He did something reckless and out of character,' I smiled teasingly. 'He said it was even against his better judgement.'

'Ooh.' She tugged excitedly at my sleeve. 'Tell me, tell me, tell me.'

'He only went and saw James and gave me a character reference.'

Her jaw dropped and she stared at me. When, after a moment or two, her expression was unchanged and she still hadn't spoken, I said, 'It's OK. I was horrified initially too, but then I was fine about it. I know it was a really kind thing to do.'

She nodded wordlessly and closed her mouth.

'The only slightly iffy bit,' I continued, 'is that *Gavin* went round, the next day. Completely off his own bat. Neither knew that the other had been.'

Simone's jaw dropped for a second time.

'I know,' I said sadly. 'That's a bit cringey, isn't it? It occurred to me afterwards that James might've thought I'd asked them to go — or told lots of people exactly what had happened. He's so private. That wouldn't improve his opinion of me, would it? But anyway,' I shrugged, 'it makes no difference now. So there's no point in worrying about it, is there?' I concluded quietly.

I looked questioningly at Simone, waiting for a verbal reaction. When none came, I began to worry. 'Are you OK?' I prodded her upper arm. 'You're allowed to laugh about it, you know.'

Her response was to shake her head, stop walking and then hide her face in her hands. 'Oh Grace.'

'What?' I laughed uncertainly. 'Don't be silly. I've told you, I'm fine about it, Sim.'

She looked up, all hint of habitual rosiness gone from her face. I hadn't seen her so ashen since a bout of flu eighteen months earlier. 'I went to see James,' she whispered. 'I've been waiting for an opportunity to tell you.'

I stared at her. 'For a moment there I thought you said you went to see James.'

She nodded silently, biting her lower lip, her eyes filled with anxiety. 'I did,' she mouthed soundlessly, 'say that.'

I closed my eyes and allowed my head to drop.

'And then…' she continued.

'Oh my God, there's more,' I murmured.

'And then Guy…'

I looked up sharply. 'Please do not tell me that Guy went to see James. Please do not tell me that. If that happened, I do not want to know.'

She looked up at me, now apparently on the verge of tears, her mouth firmly downturned.

'Well?' I asked impatiently. 'Did he? Did Guy go and see James?'

'No.' She gave her head a small, anxious twitch of a shake.

I put a hand to my forehead and heaved a sigh. 'Thank God for that.'

'He Skyped him,' she said quietly.

I took a deep breath and nodded, slowly and resignedly. 'Of *course* he did. And I'm sure James really appreciated the variety in approach.'

Simone reached out and gently rubbed my upper arm. 'I'm sorry, Grace. We were just trying to help. I saw James on Monday afternoon and then Guy Skyped him on Tuesday morning after setting it up with his secretary. He did it because I was in a mess, wondering if I'd done the wrong thing, and also because he thought it was all his fault in the first place. He just wanted to explain to James that he hadn't been up to date with what had been going on and also to tell him how lovely you are. You know what he's like.' She stopped rubbing and allowed her arms to hang limply by her sides. 'I'm sorry,' she repeated. 'I can see how embarrassing it must be for you.'

I shook my head. 'No, no, *I'm* sorry. For being ungrateful,' I said, stepping towards her and giving her a hug. 'That was an amazing thing you and Guy did for me. And, of course, you actually beat Neil and Gavin to it, so I'll be sure to rub their noses in that over Christmas.'

I was aware of a combined sniff-giggle against my shoulder. 'Do you want to hear about my conversation with him?' she asked after a moment.

I released her from the hug and shook my head. 'Not if it involves personal circumstances which make a relationship with me impossible.'

She nodded sadly.

'Heard it all before, you see.' I smiled ruefully.

She took a tissue from her sleeve and blew her nose. 'A Danish, then?' she asked.

'Definitely,' I said. 'And while we eat, you can cheer me up by telling me more about your vegan Christmas.'

Chapter 40

'B6,' I said.

'Are you cheating?' asked Gavin, eyeing me with suspicion over the top of the board and reaching for a peg.

'No, I am not!' I protested. 'How could I cheat, unless I had X-ray vision?'

'I don't know, but you haven't had a miss yet,' he said. 'And that's so improbable.'

'Yes, well, so are you and Neil, and yet here we all are,' I said brightly. 'Isn't life strange?'

'Enough!' called Neil, re-entering the living room carrying three glasses. 'Come and have a Baileys break, you two, before things get physical.'

'Baileys!' I said excitedly, standing up and heading for the sofa at the other end of the through-room.

Neil placed the glasses on the wooden coffee table in front of the fire and sat down in the cream armchair next to it. 'I'll put some carols on,' he said, reaching out and pressing a button on the hi-fi, which sat on a bookcase to his left.

'And I'll come and sit next to you, Grace,' said Gavin curtly, following me to the sofa.

'To make sure I don't get out my binoculars and peek at the Battleships board?' I asked.

'Got it in one, love,' he said, flopping down next to me.

I laughed and leaned forward, picking up two glasses of Baileys and passing one to him. 'Thank you for sharing your Christmas with me,' I smiled, nudging him affectionately and then smiling at Neil, 'both of you. You're so kind.'

Gavin kissed the top of my head and Neil raised his glass. 'And thank you for our Christmas Eve pyjamas. These are great.' He looked down admiringly at the navy, silk-sheen cotton pyjamas I had given him and which he was already wearing, despite it being not quite eight-thirty. 'I feel like Cary Grant in *Indiscreet*,' he said.

'That is exactly who I had in mind when I bought them!' I exclaimed happily.

'Er, and what was running through your mind when you bought mine?' asked Gavin, tugging at his snug-fit, jersey pair, which were covered in pictures of Royal Navy frigates. 'I'm guessing prescription meds.'

I punched his upper arm. 'Have you *any* idea how hard it was to find a pair of adult-sized PJs covered in battleships?'

'Really?' His eyes widened in mock surprise. 'It's almost like there's absolutely no demand for them, isn't it?'

I laughed and he joined in. 'I love 'em,' he said. 'Especially the elasticated cuff at the ankles. It's been a good thirty years since I've had a pair of jammies with elasticated ankles. Makes me all nostalgic for *Grange Hill* and Debbie Gibson. But tell us about what you're wearing,' he said, pointing at my cream sheep onesie, complete with a hood with ears and fluffy black hooves. 'I love that too. Might nick it before Boxing Day is out.'

'Well, you know my mum always used to give me Christmas Eve pyjamas when I was growing up,' I began, smiling.

Gavin popped an arm around my shoulders and squeezed. 'Yes,' he said.

'Well, when she died, her sister, my Auntie Barbara, kept up the tradition and she still gives me a pair each year. I usually see her and my cousins around Christmas, but this year she posted them. Or it.' I looked down at the onesie. 'This is really left-field for her, actually. I'm wondering if one of my cousins picked it up for her.'

'It's a great tradition,' said Neil. 'I think we should adopt it, Gavin.'

'Me too,' said Gavin, giving me another hug.

'This room is so festive,' I said, contentedly sipping my Baileys whilst taking in the candles dotted around the room and the Christmas garlands running across the fireplace and bookshelves. The *pièce de résistance* was a perfectly decorated seven-foot tree which took pride of place in the front bay of their immaculate, but warmly welcoming, Edwardian terraced home. 'It could grace the cover of *Homes and Gardens*,' I said.

'It's all Neil,' beamed Gavin proudly. 'He really knows how to do Christmas.'

Neil smiled in an endearingly self-conscious way and was just about to reply when the doorbell rang. 'That'll be the carollers,' he said, jumping up from his chair. 'I'll get the mince pies from the Aga. Do you two want to come and listen?'

'Er, no, you're OK, thanks,' said Gavin casually. 'We're toasty warm here by the fire and we'll still be able to hear them, won't we, Grace?' He turned to me, rolling his eyes affectionately as Neil left the room. 'I know he has this cool, calm, collected professional persona, but he's a big softie really. Those carollers are from St Peter's. They collect for charity and know they're on to a winner with Neil. He throws tenners at them like they're going out of fashion. *And* he feeds them. Every Christmas Eve they come round – it's why he never wants to go out. He loves it and they always do him a special little medley.'

'Ah, that's so lovely,' I said, smiling and sinking further into the sofa.

Gavin shook his head. 'They're crap. You know that bit in *The Goblet of Fire* when Harry Potter opens the golden egg and people's ears start bleeding?'

I nodded.

'That's what they sound like,' he said. 'It's like they're screaming. They "sang",' he drew the inverted commas in the air, "Mary's Boy Child" last year, and even the bloody tambourine was out of tune. I don't like going to the door because I just can't make my face do the right thing. Last year Neil said I looked constipated.'

I laughed. 'Oh, I really want to hear them now,' I said, sitting up and leaning over the back of the sofa to listen. 'Can't hear anything,' I said after a moment. 'Am I going deaf?'

Gavin frowned and looked over his shoulder towards the living room door. 'No, I can't hear them either. Probably not finished their mince pies yet.'

At that moment, Neil re-entered the room.

'It wasn't them, then?' asked Gavin, pulling a sad face before adding, 'What's wrong? You look…'

And that was as far as he got before James walked in.

I was immediately overwhelmed by the same sense of uncertainty, inertia and pure terror I had experienced forty-eight hours earlier, when he had stepped into Percy's hallway. He, however, was much better prepared this time. 'Hello and happy Christmas, Grace,' he said, looking at me and smiling, 'and Gavin,' he added, turning towards him.

I stared at him, aware that Gavin was staring at me.

'Gavin,' said Neil, stepping forward, 'James has come to talk to Grace.'

Gavin gasped and put both hands to his mouth before throwing his arms around me, enveloping me in a crushing hug.

'Gavin,' said Neil quietly.

'Sorry, yes.' Gavin released me and stood up, walking round the sofa and solemnly holding out his hand to James. 'Happy Christmas, James,' he began, his voice full of emotion, 'and may I just say—'

'Maybe later, Gavin,' said Neil, taking his outstretched hand and leading him from the room. 'Come and help me in the kitchen. The carollers will be here soon. James said he passed them a little way down the street.' They exited, closing the door behind them.

I continued to stare up at James, whose smile, whilst still just about in place, had now faded somewhat. Tormented by the silence and desperate to end it, I said, 'This is my new sheep onesie. It's from my Auntie Barbara, but I think maybe my cousin chose it.'

I was aware of my small, internal Neil-voice querying why I always spouted such utter rubbish at the worst possible moments.

James glanced towards the door and I realised that the voice wasn't internal at all, and that Neil was actually talking to Gavin. This was followed by the sound of Gavin murmuring the word "Tourette's", and then two sets of footsteps heading down the hallway to the kitchen.

James turned back towards me, apparently unfazed by the overheard exchange. 'Can I sit down?'

I nodded and he made his way around the sofa and sat down, well outside my personal space.

'I've had lots of visitors this week,' he said after a moment, staring straight ahead, addressing his comment to the fireplace.

I nodded again, joining him in his study of the flames.

'They all told me what a wonderful person you are: Simone, Guy, Neil, Gavin, Rose, Percy – all of them.'

I turned to look at him. 'Rose and Percy?'

He didn't blink, or turn; just nodded. 'Gavin is Percy's hairdresser.'

I returned my attention to the fire. 'I didn't know that,' I said quietly.

'They had a conversation during her appointment on Friday morning. Percy then had a conversation with Rose and together they paid me a visit yesterday afternoon. They were a formidable delegation.'

'I can imagine.'

'Rose even brought supporting documentation with her, in the form of emails and texts, but I didn't need to see those. I just told them what I had told everyone else: that I didn't believe you would ever do, say or write anything to intentionally hurt.'

I took a deep breath and forced myself to focus, keen to perfect each sentence before uttering it. 'You didn't seem to believe that last Saturday,' I said, now looking at him. 'It's a shame, and not hugely flattering, that it took you so long to reach that conclusion.'

He at last turned and looked at me steadily. 'It took me five minutes,' he said. 'Possibly less.'

'Then why didn't you tell me that?' I asked, feeling suddenly irritated. 'Instead of running off home in a big tizzy.'

His mouth twitched, as if suppressing a smile, a reaction which served only to annoy me further. Was this a joke to him? Had he spent a week pretending to be angry and hurt when in fact he found the whole incident highly entertaining – an emotional game played with the same enthusiasm with which Gavin played Battleships?

'I'm glad you find it all so funny,' I said. 'And it's good to know that your feelings have such depth.'

He frowned at that. 'I don't know what you mean.'

'What I mean is that a person with any kind of feeling would have returned to that restaurant to reassure me. They would not have left me upset and alone and feeling absolutely awful about absolutely everything and very nearly ruining my Christmas.'

He nodded slowly. 'I agree,' he said calmly. 'That's why I returned to the restaurant. I was back there in a little over ten minutes, but they said you hadn't wanted to wait for the cab and had left only a matter of moments after I did.'

'Oh,' I said, feeling slightly put out that my accusation of insensitivity and superficiality had been so rapidly shot down in flames. 'Ah, but,' I said, recovering quickly and raising a finger, 'why then did you not come after me? A matter of ego? Of pride, perhaps?' I asked, in the manner of a triumphant prosecuting lawyer.

He looked at me impassively for a moment. 'If ego or pride were a factor, I wouldn't have returned to the restaurant,' he said simply. 'In fact, I hailed a taxi and headed immediately for your flat.'

'Oh,' I said a second time, experiencing a strange and highly unsettling mixture of dissatisfaction at once again having my argument torn to shreds, and delight at the thought of being pursued by James. I looked up at him, feeling increasingly confused. 'Auntie Barbara buys me new pyjamas every Christmas,' I said.

He nodded. 'Are they from John Lewis, perhaps?'

I shrugged. 'Not sure.'

He took a deep breath. 'OK, well as you seem to have gone into panic mode, shall I tell you what happened after I hailed the cab?'

'OK,' I said quietly.

'I asked the driver to take me to Henleaze,' he said, 'and I arrived at your flat…'

I gasped and put a hand to my mouth as I suddenly understood. 'You arrived at my flat at exactly the same time I did!' I exclaimed, my eyes wide with comprehension.

'That's right,' he nodded. 'I did.'

'And you were in a Bristol blue cab!'

'I was.'

'And I…' I leaned back on the sofa and stared once again at the festive flames dancing in the hearth.

'And you were with Aiden,' he said quietly. 'More specifically,' he continued, 'you were in Aiden's arms.'

I nodded slowly. 'Yes.' I looked up at him. 'Was that the circumstance which made a personal relationship with me impossible?'

'It was clear to me that you still have a very close relationship with him. And as we drove away, you were heading towards your flat.'

I frowned and shook my head. 'If you had told any of this to Simone, or Guy, or Neil, or Gavin, or Rose, they would have—'

'I couldn't discuss it with anyone else,' he interrupted. 'I might have been revealing something which would hurt you, and others, very much.'

I threw up my hands. 'Then why not ask *me*? Why not tell me what you saw and ask me to explain?'

He smiled sadly. 'I'm not made of wood, Grace. If you prick me, I do bleed, you know. Asking you to dinner was difficult because it was important – you had become important… to me. So when I saw you with Aiden, it felt right to step back for everyone's sake, including my own.'

'So why are you here now?' I asked. 'To give me an opportunity to prove to you that I'm worthy? To let me try to explain everything and convince you that I wouldn't have an affair with another woman's partner, no matter what the past?' I looked up at him and shook my head. 'I don't think I want to do that.'

'And I wouldn't ask you to,' he said. 'Although I do feel I have to point out that a moment ago you were frustrated that I *hadn't* requested an explanation of the situation from you.' He looked at me and raised an eyebrow.

'Oh for goodness' sake,' I sighed, beginning to despair of ever winning an exchange in this conversation. I leaned back on the sofa, feeling suddenly exhausted. 'So why *are* you here?'

'Because,' he said, 'after Simone and Guy and Neil and Gavin and Rose and Percy had been to see me...' he paused and took a deep breath, 'Aiden came.'

'Aiden?' I echoed quietly. His was not a name I had expected to hear.

'Yes, this evening, Aiden came,' he repeated. 'He didn't know that I had seen you both on Saturday. All he knew was what you had told him that night, on your doorstep, before you sent him home to his family. And, like everyone else, he wanted to make sure that I understood and accepted that you were not a person who would intentionally hurt anyone. Even the woman who had contributed so materially to the collapse of your marriage.'

I looked up at him, overwhelmed by what Aiden had done. Not for himself, but for me. 'Aiden...?'

He nodded.

'But that's so not...' I began, before losing the ability to express in words the feelings I was experiencing. I couldn't think of another occasion in our entire relationship, as partners, as spouses, as exes, as friends, when Aiden had done anything so selfless. Not only had going to see James been of no benefit to himself whatsoever, it must have been professionally difficult, personally humbling and emotionally painful.

'I can't believe he did that for me,' I murmured.

James shrugged. 'You are loved, Grace,' he said simply.

I nodded.

Neither of us said anything more and, after a moment, James rose to his feet. 'I think I had better be going,' he said.

I stood up and managed a polite smile. 'Right, yes. Of course,' I said, feeling a little dazed as I struggled to disentangle my feelings and digest what I had just been told. 'I'll show you out.'

I walked ahead of him out of the lounge and down the hallway. 'Thank you for coming,' I said, as I opened the front door, 'and for explaining everything.' I looked up at him and, suddenly experiencing an almost overwhelming sense of well-being, my smile broadened into one of genuine happiness. 'It's just wonderful. Merry Christmas, James.'

He nodded and, smiling somewhat uncertainly, stepped outside.

'Bye!' I said cheerily, closing the door and hurriedly padding back down the hallway.

I burst into the kitchen to find Gavin and Neil sitting at the table, glasses of Baileys in hand and a plate of mince pies between them. They looked up enquiringly as I clapped my hands. 'It's all absolutely fine!' I exclaimed, walking towards them, giving them each a hug and then pulling out a chair and sitting down. 'Aiden went to see James and what he told him made it clear that there was nothing going on between us.' I spoke rapidly, aware of Gavin and Neil's puzzled expressions and anxious to explain. 'James had got the wrong end of the stick, you see, because he had seen me hugging Aiden outside my flat late Saturday night. And to be fair to James, it was a very emotional moment and, if I'm completely honest, I did actually think about snogging Aiden, but not because

I fancied him,' I reassured hastily, 'just because I felt so low and because it would have been one in the eye for Summer. But oh my goodness,' I gushed, 'I'm so pleased I didn't do that, because James was sitting in the cab and if I had kissed Aiden who knows what might have happened? And I'm so over the whole Summer and Aiden thing anyway. I don't need that kind of petty, pointless revenge. Especially not when there is lovely, gorgeous James. I'm so grateful to Aiden for what he did. I'll have to email him. And James is just...' I placed my elbows on the table, rested my head in my hands and sighed contentedly, 'lovely-gorgeous. He pursued me, you know,' I added happily. 'Me!'

I smiled at Gavin and Neil, but was a little deflated to find that neither was smiling back at me, but were instead looking confusedly at each other. 'What?' I asked, prodding them each in turn. 'What's the problem? Aren't you happy for me? Am I missing something? Everything's sorted, isn't it?'

'She's unreal,' Gavin murmured, massaging his temples, as Neil looked at me somewhat despairingly over the top of his glasses and placed his hand on my arm.

'Where is he, Grace?' he asked gently.

I laughed and then shrugged. 'Where is who?'

'James,' said Gavin. 'You know, the lovely, gorgeous man? Where have you put him?'

I laughed again. 'Well, he...' I began, before my face suddenly dropped. 'Ooh.' I put a hand to my mouth. 'He... I...' I turned and looked out into the hallway.

'Exactly,' said Gavin with an exasperated sigh. 'For some reason, instead of ripping all the lovely, gorgeous man's clothes off and then inviting him to stay for a drink, you showed him the front door. Did you at least tell him that he was lovely and gorgeous before you waved him off?' he asked.

I turned back towards him. 'I… I wished him a Merry Christmas,' I said uncertainly. 'But that's not quite the same thing, is it?' I concluded in a whisper.

They shook their heads silently and simultaneously.

'Did you say *anything* to indicate, even obliquely, that you're still attracted to him?' asked Neil.

I thought back over my conversation with James. 'Shit,' I said after a moment.

'It's fine,' sighed Neil. 'You can call him later, or tomorrow morning.'

I stared down dejectedly at my onesie for a moment and then jumped up. 'Can I borrow some big boots or shoes?'

'Some what?' asked Neil, frowning.

'Yes!' said Gavin, leaping from his seat and grabbing a pair of black wellies from beside the back door. 'Here, these will go on over your sheep feet!'

Neil looked horrified. 'Do not do this,' he said. 'Leave it an hour or so, then pick up the phone. That way you can plan what you—'

'Oh hush up, Cary!' said Gavin, steadying me as I leaned on him and attempted to force my onesied foot into a wellie. 'Where's your sense of romance?' He reached down and grabbed my leg. 'Just shove it in, Grace. Stamp hard!'

'They're a bit snug,' I said breathlessly, now struggling into the second wellie, 'but I'm in.'

'Fabulous,' beamed Gavin. 'Now, off you go. He can't have got far, and if he's gone, well, we can always revert to Billy Boring's plan B.' He jerked his head disdainfully towards Neil.

He ushered me out into the hallway before overtaking me, squeezing past to open the front door. 'Can't you go any faster than that?' he asked as I hobbled down the hallway. 'Long John Silver could have you in a race.'

'The wellies are really tight over my hooves,' I protested. 'I'm doing my best.'

'I know, I know,' he said soothingly, helping me into Neil's grey herringbone overcoat as I shuffled past him. 'Keep that on. And don't go too far. Just step outside the gate and look up and down the street. And put your hood up,' he called, before running after me to pull it over my head. 'It's cold.'

'Thanks,' I said breathlessly, raising a hand as I opened the gate. 'Now go inside. You're in your pyjamas and slippers.'

'Run, Forrest, run!' he laughed, and then hurried back up the path. I heard him shut the front door as I stepped out onto the pavement.

The street was deserted and silent. Looking left and right, I decided to go as far as the bend in the road, in the direction that James would have taken to walk home. I set off as fast as my severely squashed feet would allow and it took me less than a minute to reach the bend. From there, I could see all the way to the end of the street, but there was no sign of him.

In desperation, I decided to limp back the other way, just in case he had decided to, say, detour to Waitrose on his way home. It was a pretty forlorn hope, I knew, but unwilling to give up just yet, I whirled around and did my best to hurry. Discovering that longer steps were more efficient and less painful than shorter ones, I slowed my pace but lengthened my stride to the max, in the manner of Neil Armstrong departing Apollo 11. I was back at Gavin and Neil's gate in what I considered to be rather impressive time in the circumstances and, ignoring the twitching of their front curtains, I kept going, soon reaching the point from where I could see the other end of the road.

I sighed and hung my head. There was no James. There was, however, a group of about half a dozen adults and three or four children, carrying a variety of instruments. They waved and smiled as they approached, looking impressively unperturbed by the sight of a sheep wearing wellies and a Ted Baker overcoat. I managed a weak smile and a half-hearted 'Happy Christmas' in return, before turning and walking slowly, painfully and somewhat dejectedly back up the street.

On reaching their garden gate for a second time, I noted with relief that Gavin and Neil were no longer at the window. I paused to rearrange my features into a display of carefree, upbeat acceptance of the situation, keen not to give any hint of unhappiness and cast a shadow over the Christmas they were so generously sharing with me. Flipping the latch of the gate, I took a deep breath and hoisted my mouth into a smile.

I heard a car door opening behind me, but it wasn't until James said, 'Grace,' that I turned around.

He was standing beside his car, one hand resting on top of it, looking completely at ease.

My forced smile fell away. 'Have you been sitting in your car the whole time I've been running up and down the road?' I asked.

He nodded.

I threw up my arms in exasperation. 'Well why on earth didn't you get out right away?'

He walked around the car and stood in front of me, unsmiling and unblinking. 'Because it was funny,' he said.

I adjusted my jacket, looking down at my black wellies and the thick cream fabric ballooning out of them, which gave my legs the appearance of a couple of woolly chicken drumsticks. I nodded. 'OK, I can see how it might have been funny,' I acknowledged grudgingly.

'The conversation that we had in there,' said James, gesturing towards the house. 'It didn't...' he hesitated, looking down at his shoes, 'it didn't play out quite as I'd hoped.' He looked up again and, after a typical delay, he smiled. 'How was it for you?'

I frowned. 'Well, I would have liked to win some of the exchanges, but you just kept on winning them all.'

James nodded. 'OK...'

'And I would have preferred not to be wearing a sheep onesie.'

'I see,' he said, continuing to nod. 'But, other than that, you were happy with how it went?'

'I wish...' I began, looking up at him and trying desperately not to feel overwhelmed by the situation, 'I wish I hadn't shown you the door and...'

James said nothing. Instead he raised a questioning eyebrow and waited.

'And...' I continued, remembering Neil's advice to stick to simple facts and minimal information in times of crisis, 'and I think you're lovely-gorgeous, James.'

He smiled. 'The feeling is entirely mutual, Grace,' he said quietly.

'That's good, isn't it?' I whispered and then, with uncharacteristic calm, I took a step towards him, placed my arms around his neck and kissed him. His arms remained disconcertingly by his sides for a second or two before he reached up, lowered my sheep hood and, with his hands in my hair, kissed me back in a way for which I felt I had been waiting at least a week, and quite possibly my entire life.

I think if it hadn't been for a gentle tap on my back and a barely audible 'Excuse us', I might never have let him go. As it was, I was forced to release him and turned to see, of course, the carollers.

'My apologies, but whilst you are kissing him, we can't quite get past you to the gate,' said a tall elderly gentleman in a Barbour.

'Oh yes, sorry,' I said, as James and I took a step backwards. 'We didn't hear you coming. There was no screaming.'

'Screaming?' he queried.

'I meant singing,' I said quietly. 'I misspoke.'

He nodded. 'A surprising number of people seem not to be at home this evening and yet have left every light in the house on,' he said, looking back down the street in a puzzled manner. 'Oh, but I see that Neil is in, though.' He pointed at the house and at Neil and Gavin, who had, at some point in the past five minutes, thrown the curtains wide and were both now once again standing at the window, Neil smiling broadly, hands in pockets, and Gavin doing disgraceful things with his tongue and thrusting his hips, whilst giving me a thumbs-up. 'And his partner seems particularly happy to see us,' said Barbour man brightly, as the little group made their way up the path to the front door.

I was still watching, as they waited with obvious excitement for Neil to answer it, when I felt James take my hand. I turned towards him and smiled.

'I meant to say earlier,' he said, looking towards the house, 'when we were inside, that I'm sorry I left the restaurant last Saturday, even for ten minutes. That was a mistake.' He turned back towards me and stroked my hair. 'It's just that sometimes, when you're right in front of me, I find it surprisingly difficult to think clearly.'

I shook my head. 'I'm sorry for telling you to go,' I said. 'It's just that sometimes, when you're right in front of me, I find it surprisingly difficult to talk sense.'

'Really? I hadn't noticed,' he said, smiling and pulling me gently towards him. 'But in that case, perhaps we should take another break from trying to think and talk.' He lowered his face towards mine and kissed me again.

It was a good minute or so before either of us spoke.

'That was *such* a good idea of yours,' I breathed eventually. 'I think in future we should always take a break whenever we're lost for words…' I kissed him once more. 'Or thoughts.'

'Agreed,' he nodded. 'You know, this is much more how I hoped things would go,' he added, his arms still around me and his face close to mine. 'Minus the enormous wellies, maybe. I can't claim to have been keeping my fingers crossed for those.'

'I love them,' I insisted. 'They're my lucky wellies.' I held him tightly and leant my head against his chest. 'Can you come in for a drink – oh, but maybe after they've gone?' I lifted my head and looked over my shoulder as the carollers suddenly, and tunelessly, struck up. 'I'm not sure they've quite grasped the concept of a medley. They seem to be singing all their carols at the same time, rather than one after the other.'

When he didn't reply, I turned back towards him. He was looking down at me, studying me, his expression now serious. 'What are you thinking?' I asked.

He blinked. 'I *was* thinking...' he said.

'Yes?'

'I was thinking that you are loved, Grace.'

I took a deep breath and smiled up at him. 'And so are you,' I said, raising myself onto the tips of my wellied toes and kissing him again. 'So are you.'

Epilogue

Eight months later

'Hello?' I called, opening the front door and stepping inside. 'Rose?'

Receiving no answer, I closed the door and took off my cardigan, slinging both it and my bag over the bottom of the banister with a sigh and heading wearily for the kitchen.

Once there, I filled the kettle, placed it on the hob and flopped down onto a chair at the kitchen table. I rested my head in my hands and stared into space, reviewing the events of what had proved to be a physically and emotionally draining afternoon.

I moved only when the whistling of the kettle forced me to do so, hauling myself to my feet, turning off the gas and making myself a cup of tea.

'Hello, Gracie!' said Rose brightly, and incredibly loudly, as she entered the kitchen.

'Oh my goodness, Rose!' I whirled around, placing a hand on my chest. 'I thought I'd missed you. I called when I got in.'

'Sorry, I didn't hear you.' She reached into the pocket of her overall and held up the iPod and earphones Tony had bought her for her birthday a month earlier. 'Bruce

Springsteen,' she said, poking a finger in her ear and wiggling it. 'Think he's left me a bit deaf, actually. Am I shouting?'

'No, you're fine,' I smiled. 'Cup of tea? Biscuit?' I reached down the spotty tin from the shelf, removing its lid to display the contents. 'Filled it up yesterday. Look at those choccie digestives.'

'Temptress,' she said, taking one as I placed the tin on the kitchen table. 'Thank you.'

'And a cup of tea?' I asked.

'Much as I'd like to, I can't say yes please to a cuppa today,' she smiled, sitting down. 'Tony's on his way and I need to get home to finish packing.'

'I bet you're looking forward to your holiday, and seeing Violet again,' I said, fetching my cup of tea and coming to sit next to her.

'I am,' she said. 'Only two weeks, of course, but it will be so much hotter this time that I'll probably have had enough of the place by then.'

'And Violet is coming to you for Christmas this year, isn't she?'

'She is.' Rose nodded and took a bite of her biscuit. 'But quickly, tell me,' she said, holding a hand under her chin to catch any crumbs. 'How did it go this afternoon with Neil?'

I pulled a face.

'Oh dear,' she said. 'Didn't he like this one either?' I shook my head and she sighed sadly. 'Got any other ideas up your sleeve?'

'Well, I'm seriously considering killing him, if that counts.' I slumped a little in my chair. 'To be honest, Rose, if I'd known that I was going to have to traipse around

Gloucestershire, Wiltshire and Somerset with him every other week for months on end, I'm not sure I would have agreed to be his best woman.'

Rose patted my hand. 'He obviously values your opinion,' she said.

'I know, and we do get free cake every time,' I replied, attempting positivity. 'But I tell you, it's a good job he was already out of the car when he said he wondered if we should take another look at Chalke Hall.'

'Chalke Hall?' Rose frowned. 'But wasn't that the very first one you looked at?'

I nodded solemnly. 'It was,' I said. 'Fortunately, he didn't hear me swear, because he'd already closed the car door and was giving me a cheery bye-bye.'

Rose laughed. 'Did you get a chance to talk about other things? The book?' she asked.

'Oh yes, that's all fine. He loves it. And the outline of the next one.' I smiled at her. 'I've no *genuine* life moans, Rose.'

She squeezed my arm. 'You've earned your blessings, Gracie,' she said. 'The things you've gone through and managed to keep your head above water.'

I smiled. 'Couldn't have done it without you, Rose.'

She looked at me a little emotionally just as her phone buzzed. 'He's outside,' she said, peering at the screen. 'Best be off.'

We stood up and I gave her a long hug. 'Have a lovely, lovely time,' I said, 'and I'll see you in a couple of weeks.'

'Yes,' she said, as we walked out of the kitchen and towards the front door, 'and I hope by the time I get back, Neil has settled on somewhere for the reception.'

'Probably best not to hold your breath,' I said resignedly as she picked up the green National Trust tote bag she had left next to the bureau.

'Oh, and before I forget,' she said, opening the front door and pausing with her hand on the latch, 'I found an open box of Matchmakers under your bed. They're still in date, so I've popped them in the fridge.'

'Thanks, Rose, they're mine,' said James. He was standing at the bottom of the steps looking up at us. 'I was wondering where I'd left them... this time.'

'Stop your teasing, you,' said Rose, laughing and wagging a finger at him. 'Now I'd love to stay and natter but I must run because I can see my Tony looking grumpy from here.' She nodded her head towards the red Fiat parked outside Percy's house and headed down the steps, waving at me and stopping for a brief hug with James as she went. 'Bye, both!'

James smiled and climbed the steps to join me at the front door. Then, side-by-side, with his arm around my shoulders and mine around his waist, we watched Rose go. 'Hate to think how much mouldy chocolate there's going to be under our bed by the time she gets back,' he said.

'Don't worry,' I replied. 'So long as you check each time you vacuum, we'll be fine.'

'You're right.' He raised a hand and waved as Tony stuck his arm out of the open window of the Fiat and pulled away. 'I was panicking unnecessarily.'

'Don't feel bad,' I said. 'You haven't got my professional experience to draw upon.'

'Talking of professionalism... shouldn't that have been "my professional experience upon which to draw"? I

311

know I'm not an author, but I'm pretty sure that's the correct grammar.'

'Bored face,' I said, looking up at him.

'OK,' he smiled, still apparently focused on Tony's Fiat as it turned the corner before eventually disappearing from sight. 'Well, how about we go inside, pour ourselves a glass of something and sit in the garden? You can tell me all about Neil's wedding plans. Or are you as bored by weddings as you are by grammar?'

'Not at all.' I reached up to smooth his hair, then, standing on tiptoe, kissed his cheek. 'I remain a huge fan of weddings.'

He nodded slowly. 'That's very good news, because so am I,' he said, at last turning towards me, his expression serious.

'Are you really?' I asked quietly.

'Yes, Grace,' he said, looking thoughtful for a moment, as if second-guessing himself, 'I really am.' And then, suddenly smiling, he removed his arm from around my shoulders, took my hand and led me inside. 'So, let's talk.'